"Start chopping veg for eighty chicken pot pies."

Tom smiled, humoring her. "Reggie, you're preparing an Italian meal, which I happen to be rather good at, and you want me to chop veg for pot pies."

"Yes."

He nodded. "I understand." And he no doubt did. Reggie was putting him in his place.

She started to fold her arms over her chest, caught herself, and forced them back to her sides. "And I want you to be nice to Patty. For some reason her back is up."

"No problem." This time there was a note of irony in his voice, but Reggie ignored it as she led the way into the kitchen.

She pulled a list out of her apron pocket. "Here you go. I'm sure you can familiarize yourself with the kitchen. This is your station." She indicated an area of the stainless steel counter with a sweep of her hand. "Let me know when you're done." She hesitated, then added, "And be nice to Patty. I mean it."

"Yes, Chef."

Reggie left Tom standing next to the counter and went into the office. When she returned, Tom glanced up. Oh, yeah. This wasn't nerve-racking or anything, having him here.

Tom was chopping as he'd been told to do, his hand moving so quickly it was a blur. Reggie knew he wasn't showing off. He was making a point. Yes, he'd chop veg, but using him that way was a waste. He was probably thinking of how he could revolutionize her kitchen.

He'd lost that chance seven years ago.

Dear Reader,

I love to cook, but more than that, I love it when my husband cooks for me. What is it about a man in the kitchen?

I had heard that chefs are notoriously difficult to write and guess what? They are. Many chefs are bona fide alpha males, used to command and having their every order followed without question. My chef, Tom Gerard, made a spectacular career for himself by refusing to compromise, and then destroyed it in the same way. When the story opens, he has burned most of his professional bridges by refusing to bow to authority and has finally come to realize that there are consequences to his actions. And as he makes that discovery, he gets another bit of news. His former girlfriend, caterer Reggie Tremont, is pregnant—and she doesn't need any help or support from him, thank you very much.

Now Tom not only has to rebuild a career; he has to rebuild a relationship with the woman he once abandoned.

I hope you enjoy Tom and Reggie's story. While writing this book, I researched celebrity chefs, read several chef biographies and became a cooking show junkie. I guess you could say that Tom and Reggie broadened my world and, thanks to the many recipes I just had to try, I may have broadened in other ways, too.

I love to hear from readers, so please feel free to contact me via my website, www.jeanniewatt.com.

Best wishes,

Jeannie Watt

The Baby Truce
Jeannie Watt

TORONTO NEW YORK LONDON
AMSTERDAM PARIS SYDNEY HAMBURG
STOCKHOLM ATHENS TOKYO MILAN MADRID
PRAGUE WARSAW BUDAPEST AUCKLAND

Recycling programs
for this product may
not exist in your area.

ISBN-13: 978-0-373-78494-3

THE BABY TRUCE

www.Harlequin.com

Printed in U.S.A.

ABOUT THE AUTHOR

Jeannie Watt lives off the grid in rural Nevada and loves nothing better than an excellent meal. Jeannie is blessed with a husband who cooks more than she does, a son who knows how to make tapas and a daughter who knows the best restaurants in San Francisco. Her idea of heaven is homemade macaroni and cheese.

Books by Jeannie Watt

HARLEQUIN SUPERROMANCE

1379—A DIFFICULT WOMAN
1444—THE HORSEMAN'S SECRET
1474—THE BROTHER RETURNS
1520—COP ON LOAN
1543—A COWBOY'S REDEMPTION
1576—COWBOY COMES BACK
1628—ALWAYS A TEMP
1647—ONCE AND FOR ALL
1690—MADDIE INHERITS A COWBOY

Other titles by this author available in ebook.

Don't miss any of our special offers. Write to us at the following address for information on our newest releases.

Harlequin Reader Service
U.S.: 3010 Walden Ave., P.O. Box 1325, Buffalo, NY 14269
Canadian: P.O. Box 609, Fort Erie, Ont. L2A 5X3

To Gary, my personal chef.
I couldn't do it without you.

PROLOGUE

TOM GERARD CAME AWAKE suddenly, aware that something wasn't right. He reached out and found the other side of the bed empty, the sheets cool to the touch.

"Reg?"

The suite remained silent, and although he couldn't see into the living room, he felt the stillness.

"Reggie!" He got out of bed and walked out there naked. His clothes were still scattered across the floor, but hers were no longer there.

He stood taking in the emptiness, not liking it. She was gone, and he didn't think she was out getting coffee and the newspaper. That had been his Sunday morning task during the year they'd been together. Hers had been to laze in bed until he returned. Then they would drink coffee, share the paper, make love again.

Those days were almost a decade past, but when Reggie had come to his suite with him last night, he'd assumed everything would be the same. For a while anyway, until they went back to their real lives—hers in Reno, his in New York City...or wherever he got hired. So far San Francisco was a bust, but he didn't care, because, honestly, he was an East Coast chef. California cuisine didn't do it for him.

The phone rang and Tom scooped it up. "Reggie?"

"It's Pete." Tom's long-suffering business manager, who took a nice slice of his income in return for that suffering. "I just booked you a ticket to New York. You leave at noon. Jervase Montrose wants to talk about a job. It looks good."

"Great." Tom wasn't surprised to have nailed an interview with Jervase, despite Pete's concerns. Yeah, he'd gotten his ass fired a couple weeks ago—the second time in two years—but he was still one of the top chefs in the country. Jervase would be lucky to get him.

Pete gave him the flight information, then added, "Be on your best behavior."

Hey. It wasn't like he was a wild man. He simply knew his own worth and he didn't suffer fools gladly. Was it his fault that he'd run into a hell of a lot of fools lately? "I'll call you when I land."

He hung up the phone and stood regarding the empty suite.

In all the time he'd known her, Reggie had never once walked out on him without a word.

CHAPTER ONE

REGGIE TREMONT SNAPPED OFF the TV and tossed the remote onto the sofa, startling her fat cat, Mims. "Damn it, Tom."

Fired again.

Not a world event, but he was enough of a bad-boy chef to get a small blurb on the *E!* entertainment network. Volatile chef dismissed. Celebrity witnesses involved.

They'd flashed a photo that made him look more like a pirate than a chef, with his black hair pulled into a ponytail, scruffy facial hair, dark eyes glinting. She was quite familiar with that unrepentant expression—a mask he popped on when he didn't want anyone getting too close. Or when he was getting ready to walk away.

Reggie grabbed her red cardigan off the arm of the recliner, where she'd left it the night before. She slipped it on while Mims twined around her ankles.

"Yeah, yeah, yeah." She headed for the pantry, where the cat food was stored. Like she'd forget to feed the cat. Mims was as wide as she was high.

Reggie opened the can and dumped it into the ceramic dish with Meow spelled out on the bottom, wrinkling her nose as the scent of fish mixed with who-knew-what hit her nostrils. Her stomach roiled. Second day in a row. That did it. She was going back to the old brand.

She fanned the air as she retreated from the kitchen. She had to make a quick stop at the catering kitchen she ran with her sister, Eden, and her brother, Justin, to pick up her portfolios, before her client meetings and site visits. At noon she'd trade her business heels for kitchen clogs and prep for a luncheon the following day.

Full days were good days.

She glanced at her watch after pulling her hair into a barrette at the back of her neck and double-checking her makeup. *Please let the traffic be with me for a change.*

The kitchen still smelled of the awful cat food and she tried not to breathe as she retrieved her keys from the hook next to the sink. Once she got outside the house and took a deep breath of fresh, non-cat-food-tainted air, she felt better. Well, a little better, anyway. The scent of the lilacs blooming beside the house was surprisingly strong and cloying, but not nearly as bad as Mims's new food.

Reggie pressed the flat of her hand to her stomach as she walked to her car, parked on the street, since her tiny brick house had no garage. She would not, *could* not, come down with something while they were short one prep cook.

Mind over matter. That was the trick.

EDEN SWIVELED IN HER CHAIR AS soon as Reggie walked into the tiny Tremont Catering kitchen office. "We have three applicants for the prep cook position!"

Finally. The employment agency they used for catering temps had taken its sweet time. Eden and Reggie had been fighting to keep their heads above water after their last employee quit.

"Have you set up interviews?" Reggie asked, dropping her tote bag on the floor next to her small workstation. She was still fighting queasiness and now her forehead felt damp.

"Day after tomorrow. Back-to-back, starting at one o'clock."

"Great."

Eden slipped an elastic band off her wrist and gathered her dark blond hair into a haphazard knot, then pulled a clean white chef's apron off one of the hooks next to her station. She wrapped the strings twice around her before she tied them. Eden was petite, but...

"I think that's Justin's apron," Reggie said.

"It'll do," she replied distractedly. "After the agency called about the applicants, I got news that the Dunmores have an unexpected guest this week, so I have to figure how to stretch what I made yesterday and add a couple more dishes. Then I still have all the morning prep for that luncheon."

Reggie glanced at the handwritten schedule she kept next to her computer. "Justin's coming in at nine?"

"New cake order and he wanted to get started."

"Of course," she murmured. He wasn't quite overextended enough and had to take on that one extra project to tip the scales.

When they'd first started Tremont six years ago, all three of them had worked extra jobs to keep the business afloat. Reggie, who like many would-be restaurateurs and caterers, had taken business and accounting classes along with her culinary courses, did the books for a couple small firms. Eden worked as a personal chef and Justin had snagged a part-time job as a backup cook for a resort at Lake Tahoe.

Reggie had long ago given up the book-keeping to run Tremont full time, but Eden still cooked for three families on a weekly basis and Justin was a backup pastry chef and fill-in cook at the same hotel. And he made cakes. Exquisitely crafted and gloriously expensive cakes that were gaining popularity and bringing some serious money into the business. At the same time they were forcing him into a ridiculous work schedule that didn't involve a lot of sleep.

"I saw that your ex got the ax again," Eden said.

"I saw it, too," Reggie said, without looking up. She tucked her site notes into the wedding portfolio.

"I guess he should have kept his mouth shut." Eden breezed by her and disappeared into the kitchen.

"A lesson for all of us," Reggie muttered. A lesson Tom wasn't learning.

She shut off her monitor before shouldering the leather portfolio. Her stomach tightened as she walked into the kitchen, where Eden had beef stew simmering.

"There's something wrong with your stew," Reggie said, wrinkling her nose. She stopped a few feet away from the stove.

"What?" Eden lifted the spoon and sniffed.

"Can't you smell it? It's…off."

Eden sniffed again, then tasted. "No, it's not."

Reggie came closer, took a deep whiff of the rich brown broth, and her stomach roiled violently. She clapped a hand over her mouth.

"Reg?"

The leather portfolio hit the rubber floor mat in front of the stove as Reggie turned and raced for the bathroom, barely making it before she heaved. She pushed away from the porcelain bowl as sweat broke out on her forehead. Then pulled herself closer as she heaved again.

"Reggie!" Eden knelt beside her, one hand on her back, offering her a wad of toilet paper.

"I'm fine," Reggie said automatically, taking the tissue to wipe her mouth.

"Oh, yes. Totally fine."

"No. Really." Reggie focused on her sister. "I feel better."

Eden regarded her for a moment. "Could you stop by the seafood shop right now?"

Reggie's stomach convulsed at the mere thought of fish. It must have showed.

"Uh-huh." Eden helped her to her feet. "You need to go home and lie down before you get really sick."

"This was just a fluke. Besides, I have meetings." That she couldn't afford to throw up in.

"How long have you been feeling like this?"

"A couple days," Reggie said. "Just a little out of sorts. Kind of sick in the mornings."

"Morning sickness?!"

Reggie met her sister's eyes, then slowly started shaking her head. "No. I feel sick in the morning. There's a difference."

"Oh, yeah? And what is that difference?"

"I believe what *you're* talking about is called pregnancy," Reggie said.

"No chance...?" Eden asked.

"*Who* are you talking to? I never take chances."

Eden merely stared at her in a decidedly unconvinced way.

"Ever," Reggie added. She glanced down at

her shoes, which, thankfully, hadn't suffered any damage.

"You've been damned cranky lately and now you're puking in the morning." Her sister lifted her chin, looked Reggie in the eye and asked flatly, "You swear there's no chance at all?"

Next she'd have her putting her hand on the Bible.

"None," Reggie replied. After all, she and Tom had used condoms.

TOM WALKED DOWN FIFTH AVENUE, hands shoved deep in his pockets, chin tucked low to his chest against the pelting rain. He hated rain.

Right now he hated just about everything, and especially Jervase Montrose. It was one thing to get canned, and another to get canned in front of his kitchen brigade just after service. Jervase had planned it that way. He'd all but called in a news crew. And he'd made such a fricking big deal about having taken a chance on him. What chance? Tom had delivered everything he'd promised. The number of covers had increased exponentially since he'd taken the helm of Jervase's restaurant.

Ungrateful bastard.

Tom climbed the four stone steps to the

entryway of Pete's office building. The security guard nodded at him as he passed on his way to the elevator. His business manager's receptionist did the same, then ignored him during the twenty minutes Pete kept him waiting. He hadn't even sat down in one of the sleek ebony chairs on the opposite side of the equally sleek but cluttered desk when Pete announced, "It was your fault."

Tom didn't bother sitting after that, since it was going to be one of those kinds of meetings. Pete might be a good six inches shorter than Tom and generally soft spoken, but he didn't take crap from anyone. "My fault? How the hell did you come to that conclusion?"

"Eyewitness reports."

"What? Who? Because anyone there last night could tell you—"

"Not last night. The night before. When you told the group of diners how ridiculous upper management was."

Tom shifted his weight impatiently. "I didn't say anything that wasn't true." Rampant inefficiency was making it damned hard for him to do his best work, and it wouldn't have been that tough to fix it.

"But unfortunately, you said it to one of the men responsible."

Tom snorted. "All the more reason to say something. If they would have listened to me weeks ago—"

"Play the freaking game, Tom! Other people do. Why can't you?"

He placed his palms on Pete's desk and leaned closer. "Because the game bites. If there's a problem, you identify it and fix it."

"Well, apparently Jervase has identified the problem and fixed it."

Tom had no answer for that. Jervase was within his rights to fire him. He was stupid to, but within his rights.

"What now?" he asked.

"What the hell do you mean, what now? You're burning bridges faster than I can build them."

"Build faster."

Pete slumped back in his chair. "Jervase is well respected. I hate to say this...but you may have burned your last bridge. For a while, anyway."

"Meaning?"

"If he wants to, he can blackball you."

Tom's chin came up. "He's a money man. He doesn't know squat about running a restaurant—or creating a menu." One of their first bones of contention. "I mean, seriously."

"Money talks." Pete got out of his chair and came around his desk. "Consider an apology. Possibly even a public one."

"An apology?" Tom almost choked. "Give me one frigging reason why I should apologize to him when his head is so far up his—"

"He can do you some major damage, no matter how good you are." Pete paused, then added significantly, "Even *more* damage than you're causing yourself."

"*I* am not the problem."

"So this has all been what?" Pete asked calmly. "A run of bad luck?"

Tom slapped his hand down on the desk. Why in the hell couldn't the man see what was going on? "It's been a run of idiots with money thinking they know more than the experts they hire. Assholes who can't handle hearing the truth because they didn't think of it themselves."

"Assholes who do the hiring and firing." Pete pointed a finger at him. "Assholes who hold your future in their hands."

"They don't hold *my* future," Tom said. "*I* hold my future."

"Don't be so sure of that."

Tom's head started to pound. Pete was missing the point, and Tom needed to get the hell out of there before he really blew. He turned and headed for the door. "I've got to go."

"Don't do anything stupid," Pete said. "Or should I say stupider."

"Wouldn't dream of it." Tom yanked the heavy paneled door open and strode out into the hall. "I'll check back with you."

Pete didn't answer. Tom didn't know whether that was good or bad, and didn't care. Pete had been his manager since he'd been a candidate for the James Beard Upcoming Chef awards, and once they weathered this particular storm, things would be good again.

He could see why Pete wanted to make nice with Montrose—after all, Tom wasn't Pete's only client. But he was his biggest name, and Tom would pound nails with his knife before he'd apologize for speaking the truth.

Let the man do his worst.

THE UNOPENED PREGNANCY TEST stood like a sentinel on Reggie's kitchen island. She walked slowly around the granite-topped fixture, not quite ready to take the plunge, mainly because she couldn't be pregnant.

No. Way.

She and Tom had used condoms. Both times.

So why didn't she just pee on the stick and get it over with?

Because the possibility of being tied to Tom for the next eighteen years was simply too much for her to handle. Yeah, she'd once loved him. But that wasn't why she'd slept with him.

Never sleep with someone you don't want to raise a kid with—no matter how hot they are. Her ninth-grade health teacher's words, which had been repeated at least fifty times during the semester.

No question about Tom being hot. And if Reggie pushed aside her resentment about how he'd walked out on her, how he'd chosen a high-risk job on the other side of the ocean over staying with her and starting the catering business that had become Tremont, she could concede that he had good points besides hotness. But he wasn't father material. Fathers needed to be steady. And there.

Reggie grabbed the box and opened the top. Enough. She was settling this once and for all.

It took Tom a long time to wake up enough to realize that the constant ringing was not in his head. He pushed himself upright on the sofa, stared at the cell phone he held in his hand, then answered.

"Are you crazy?" Pete barked into his ear, making him wince.

"According to you, I am," Tom said, his voice thick. He cleared his throat twice, trying to ease the cotton mouth. "Why?"

"Do you recall talking to any reporters lately?"

Tom planted a palm on his forehead, trying to hold in the pressure. "Why in the hell are you calling me about reporters?"

"Because of what greeted me in the paper this morning!" Pete, normally the most patient of men, even when Tom was on a rampage, sounded utterly pissed. "I sent you the link. Take a look once your vision clears enough to read it." The phone went dead.

Tom let his head fall back against the sofa cushions. Closed his eyes. His head was throbbing. Mescal? Was that what he'd drunk? He remembered demanding something strong to kill the disappointment of having everyone he'd called for a job lead give him a helpful suggestion as to somewhere else he might want to call.

Whatever he'd drunk, it'd been a killer

night. But he hadn't talked to any reporters. He was certain of that.

The room spun as he got to his feet and trudged naked to the bathroom. A woman's red sequined top hung on the doorknob by one strap. He stared at it for a moment, then continued into the john, closing the door just in case. When he came back out, he looked around the apartment, which didn't take long since it was only four small yet highly expensive rooms. No woman.

He sat in front of the computer, brought up his email and clicked on the link Pete had sent. Obviously some tabloid had manufactured a few lies, twisted a few truths.

And that tabloid was called the *New York Times*.

Oh, shit.

In a small but clear photo he had one arm draped over a woman wearing a sequined top very similar to the one on his bathroom doorknob. With the other hand he pointed directly at the camera, his mouth open as he obviously expounded.

And how he'd expounded, according to the article beneath the photo. The text wasn't long, but it was colorful and explained exactly what he thought of Jervase Montrose and his restaurants, plus his feelings on all corporately managed eating establishments. The reporter had also helpfully included Tom's insights into the personal habits of several food critics. There were many, many quotation marks.

Tom slammed the laptop shut and jumped to his feet, needing to move.

He sensed the need for some damage control.

He punched Pete's number into his phone. The business manager answered on the first ring. "You read it?"

"Yeah."

"Then you'll understand what I'm about to say next."

"Which is?"

"I quit. Please seek other management."

REGGIE HAD HEARD OF WOMEN IN denial buying three and four different pregnancy tests, just to make certain the first two or three were correct. She was about to join their ranks. The only thing that stopped her was the landline ringing as she went for her purse and keys. Ignore her sister or get it over with?

If she ignored her, Eden would show up at her door.

"Well?" Eden said when she answered.

"I don't want to talk about it."

"No!"

"I said I don't want to talk about it." Reggie planted the palm of her free hand on her throbbing forehead, trying to ease the tension there. "I'm going to buy another test. This one may have been old."

"Old?"

"Or compromised in some way."

"Or the reason you're throwing up is because you're pregnant." Reggie dropped her hand. She couldn't bring herself to respond. "I'll be right over," Eden added.

"Don't tell Justin," Reggie said through gritted teeth. Her brother did his best to appear as if nothing bothered him, but it was a front. Justin was the most protective male of her acquaintance, and right now she didn't need protection. She didn't need to hash this through with Eden, either, but better to get it over with now, while she was still numb.

"Wouldn't think of it," Eden said. "See you in twenty. Just...stay calm."

Reggie rolled her eyes and hung up. Stay calm. Oh, yeah. She headed for the door. She had just enough time to get to the nearest drugstore and back again.

No. She'd wait for Eden and then go to the

drugstore. They could go together. Reggie stopped in the middle of the room and pressed her palms against her abdomen. How? How could there possibly be a baby growing inside her?

When Eden showed up twenty minutes later, Reggie was sitting on the sofa, holding Mims on her lap and staring at the opposite wall. This was real. She had accidentally become pregnant at the age of thirty.

Unless, of course, the test was wrong. It happened.

Reggie stood as Eden let herself in with her own key. They were dressed almost identically in white T-shirts and jeans…and Eden's jeans were going to fit her in six months. For a moment the two sisters simply stared at each other, then Eden crossed the room to wrap her arms around Reggie and hug her tightly. "You're not alone in this. All right?"

"I know."

Eden released her and stood back. "It's none of my business—"

"Tom." No sense being coy.

"Gerard?" Eden's mouth fell open. She waited, as if expecting Reggie to say, "Just kidding." That didn't happen. "When… where…? Isn't he in New York?"

"Sommelier class. San Francisco. He was staying at the hotel while interviewing for a job. We ran into each other the first day of class."

"So you slept with him?"

Reggie gave her sister a weary look. *Obviously.*

"You—"

"We used protection," Reggie said. "It didn't work."

"But…Tom?"

She wasn't going into the wherefores and the whys—mainly because they sounded lame. And she didn't want anyone to know that she'd gotten pregnant proving to herself that she was over a guy; that she could walk away, just as he had.

Especially when she'd made the rather startling discovery that physically, at least, she wasn't over him. Regardless of what her very logical brain was telling her. Sleeping with Tom after all these years had been…something. And if it hadn't been for her realization that she still had issues with him, she would have pushed back her departure. Had another night with him.

"Yes, Tom." She picked up a squirming Mims, who'd had about enough of being used as a security pillow. "And now I have to tell him."

Eden's expression became closed. "Why?"

Reggie hugged Mims tighter, holding the cat's plump gray body against her chest. "What do you mean, why? Because he's the father. He has a right to know."

Eden let out a sigh as she reached up to pat Mims, who escaped to the back of the sofa after Reggie released her. "It's just that he made you so damned unhappy when you guys broke up, and now…" She gave a small shrug. "But it isn't like he's going to want to settle down or anything."

"No." Again, obviously. He hadn't settled into anything since leaving her, moving from job to job, city to city. Her kid was going to have a normal life, and Tom's life was anything but normal.

Her kid. What a concept.

"And I guess he should pay support," Eden added.

"I don't know that I want him to." Because if he paid support, he'd have a say in the child's upbringing.

But would he want a say?

She'd been officially pregnant for all of

an hour and was already drowning in unanswered questions and potential complications.

And she was still grappling with the thought of a tiny being growing inside her. "I guess the smart thing to do, after I go to a doctor and make sure I'm really pregnant, is to see a lawyer." She sat on the sofa, reaching up to stroke Mims on the cushion next to her head. "It's going to take a while to get used to this idea."

"For all of us."

Reggie dropped her hand into her lap and looked up at Eden, who still stood next to the recliner. "I always figured that if one of us got into this mess, it would be Justin."

Eden's mouth twisted in ironic acknowledgment. "Instead, it's the responsible Tremont. Go figure."

The responsible Tremont who had no idea what to do next.

CHAPTER TWO

REGGIE TOOK TWO MORE PREGNANCY tests early the next morning before work. Just to make sure.

Her body and three different pharmaceutical companies were in agreement. She was pregnant.

After the last test went into the trash, Reggie poured a big glass of orange juice, took two sips before deciding it tasted off, then put the glass on the counter.

She sat at the kitchen table and laid her head on her folded arms. Mims jumped up on the off-limits surface and butted her with her head, trying to remind her that the Salmon Soufflé was still in the can. Reggie shooed her off, then closed her eyes. Maybe she could sleep here, shut out the world and all the issues she had to figure out fast.

Issues she didn't think Eden would fully understand, because *she* hadn't understood until she'd found herself in this position.

The questions about her future, the sobering reality of being responsible for a child. The fear that Tom's gypsy lifestyle would forever warp her kid, coupled with the lingering sense of unreality about the entire situation. She wanted nothing more than to slip into denial, pretend none of this was happening— at least until she vomited again.

Mims was having none of being shooed away. She threw her body hard against Reggie's legs and then, when she had her weary owner's attention, raced for the pantry. Reggie got to her feet and followed, wishing she'd thought of picking up the old brand of cat food when she'd gone to the store for more pregnancy tests.

A few minutes later, she took a deep breath, held it as best she could as she opened the can and dished out the food. She tossed the can in the trash on top of the pregnancy tests, then fled the kitchen for the relatively fresh air of the living room.

When she arrived at work twenty minutes later, Justin was there alone, leaning against the counter at the opposite end of the room, not moving at high speed for once in his life...almost as if he was waiting for her.

"Justin."

"Reggie."

Oh, yeah. He knew. She didn't know whether to be angry at Eden for spilling the beans, or grateful that she herself didn't have to. The three siblings hadn't kept many secrets from one another while growing up. They'd been in the odd position of practically raising each other while their long-haul trucker father had been on the road, after their mother's death. Oh, Justin had tried to hold secrets, but the neighborhood grapevine was quite effective at keeping Reggie and Eden up to date on his activities.

But this time it wasn't Justin who was in hot water. Nope. Tables turned.

Reggie walked the short distance from the back door into the office as if nothing was wrong, put away her purse, smoothed her hair, tied on an apron. When she left the office, Justin was right where he'd been when she'd entered the building, leaning against the stainless steel counter, gripping the metal on either side of him. His usually warm expression was cold. Was he ticked because this had happened to her after all the lectures she'd given him?

"Been talking to Eden?" Reggie asked, giving him an opening so they could get this discussion over with fast.

"Yeah." Still cold. Still closed off.

"Well." Reggie shrugged, less than comfortable discussing this matter with her younger brother. The one she'd threatened with annihilation as a teen if he wasn't sexually responsible. "I don't know what to say."

He nodded as he regarded her. "Have you… made any plans?"

"Like…?"

"Keeping the baby?"

Reggie raised her eyebrows. "I'm keeping the baby." Of course she was keeping the baby. She wasn't a pregnant teen. The thought of giving it up hadn't even crossed her mind.

Her brother's face relaxed an iota, but his voice was still stern when he asked, "Told Tom yet?"

"No."

"You gotta do that."

Reggie frowned. "I will." Justin appeared as if he was on a mission. But what mission? She hadn't a clue. "I'm going to phone him."

Her brother glanced down at his feet. He was wearing flat skateboard shoes. He hadn't changed yet, which meant talking to her had been his first order of business. "I can be there when you make the call."

Justin was returning to protective form—a good sign.

"I'll handle it." It wasn't a conversation she wanted anyone to hear. She met her brother's blue eyes. "If I need propping up afterwards, I'll hunt you down."

He smiled slightly. "Just…don't put it off too long. All right?"

"All right." Reggie smoothed her hands down the sides of her apron. "Well, I guess I'd better get going on the chops for the dinner tonight." She started for the cooler, then glanced back over her shoulder. "Will you be here for the interviews this afternoon?"

"I got called in to the lake early." His mouth tightened. "Sorry about that."

"No, I understand." Justin's job at Lake Tahoe brought in a lot of contacts and potential business. "Eden and I will be fine."

"Don't settle," he said. "Because, well, there's a chance whoever we hire might end up full time for a while. You know?"

Reggie knew.

Tom gave Pete a week to cool off, then phoned. Pete was out of the office. The next time he called, a day later, Pete was once again unavailable. By the third call Tom understood that he was never going to be available. Tom was on his own.

And that sucked, because while he could cook, he knew squat about business.

He'd already called everyone he knew in the city, tried to pull in a few favors, but so far no luck. Even people who said they wanted to help indicated they couldn't. Not right now. Lower-end restaurants were more than willing to take a chance on him, hoping his notoriety would bring in business, but that wasn't a career move Tom was ready to take. He wasn't into notoriety. Not on purpose, anyway. He was into making good food the only way he knew how. His way.

The *Times* article had done him some serious damage. He spent an evening writing a blistering rebuttal, but realized after an hour of slamming thoughts onto paper that he wasn't in the most defensible position. In fact, he was pretty much in the juice.

Memories were short, though. Given a month or two, a new scandal, people would forget. He'd be back at the helm of a new restaurant, and this time he'd choose more wisely—choose a place where he approved of the management style, rather than the name. He had savings and investments. Although he knew very little about them, since he'd trusted Pete implicitly.

But what to do now? Continue pounding the pavement, trying to get an interview? Call Lowell and hear the guy rant about how Tom had screwed himself?

Not yet. Lowell Hislop, who'd gotten Tom the job in Spain that had ultimately jump-started his career, was the closest thing to a mentor he had. He was also unpredictable and hard to deal with. A veritable force unto himself, and at the moment as unemployed as Tom was. But in Lowell's case it was by choice, while he hammered out a divorce agreement with his French wife, Simone. They'd split innumerable times in the past, but this once it appeared to be for real. Lowell had sold his restaurant, dumped his investment properties and quite likely stashed a bunch of cash in odd places. He was nothing if not savvy, but the last Tom had heard he was up to his ass in his wife's lawyers.

Yeah, Tom would call him, but first he'd see what he could do on his own. There were still a couple avenues left to him.

He hoped.

He was halfway up the stairs to his apartment when his phone rang. It wasn't Pete, as he'd hoped, but it wasn't Jervase telling him the town wasn't big enough for the both of them, either. It was a Nevada number.

"Reggie?"

"Hi, Tom." There was an awkward silence, then she said, "I, uh, have some news for you."

"All right." A lead on a job, maybe? The Associated Press had picked up his "interview" with the *Times* and it was all over the country. No doubt she knew he was out of work. He didn't really want a job in Reno, but he'd consider it. For a while.

"Before I start, I just want to tell you that you don't have to be involved in any way. I plan to handle everything myself."

"Handle what?" He balanced the phone on his shoulder while he dug his keys out of his pocket.

After another short silence, she said, "I'm pregnant."

He almost said congratulations. Then her meaning struck him. "How pregnant?"

"Almost two months."

He dropped the keys on the carpet between his feet. "We...used protection."

"I haven't slept with anyone but you."

"We...used protection," Tom repeated. He

pressed the heel of his palm into the solid wood door. Blood hammered in his temples, making it damned hard to think.

"Like I said..." She hesitated. "I thought you should know, but...I don't need anything from you."

"Well, aren't you brave?" he snapped.

"Yes. I am. I lived with you for a year." The phone went dead.

Tom stood for a moment without moving, then reached down and picked up his keys. It took him two tries to get the right one into the lock, mainly because his hands were shaking.

Pregnant?

Call her back, you jerk.

Not yet. Soon, but not yet.

He needed time in the worst way.

Once inside, he dropped the keys on the table, set the bag of produce beside them.

He was going to be a father.

Out of a job. Living on savings. About to be a dad. This was not the way his life was supposed to work out.

Tom rubbed his temples with his fingertips. Then he went to the cupboard and pulled out a bottle, the first one he touched. He didn't even look to see what it was. He poured a healthy amount into a glass and downed it in one swallow.

Bourbon.

He poured another, then went to the window and stared out at the building behind his, swirling the amber liquid in the glass. This time he sipped, allowing the alcohol to warm his throat slowly. The tension started to ease out of the muscles of his neck and shoulders, but his mind was still whirling.

If Reggie was two months pregnant, then he had seven months to figure this all out. He'd be employed by then. Have a new business manager, be able to set up a college fund, or do whatever dads did. His father had done two things—hauled him around the world with him when he could, or sent him off to boarding school when he couldn't. Not the most normal of upbringings. His dad had been more like a friend than a father...when they'd been together.

So what the hell did Tom know about fatherhood?

"Damn." He tossed the bourbon back, then reached for the bottle and poured another shot.

TWO INTERVIEWS DOWN AND ONE TO go. So far, not so good.

Eden and Reggie exchanged glances as

the second of their three candidates walked out the door. Reggie's stomach was in a tight knot, but this time it had little to do with morning sickness.

The first candidate hadn't known how to hold a knife and, when shown, had preferred to do it her way. That was fine. She could do the wrong thing in her own kitchen, but not the Tremont kitchen. Oh, and she couldn't work on weekends.

The second candidate had skills, but also had a schedule Tremont would have to work around. That kind of defeated the purpose of having a prep cook, who had to be able to prep when they needed her, not when she was free from her other job.

If these were the top candidates, Reggie didn't hold out much hope for numbers four, five and six.

"If this person can breathe and work our schedule, I say we hire her," Eden whispered to Reggie as a roundish woman in her mid-forties, with short brown hair and a no-nonsense expression—candidate number three—walked in the door exactly five minutes before her interview.

She approached the desk where Eden and Reggie were sitting and set a bound résumé before them.

"I'm Patty Lloyd. How do you do?" she said. "I'm here for the interview. I realize that I have large gaps in my employment history, but I assure you, I can cook."

Eden met Reggie's gaze with raised eyebrows as Patty took her seat on the other side of the desk.

The interview went well. Despite her somewhat arrogant, take-charge attitude, she'd been employed at a private care facility kitchen for the past two years and proved to be slow yet meticulous. And part time was fine with her for now. What the woman didn't know they could teach her.

The only problem was that Patty was very, very serious, in her speech, in her dress, in her attitude, which made Reggie wonder if the woman could handle Justin. Justin, when not dealing with pregnant sisters, tended toward irreverence.

Eden obviously had the same concern. She smiled up at Patty and said, "I want you to meet my brother for a second interview tomorrow, and then we'll have you make a couple standard dishes on our menu. Would that work for you?"

"Certainly. Let's say ten?" Patty stood, extending her hand.

"She scares me a little," Eden said after the door shut behind her. They watched through the front window as she got into a small blue Ford that had to be twenty years old, yet appeared almost new.

"That," Reggie said, carefully setting down her pen, "makes two of us. But if we keep her in the kitchen and away from clients, I think she'll do fine."

"We'll have to tell Justin to behave."

"That goes without saying. I'll get going on the tapenade," she added, because Eden had that touch-base-to-see-how-you're-feeling look, and Reggie wasn't in the mood.

She was still recovering from her phone conversation with Tom, would most probably have to have another in the near future, and wanted time to stew. Alone.

Tom went to the window of his apartment and leaned his forehead against the cool glass, watching the people on the sidewalk five stories below. A lot of them were probably going to work. The bastards.

It was hard to believe, but Montrose appeared to have him by the short hairs. As near as he could tell, he *was* blacklisted.

But for how fricking long?

Tom left the window and stepped over the

clothes he hadn't bothered to pick up during the past few days. It was time to call Lowell, admit that he needed his help.

"You're totally screwed," Lowell said shortly, after hello. "I've been keeping tabs."

"I don't buy 'totally screwed.'" Maybe he was temporarily screwed, and for the zillionth time Tom wondered how getting fired for stuff that had nothing to do with his cooking ability could interfere with his ability to get a job cooking. "What do you suggest I do about that?" he asked with more patience than he was feeling.

"Keep out of trouble for, say, a day or two and let this blow over."

"It's *been* a goddamn *day or two*."

"Calm. Down."

"This is your advice? Calm down and what? Helpful, Lowell. Really helpful. At least tell me if you hear of anything…"

"Yeah…but like I said. Right now? Screwed. Hope you have some savings."

Tom hung up so he didn't have to tell Lowell what he could do with his bloody useless advice. One thing about Lowell—you might not know what he was going to do next, but you knew where you stood with him.

Staring at the phone, Tom became increasingly aware of an unfamiliar feeling unfurling inside him. Desperation. Coupled with fear.

He grabbed the phone and threw it across the room, where it smashed into the wall. That felt satisfying. He refused to give in to fear.

He had to plan for this baby.

Tom had no idea how to handle fatherhood, but regardless of Reggie's glib assurance that she would handle everything by herself—or maybe because of it—he'd have some say in his kid's life. Even if that kid didn't seem real. Yet. Seven more months and he'd be real. A new Gerard in the world.

Tom went into his kitchen, bypassed the bottle of bourbon for a glass of tap water, which tasted of metal, then went back to his phone and called Pete at home. He was getting his business manager back and his life on track. All he wanted to do was cook and cook well—for someone other than himself. And get himself into a position where he could at the very least support his kid.

CHAPTER THREE

THE DOCTOR WAS RUNNING LATE BY almost an hour, and if he didn't hurry, Reggie was going to have to abandon ship in order to make a meeting with a prospective client. A bride.

Several other women sat in the waiting room with her, most very pregnant, and she studied them out the corner of her eye while pretending to read. What did it feel like to no longer have a waist? Or in some cases ankles? Oh, she hoped she got to keep her ankles.

How did seat belts work when one didn't have a lap?

Was she going to have to get a special order chef's jacket? Hers was roomy, but judging by the slender-except-for-her-belly woman who was just called from the waiting area by a nurse with a chart in her hand, not roomy enough. Maybe Reggie could wear Justin's jacket? Not working wasn't an option. Working kept her sane. It also kept the business afloat and money in the bank.

Her heart gave a mighty thud when her

name was called and she followed the nurse to the room where she was weighed and her blood pressure taken.

"First pregnancy?" the nurse asked.

"Yes." Reggie stared at the opposite wall, at the collage of happy babies.

"We'll have to run a blood panel," she said briskly.

Reggie automatically pushed up her sleeve to expose the veins in her arm. "How often will I have appointments?"

"First we have to make certain you're really pregnant."

Her heart skipped a beat. "I took three pregnancy tests."

"We'll just run a blood test anyway," the nurse said.

What if she wasn't pregnant? What if she'd been so afraid of becoming pregnant, of tying herself to Tom, that she just showed the symptoms?

"Do you get many false positives?"

"Not with three positive home tests, but we have to follow procedure." The woman slipped the needle into Reggie's vein, filled first one vial, then another. "Was this an unplanned pregnancy?" she asked as she labeled the small containers.

"You could say that."

"Do you want to make an appointment to speak with our wellness counselor?"

Reggie frowned.

"About the pregnancy." The nurse popped the needle into the sharps container. "Unplanned pregnancies cause stress. Especially if the mother is going through it alone."

Did she have the look of someone going through her pregnancy alone?

"I want the baby," Reggie said coolly, not taking a particular shine to this nurse. "I just hadn't planned to become pregnant. It happens."

"Boy, does it," the nurse muttered. She smiled at Reggie, though. "I didn't mean to offend. If a woman isn't comfortable with her pregnancy, she needs to confront the issues both for her health and the health of the child. I offer the service to all mothers-to-be."

Reggie didn't believe her. Or maybe she was just nervous and cranky.

The doctor was a very likable, if somewhat harried man. He did a quick exam, pronounced Reggie fit to have children without a C-section, and prescribed vitamins. "Now, do you have any questions?"

"About five hundred," Reggie said.

He laughed. "I'll answer what I can and point you to some excellent online sources for the questions that pop into your head as soon as you leave."

Reggie left the office with a handful of literature and web addresses, a prescription for vitamins and a November due date.

"Well?" Eden said, looking up from the manicotti she was filling when Reggie walked into the kitchen.

"Everything's good."

"No pictures? No boy or girl?"

"Not yet. Several more weeks before they can tell."

"Hope it's a girl," Eden said.

Obviously the aunt was settling into this pregnancy better than the mother.

PATTY PASSED HER SECOND interview with flying colors, because Justin was more than happy to rein in the irreverence if they could get some additional help. She started work the day after Reggie's doctor's appointment, bustling in fifteen minutes early and then carefully stowing her purse in the locker assigned her. She'd brought a chef's jacket that was so stiff it seemed to creak when she put it on. Once it was buttoned to the top, she rolled her shoulders and asked, "Where do I begin?"

"Inventory," Reggie said, leading the way to the dry storage area.

Patty pulled a small spiral book and pencil out of her pocket. "Do you mind if I take notes?"

"Not at all," Reggie said. "Although honestly, the procedure isn't that complex."

"Everyone has their own way of doing things."

Indeed. Counting could be tricky. But Reggie reminded herself that the woman had primarily worked in hospital and care facility kitchens. There were probably set procedures for everything.

Once she and Patty were in front of the open stainless steel shelving, she said, "It's important that we have emergency stock and an adequate supply of basic ingredients, but having too much of anything is a waste of money that could be earning interest."

Patty nodded sagely and made a notation in her book.

"I have a master list here…" She went through her procedure, letting Patty do the actual inventory. "Justin's cake supplies are on a different sheet, and vary according to what he needs for the week. I take care of the orders, but he fills out this list." Reggie was just flipping to it on the clipboard when the phone rang.

"When you're done here, move on to the cooler. The sheet is on the very bottom of the stack."

"Will do." Patty didn't salute, but Reggie had the feeling she wanted to. *Please relax,* she wanted to say.

The call was from Eden. She was leaving the site for the Italian dinner party they were giving that evening and heading for the linen supplier. She'd discovered that the order was short. "Be sure you make a notation on the invoice," she said. "How're you feeling?"

"Like I'm tired of you asking that every morning."

"Better?"

"Good enough."

It had been only two weeks since Reggie had found out she was pregnant, but her body had definitely become different. Not her own. It was acting on autopilot, responding to ancient signals from deep within her DNA. She only wished those signals would stop making her feel queasy because she wanted the Italian dinner, not to mention the bridal shower the day after tomorrow, to be perfect. Or if not perfect, to at least give that impression.

Funny how the success or failure of Tremont Catering had taken on a whole new significance since discovering she was pregnant. Yes, she'd been driven to make the business a success, but it had been because she loved to cook and cater. Because she enjoyed the challenge and thrill of running her own company and enjoyed working with her brother and sister.

Now success was a matter of necessity, because she was going to have a child to support.

As soon as Patty finished the inventory, Reggie put her to work chopping veg for the salad and vegetarian courses for that evening's dinner. Reggie waved at the mail lady from the kitchen, as the woman came and went, and minutes later Justin walked through the front door. Reggie kept her eyes on her knife as she sliced mushrooms, but she heard her brother sorting through the mail, envelopes hitting the bottom of the metal trash can every few seconds, then silence.

He was yawning as he walked in, and Reggie was about to say something along the lines of how much sleep did you get last night, despite her intentions not to, when he held up an envelope with a distinct blue-and-green design.

Reggie almost dropped her rolling pin. "Is that…"

"I hope it's not bad news," Patty said.

"Bad news doesn't come in a blue-and-green envelope, Patty." The prep cook turned a little pink at Justin's tone.

"Are we in?" Reggie asked, stunned. The deadline for acceptance into Reno Cuisine had passed two weeks ago—just about the time she'd discovered she was pregnant, and hadn't given two hoots about a catering competition. Not even a big one.

Justin pulled the contract and a letter out of the envelope and handed them to her. "We're in. Sutter's Catering had to drop out and we're first on the waiting list."

"I'll write the check and get it in the mail today," Reggie said, skimming the letter. This was good. Really good. Now to make a decent showing. Thank heavens for Patty. "How much time do I have? Do we have to notarize the contract?"

"They need word by the end of the week. No notarization." Justin had obviously read every word before coming in.

"Maybe I'll drop it by their office on the way home." Reggie looked up at him.

"Good plan."

"The Reno Cuisine?" Patty beamed. "How exciting."

"You have no idea," Reggie said. Tremont was doing well, but competition was tough in Reno, and they needed every edge they could get. This would help establish them.

"Exciting and hopefully lucrative." Justin smiled at the prep cook and again she went pink, even though she was old enough to be his mother.

"Patty," he added, "you might just be our good luck charm."

Tom HAD FINISHED FUNNELING HIS frustrations into a massive apartment sterilization project and was packing laundry into bags for his weekly trip to the cleaners when the phone rang.

"Tom Gerard," he answered as he cinched a bag shut.

"Mr. Gerard? This is Debra Banks from the Letterbridge Hotel Corporation."

Tom dropped the laundry bag on the sofa and stood up straighter. Finally. He'd turned down an offer from them two years ago, but now he wasn't turning down anything. Maybe they knew that.

"Would you be interested in flying to our corporate office in Seattle for a meeting and interview with our culinary vision team?"

"Yes, I would," Tom replied without hesitation. "When?"

Many fine chefs worked for hotels. It was exactly the kind of corporate, don't-color-outside-the-lines environment that had gotten Tom in trouble in the past, but things had changed since he'd found out Reggie was pregnant. He was going to have to learn how to survive in a corporate environment. There weren't many other options. He could give them a year or two, then try to move into a more creative kitchen.

"I know it's short notice, but next week, if you can work it into your schedule."

"I, uh, think I can do that."

Ms. Banks went on to describe exactly what they were looking for—three chefs to head operations in three different areas of the country. They had a short list of four chefs for each region. "Does that sound like something that would interest you?"

It sounded like an answer to a prayer.

"I'll email you the meeting, flight and hotel

information. Please call if you have any questions or conflicts at all with the time."

"Sure thing. Thanks."

"No. Thank you. I certainly hope you become part of the Letterbridge Hotel team."

So did Tom.

REGGIE GOT INTO BED AT NINE, still making plans for Reno Cuisine. She and Eden had made some preliminary decisions that afternoon, decided on a French bistro theme, since it hadn't been well represented in the last competition—unlike luau and garden party. They had a ton of work ahead of them and Reggie was supremely grateful. She wanted her plate full. Loaded to the brim. Anything to keep her from obsessing full time over how to handle the baby situation. So far, she'd had no word back from Tom.

But she'd hung up on him. Maybe that was that.

She knew it wasn't.

Mims was curled up on her chest and she was just nodding off—finally—when her cell phone rang, startling her awake. "Great," she muttered, automatically snapping on the beside lamp before she answered.

"Reggie." Speak of the devil… There was

no mistaking Tom's voice. "I'm flying to Seattle and routed the flight through Reno. I'd like to see you."

"When?" Realizing she was holding the phone in a death grip, she forced herself to relax her fingers.

"Day after tomorrow."

Damn. Kitchen prep and nothing else. She was so tempted to lie and say she was booked, just to buy some time, but it would only put off the inevitable. Better to man up, get this first difficult meeting over with.

"Yes. I can see you then," she grumbled.

"You don't need to sound so thrilled about it."

Reggie ignored her irritation. Anger would get her exactly nowhere with Tom. He dealt with high emotions every day in the kitchen. A master. "Will you have enough time between flights to go in and out of security?" she asked politely.

"I'll take a later flight if I have to."

Oh, joy. "All right. Any idea what time?"

"Around noon as things stand now."

"I'll meet you at the airport. McDonalds. It's on the lower level."

There was a moment of silence, then Tom said, "McDonalds it is."

REGGIE TOLD EDEN AND JUSTIN about her imminent meeting with Tom the next morning in the kitchen as they drank the lattes Justin had bought.

"Maybe I should go with you," Eden suggested.

Reggie appreciated what her sister was trying to do, but she'd gotten herself into the situation and she'd take care of it on her own.

"No need," she said. "We're going to start a dialogue. Nothing more." Because she wasn't ready for anything more. Just a civil meeting with the father of her child. In a public place.

Damn, but she was nervous.

Justin said nothing as he drank his coffee. Which wasn't like him. And he wasn't meeting Reggie's eyes, which in the old days meant he either had or was planning to pull a fast one. Nowadays it meant he had something to say and was biding his time.

Reggie finished her drink and tossed the paper cup into the trash. "Are you meeting with the birthday people this morning?" she asked Eden.

"They're coming here to sign the contract and finalize the menu. Which means I'd better get it printed out."

She headed to the office and Reggie turned

to face her brother. "What?" she said softly, perplexed by his attitude.

"I'm concerned," he said flatly. "About you. And the kid." He crumpled his cup in one hand. "You've spent so much of your life raising us, and now you're going to be raising a kid you didn't expect to have. Probably without a father around."

Without a father around.

They'd basically grown up without one around and it had left a mark. Especially on Justin, who'd idolized their dad until he'd let him down one time too many. Hero worship had turned to bitterness.

And now Reggie was about to reenact the crime.

She wanted to say, "The kid will have a great uncle, though," but she didn't wish to put that burden on Justin.

"We'll do all right," she stated.

He had more to say. She could see it, but he was holding back. "If you change your mind about having one of us come with you, pick me. Okay?"

Reggie reached up and patted her brother's cheek, then smiled. "First on the list."

REGGIE ARRIVED AT THE AIRPORT McDonalds early because she wanted to make sure the smell of food wasn't going to trigger any bouts of nausea. So far, so good.

She chose a table close to the edge of the seating area, where she could watch the escalator, see Tom before he saw her.

She didn't have long to wait. Less than fifteen minutes after she sat down, he came down the escalator. Tall, dark, striking. Two women traveling up on the opposite side gave him second glances, but he had zeroed in on her.

Reggie swallowed.

This is Tom. Just...Tom.

But they had so much to hash out, and were undoubtedly coming at it from two different angles. Tom was probably wondering what this would do to his career, and Reggie was wondering what his career would do to the kid.

"No bag?" Reggie said before he could speak. She wanted to take control. Now. Always.

Good luck to her.

"I checked it."

"So if you take a later flight—"

"It'll be waiting for me. Do you want something?" he asked, gesturing at the counter.

"I already had orange juice."

"Been here long?" he asked, looking at the table, empty except for her napkin. The napkin was to give her something to do with her hands.

"Not really."

Tom sat opposite her and for a moment they regarded each other coolly. Warily.

"How are you feeling?" he asked.

Distraught. Confused. Nervous.

"A little sick in the morning, but not as bad as last week." There was no way she was going to pour her soul out to him, count on him to make things better, help her through this.

"Me, too," Tom said. Reggie smiled. Or tried to. "We have some stuff to work out," he added softly. But Reggie heard that underlying steel she remembered so well.

"Yes."

"I have no idea where or how to begin."

Reggie reached for the napkin. "You don't have to do anything."

"I remember that part from our phone conversation."

She didn't answer immediately, not wanting to make any more errors at this point in the game. "What exactly do you see as your role here?"

"Father?"

Reggie briefly twisted the napkin between her fingers, then realized what she was doing and made herself stop. "How much contact do you want with the baby?"

"Jumping right into it, aren't you?"

"Isn't that why you're here?"

Tom put both his palms on the table in front of him and Reggie focused on his long, strong fingers, with the small nicks and scars from past culinary adventures. He had wonderful hands. There was a lot about him she'd found wonderful...and yet something had prevented him from fully giving himself to her. And that had made it possible for him to walk away from her—from their plans—pretty much devastating her.

"I'm here as a first step only."

"Agreed," Reggie said. "We can't arrange custody until the baby is born, but I'd like to understand our roles beforehand."

Tom nodded, lightly moving the tips of his fingers over the tabletop.

"Do you want custody?"

He looked up at her point-blank question, his dark eyes unreadable. "That's what I'm here to figure out."

"If you have any doubts about it...err on the side of caution," Reggie said.

He cocked his head, his eyebrows moving together. "Meaning?"

"A kid needs a steady father, Tom. I know that because I didn't have a steady father."

"What makes you think I wouldn't be steady?"

Reggie gave a short laugh, crumpling the napkin. "What makes me think you *would* be?" She hadn't meant to be cruel, but it was oh so true. He had no record of steadiness, and she *was* justified in pointing that out.

His expression darkened, the first sign that his temper was taking over. Reggie had never been intimidated by his moods, and when they had argued in the past, she'd merely stuck to her guns and eventually the storm would peter out. But sticking to her guns took time, and today she didn't have time.

"I'm sorry, Tom. That was uncalled for."

"But somehow it seemed to come from the gut," he said.

Reggie leaned back in her chair and studied his face. With the exception of the longer hair and the beard, which was little more than a neatly trimmed five o'clock shadow, he looked almost the same as he had seven years ago. But he wasn't. Her Tom was there—she'd seen glimpses of him the night they'd slept together—but he was buried under a heavy layer of Chef Tom Gerard. The dog-eat-dog world he had embraced had changed him.

But why had he chosen it over her? Why couldn't he have stayed with her?

"Maybe it did," she allowed. She put a hand against her flat abdomen. "I'm concerned about the baby."

"And I'm your biggest concern."

"In a way, yes."

"Why? This has got to be as life altering for you as it is for me."

She had a feeling he knew exactly what she was going to say. That he wanted her to say it so he could contradict it. Fine.

She leaned forward again. "I'll spell it out, Tom. Once upon a time I loved you. We were supposed to start a catering business. Papers were signed. We had a plan."

His eyes flashed with sudden temper. "It wasn't carved in stone."

"Obviously," Reggie replied, unfazed. "Since you took off for the north of Spain for a job that had no future."

"It made one hell of a future for me."

"Yes, it did," she conceded. He'd taken a gamble and it had paid off. And, since he had such a valid point, she took the low road. "But which of us is still employed?"

"I will be employed," he said coldly. "I don't think Letterbridge is flying me across the country on a whim."

"Okay…and forgive me for being blunt," Reggie said, tossing the crumpled napkin past him into the trash, "which one of us will stay employed?"

He smiled. "Which one of us has had the more successful career?" he asked with exaggerated politeness.

"I rather like mine. At least I know I'll be bringing home a paycheck. It may not be as big as yours, but it's steady."

Tom hooked an elbow over his chair back. "You're *still* angry about me leaving," he said as if making a major deduction.

Brilliant, Tom. "Believe it or not, it stung when you chose a shot in the dark over me and a fairly sure thing."

"You could have come with me. Instead you gave me that fricking ultimatum."

"Which you took."

"It didn't have to be all or nothing. We could have worked something out."

"Look who's talking, Mr. Compromise. I don't think so. It's all or nothing for you. If everything isn't just so in your kitchen, you throw a fit. And now you've gone public with those fits."

"I don't throw fits!" Tom's voice rose and then he clamped his mouth shut as several people at nearby tables looked his way.

"Tizzies?" Reggie asked innocently, not above driving a point home.

His neck corded as he fought to bring his temper under control. Finally he said in a low voice, "My *tizzies* aside, here's what it comes down to." He stabbed the table with his finger. "You could have come with me to Spain. The catering business had barely started. You wouldn't because I had deviated from The Plan."

"I didn't come because you didn't ask me."

"Yes, I did."

Reggie jutted her chin out. "No, you didn't."

Sweat broke out on her forehead, always a precursor to a surge of nausea, but she was *not* going to give in to it. Not in front of Tom.

Unfortunately, as totally pissed as he was, he noticed. "Are you all right?"

"Just a little queasy."

"Are you taking care of yourself?" he demanded.

"Yes." She got to her feet, gathered her purse, holding the oversize bag in front of her stomach like a shield. "I want to come to an understanding about the baby, Tom, but obviously this is not the time or place."

"I agree," he said with an obvious effort to control himself. "It seems as though we have some other issues to sift through first."

Issues Reggie hadn't expected to come screaming out of her so rapidly. But she should have known better.

She just hoped he hadn't gotten his back up. The old Tom would have cooled off fast, seen the argument for what it was—a release of pent-up frustrations and unresolved anger. This new Tom...she wasn't so sure what he was going to do.

"Yes. Maybe we can meet again—" she glanced around "—in a different environment."

He gave her a you-picked-it-I-didn't raise of an eyebrow, but simply nodded.

"Good luck on the interview."

He stood. "I don't need luck. I'm getting this job, and when I do, we'll discuss our baby."

"Call me when you get that job, Tom." Reggie started across the lobby without a backward glance, thankful that the nausea was rapidly abating so she wouldn't embarrass herself in the terminal.

She didn't realize how rigidly she'd been holding herself until she reached the automatic doors. Her shoulders were aching. She rolled them as she started across the street for the parking garage, willing her muscles to relax.

Not the meeting she'd imagined.

She hoped she could repair the damage before it was too late.

THE AUTOMATIC DOORS CLOSED behind Reggie before Tom started back to the escalator. So much for catching a later flight. Going after Reggie would do no good. He'd have to nail this job and show her that, regardless of what he might have done seven years ago, he was more than capable of being "steady." He had no idea exactly what his role would be, but his father had always been there for him, even if it had been on the other end of a phone line, and Tom would be there for his kid.

And suddenly it was important to him to prove that he wasn't some maniac who threw fits in public—although every time he'd had a blowup, he'd been more than justified.

He got back into the security line, which was ridiculously short compared to the one in LaGuardia on the first leg of his flight. He pulled his crumpled boarding pass for the next leg out of his jacket pocket.

And what the hell was that about not asking her to go to Spain? Of course he'd wanted her to go. But she'd stuck with The Plan.

At the time he'd been stunned by her choice....

In a matter of fifteen minutes he and his belongings had been inspected, prodded and okayed, and Tom was seated alone in the one bar in the concourse, going over his interview notes. This deal with Reggie, the depth of her anger at him, was upsetting, but he would figure out how to handle it after he got this job. One challenge at a time. Surmount one, move on to the next.

Despite all the shit that had come his way, he'd never interviewed for a job and not gotten an offer. The only thing that had tripped him up over the past several weeks had been in not landing the interview. Well, he had one now and he was going to ace this sucker.

He was back.

CHAPTER FOUR

REGGIE HAD BEEN HOME BARELY AN hour when Eden showed up at the door. She knocked, then let herself in, carrying a bottle of sparkling apple cider by the neck.

"I thought you might need a belt after meeting Tom," she said, lifting the cider. Reggie tried to smile. Couldn't do it. "Bad?" Eden asked.

"I said some things I probably shouldn't have." Definitely shouldn't have.

"He's being unreasonable?"

"That's the problem...I think he was trying to be reasonable. Reasonable for Chef Gerard, that is." She took the bottle and headed into the kitchen, Eden and Mims following. Her sister went to the cupboard and pulled out two glasses, while Reggie opened. She poured two healthy amounts of cider, then looked down at her stomach with a wry twist of her lips. "Somehow I don't think sparkling cider is going to take the edge off." She raised her eyes. "I don't think anything is going to take the edge off. Tom and I trigger each other."

"That's to be expected," Eden said, sitting at the table. "You guys have got a ton of unfinished business to work through."

"I think that we both need more time. This meeting...not a good idea."

"How much time?"

Reggie shrugged. "I don't know. A decade, maybe?"

Eden smiled and raised her glass in a salute, then changed the subject. "What's with Justin?"

"In what way?"

"He's been really quiet. You haven't noticed?"

"I've been kind of preoccupied," Reggie said with a significant lift of her eyebrows.

"Yeah. So's he."

"Do you think it's...me?" She frowned as Mims got up on the chair next to Eden and put a tentative paw on the table. Her cat was pushing the limits, perhaps as a reaction to Reggie's constant tension.

Eden gently moved the chair back while Mims hung on, her eyes going a little wild on the short ride. "Maybe. Or woman trouble."

"He's a big boy, Eden. We need to let him face the world on his own."

She laughed. "I asked him if he was dating and all I got was a sour look."

"Woman trouble," Reggie said. She hoped so, anyway. Justin saw himself as the man of the family—still—and she didn't want him losing sleep over her.

"And speaking of woman trouble," Eden said, "I ran into Candy." The owner of Candy's Catering Classique, who had hired Justin and Eden in high school and had never forgiven them for starting a competing business.

"She was sweet as always, while shooting daggers at me. She wished us luck in the Reno Cuisine. She even added a 'bless our hearts for trying.'"

Kiss of death coming from Candy, who always took one of the top honors at the event.

"And Julie is working for her now." Their prep cook who had quit so suddenly.

Reggie paused, her glass halfway to her lips. "Figures. Welcome to the cutthroat world of catering."

"Well, she'd better keep her hands off Patty." Eden's jaw set. "I know we won't win, because Candy will have a booth that would put a Hollywood set to shame—"

Mims took a flying leap at the table from her chair just then, didn't quite make it and would have hit the floor if Eden hadn't caught her. "Have you been ignoring your kitty?" she asked as she set her on the floor. Mims instantly started a bath.

"Not on purpose." Reggie went to pick up the cat, but Mims walked away, tail held high, before Reggie could scoop her up. Maybe she *had* been ignoring the cat.

"Anyway..." Eden reached for the cider and topped up her glass "...I thought I could take the helm of the Reno Cuisine, since both you and Justin are so busy."

"Please," Reggie replied. They had just booked a big wedding on short notice—three weeks—and that would consume most of Reggie's time, particularly since they already had a business dinner booked that same week. "Take the helm, take the entire ship, because right now I have to make amends with my cat and battle plans for a big-ass wedding reception."

HUMILIATION SUCKED.

Numbly, Tom took his seat on the flight back to Reno. Not only had he not gotten a job, he hadn't even gotten to interview or cook. In fact, he was going back to New York sooner than he'd expected. Days sooner.

He didn't know if Jervase had gotten hold of these guys or what, but after a very short, very terse and uncomfortable meeting with three members of the Letterbridge cuisine vision team, one of them had taken him aside and explained that rather than put him through an interview for a job he had no chance of getting, they were simply going to come clean. Inviting him had been a mistake. Literally a mistake. The associate in charge of contacting the top candidates had pulled his file in error. Tom had no chance of working for Letterbridge.

"None?" he had asked, flabbergasted. Two years ago they'd offered him a damned handsome deal.

"None," the guy had said flatly.

Tom felt as if he'd just swallowed a chunk of cement. How in the hell had he gotten to the point where he was disappointed—no, make that devastated—at not being a candidate for a freaking corporate kitchen job?

The man babbled about public opinion and image, and how all members of the kitchen staff and management had to be *team* players, because Letterbridge was a *team,* from the top on down. Then he looked at Tom and said, "You have to see how we cannot possibly have someone like you on our team."

And that was when Tom, despite his vow in the Reno airport not to indulge in public fits of temper, told the HR guy exactly what he could do with his team and how.

Shortly before security showed up, Tom left the building of his own volition.

He was screwed. Royally. Just as Lowell had said.

Worse yet, he was beginning to suspect that part of it was his own fault.

So what now?

Letterbridge had arranged for an earlier flight back to New York, but he'd booked his own on their dime. He wanted to stop in Reno again. Had to stop in Reno, since he had no idea when he'd get another chance to meet with Reggie face-to-face.

What was he going to tell her after his assurances that the job was all but his?

As he stared morosely out the window, waiting for takeoff, he became aware of the woman across the aisle staring at him. He glanced at her, she looked down, then when he shifted his attention back to the window, she started studying him again.

"I'm not him," Tom said.

"Not who?" the woman asked, perplexed.

"Whoever you think I am."

"Right now I don't think you're anyone," she said curtly.

"Sing it, sister," he muttered, looking back out at the tarmac.

Right now, he *wasn't* anyone. And being someone—in the cooking world, that is—had become a huge part of his identity.

Shit. He let the side of his head rest against the cool glass of the window, closing his eyes. There was a commotion across the aisle and he glanced over to see that the woman who'd recognized him had scooted over to the window seat to let a woman with a baby sit on the aisle. A baby.

Tom leaned his head back and rolled his eyes heavenward.

I get it. I'm going to be a dad. I have a responsibility here. I don't need it hammered home.

His not so prayerlike prayer didn't make him feel any less tense. He watched out of the corner of his eye as the mother settled the child on her lap. What was it? A boy? A girl? Whatever, it was totally bald. The baby looked around, wide-eyed, trying to make sense of his surroundings. Then his mouth opened and he let out a howl. Every muscle in Tom's body tensed.

The mom pulled her child closer, but he pushed away with his chubby fists, turned his mouth upside down and wailed again.

"I know, I know. It's all right," she murmured, jiggling him on her knees, rubbing his little shoulders and neck. The kid howled some more. Tom turned to the window.

How on earth was the mother dealing with this?

The hiccuping sobs continued, and when Tom looked back—because he couldn't help it—the kid's gaze fastened on to his. One fist clutched his mother's collar and she continued to soothe the baby until finally he slumped against her, pulling in shaky little breaths. But his eyes stayed on Tom until they finally drifted shut.

Asleep.

He'd fallen asleep. Just like that.

The mother smiled at Tom and he made an effort to smile back. Then she took advantage of the moment to shut her eyes, too. But her arms stayed wrapped tightly around her young son, until the attendant arrived with a travel seat and the kid woke up again. Wonderful.

This time he didn't cry. He watched in fascination as the attendant put the seat in place. As soon as she was done, a person sat in the aisle seat next to Tom, blocking his view.

The plane started to back away from the terminal, then slowed to a halt with a slight jerk. A moment later, the captain's voice came over the intercom.

"Ladies and gentlemen, there'll be a slight delay before takeoff. Shouldn't be more than a few minutes."

Tom wasn't a huge believer in signs—well, other than the baby, perhaps—but he did believe in opportunity. He pulled his cell phone out of his pocket and turned it on, shielding it with his hand in case the attendant went militant. He needed to make this call now. Because he didn't know what else to do, and he suddenly felt as if he was running out of time.

He had seven months, which wasn't very long at all. He didn't want to be an unemployed bum of a chef when his child was born.

By some miracle Pete answered his call.

"Pete...I need advice."

"No."

"Can you at least give me the name of a decent manager?"

"No, because you'll tell him I sent you."

"I won't." There wasn't a hint of irony or amusement in his voice. "I, uh, need some advice here."

"You're a talented guy, but that talent's a waste if your opinion of yourself is so high that you don't think anyone else knows jack."

Tom almost said, "They don't," but managed to hold in the words. Progress. He was making progress.

"You cut your own throat, Tom. No one did it for you."

"I know. I know." He didn't want to hear about cutting his throat. He wanted to hear about saving his ass. "What can I do to *uncut* my throat?" That didn't involve a lot of public kissing up.

"Nothing. And I mean that literally."

"Nothing."

Pete exhaled wearily. "If you can stay out of the limelight for, say, a year without blowing up or quitting or criticizing your bosses in public, then maybe I can do something for you."

Tom tapped the tips of his fingers on his thigh impatiently. Pete was missing a fairly big point here. The job, or lack thereof, was the problem. Unless...

"What am I supposed to do? Wear a paper hat?" And he wasn't talking a chef's toque.

"It might do you some good."

The flight attendant walked up the aisle, and Tom turned in his seat, shielding the phone from her. "It would kill my career if I settled for some mediocre job now." In his gut he knew this was true, and Pete had to know it, too. Maybe he'd given Pete so much grief that he wanted him to die a culinary death. Disappear from the radar.

"Well, you might have to settle. Your only other option would be to find the backers to open your own restaurant, and with this economy, and your track record, I don't see that happening."

Neither did Tom. "That's it?"

"You asked for my advice. I gave it. Work for a year without raising hell, and people might be ready to take a look at you again."

"What kind of work, Pete?" Tom muttered in frustration.

"Hell, it could be a school cafeteria. You simply have to behave and make good food. One of those won't be a problem."

Tom shoved a hand into his hair. There

were many other business managers out there. Ones he hadn't yet contacted.

"Six months," Pete said.

"Six months?" Tom repeated as the plane lurched forward and the captain's voice came over the intercom, announcing that they'd been cleared for takeoff. He covered the phone with his free hand.

He sighed. "It's like chef rehab. Work sedately for six months, prove that you can do it, and I'll see what I can do. Screw up and you can find yourself a new manager. Although right now, Tom…I don't know of a reputable guy in the industry who'd take you on."

SIXTEEN GUESTS SHOWED UP FOR A sit-down meal booked for twelve. Tracy Bremerton, the hostess, dressed about a decade too young for her age, didn't understand why this was a problem, apparently expecting Eden and Reggie to manufacture food out of thin air. Which they did, of course. Reggie cut the rolls in half; Eden raced to the store to buy ingredients to stretch the salad. Patty, who was there to watch two of Tremont's regular temp waiters serve, and learn the ropes so she could fill in if someone didn't show, ended up taking Eden's place in the kitchen while she was gone.

Thankfully, they had plenty of soup, and the entrée was a pasta dish, so it was easy to stretch. Dessert was not so easy to stretch. Reggie was not at all happy with the size of the tiramisu servings, and neither was the hostess, from the expression on her face.

When dinner was over and the van was packed, Mrs. Bremerton stepped into the kitchen and gave it a critical once-over. It was spotless, because Reggie and Eden never left a place in any other condition.

"Are the leftovers in the refrigerator?" she asked.

"There are no leftovers," Reggie said, wondering how the woman could possibly expect any under the circumstances. Even if there'd been extra food, the contract clearly stated that Tremont did not leave leftovers. They'd had a bad experience early on with a host not storing the food properly, and then getting sick days later—and threatening to sue. It'd taken months to move past the rumors he'd started. After that they'd rewritten their contract.

"There was extra pasta and bread. I saw it." Not much. Reggie was about to explain about the leftover policy when Mrs. Bremerton added, "I was a bit embarrassed at the size of the desserts you served."

"It couldn't be helped," Reggie said as tactfully as possible. Finesse was part of the game. But this was the time to be blunt. "I had a final count of twelve. We served sixteen." *And worked our butts off to do that.*

"I called as soon as I found out my friend and her family would be able to make the dinner, after all," the hostess said, taking hold of her long string of definitely not fake pearls and running them through her fingers.

"The call came a little late." As in while they were driving to the Bremerton house high on the hill overlooking Reno.

"It seems to me that caterers should be prepared for this type of emergency."

"Yes—as long as you don't mind paying for the extra food."

"Which you refuse to leave. Very unreasonable."

"I'm sorry you feel that way. Perhaps we can get together and discuss ways to avoid this in the future?"

Mrs. Bremerton sniffed. "I don't foresee a future."

"Well, good night, then."

Reggie made one final visual sweep of the spotless kitchen, nodded at the hostess, then left through the back door, a smile frozen on her face until the door closed behind her.

"Not a happy hostess," Reggie said as she got into the van, where Eden and Patty were waiting for her.

"I don't see why not," Patty said stiffly. "It was a lovely dinner."

"Because we couldn't read her mind and guess that she had extra people coming." Eden put the van in gear. "I'll do some damage control tomorrow."

"Good luck with that." Reggie leaned her head against the window.

She was so very tired. More tired than a catering event and disagreement with a host should have made her.

Pregnancy, coupled with the unfinished business with her baby's father, was wiping her out.

Reggie hoped Tom got this job so their personal negotiations could begin.

IT WAS RAINING. OF COURSE. HE comes to Nevada, one of the driest states in the union, and it rains on him. And not just a little. It rolled down his cheeks, into the corners of his mouth, collected on his lashes and got into his eyes when he blinked.

And Reggie wasn't answering her door. Finally, he heard a shuffling noise and then the peephole went dark. The door swung open.

"How did you find me?" she demanded.

"Could you please change that to 'Come on in. It's wet out there?'" And it had been easy to find her, thanks to the internet.

Reggie looked past him at the cab idling on the wet street, then stepped back so he could come inside. "Why are you here?"

She wasn't any more welcoming now that he was under her roof, but he was going to be a damned sight warmer.

"Did you get the job?" she added with a frown, since they'd met less than two days ago.

"Do you mind if I take my coat off?" he asked, buying time.

Reggie gave him a pained look, but nodded. He couldn't help but glance at her abdomen under the form-fitting T-shirt she wore. There was no sign of pregnancy.

"I've gained four pounds," she said, interpreting the look. "But I probably won't start showing until next month. Why are you here?"

"We did well together once." Reggie stiffened at his opening words, delivered as if they were part of a memorized speech. That's what he got for not practicing.

She casually folded her arms, shutting him out. "Agreed. Then one of us changed."

"I want another chance."

Reggie took a half step back, bringing her hand up to the base of her neck in a way that totally pissed him off. "With me?"

"Don't look so horrified." *Plan B, Plan B.* "I didn't get the job in Seattle."

"I'm sorry," she said without too much surprise, which kind of stung.

This was the tricky part, the part where he was feeling his way along, since he wasn't used to making requests so much as giving orders.

"I need to disappear for a while. I'll go insane if I kick around my apartment. I can't see taking some lower-level job." He'd probably blow up and destroy what he was working for—an uneventful six-month stretch of employment. "You and I have to develop a relationship to plot a future for the baby."

If anything Reggie looked even more horrified as he laid the groundwork for his proposal. He surged on anyway. "Could I work in your kitchen?"

Reggie's mouth fell open. He didn't know what she'd been expecting, but it obviously hadn't been a request for employment.

"You're delusional."

Tom shoved his hands into his back pockets and forced himself to wait until Reggie processed, thankful that she was a quick study, since his patience level was never very high. Her expression slowly shifted from horror to caution.

"Forgive me," she said, "but this is not normal. Guys like you do not go to work in a catering kitchen." She leaned forward and took a small sniff.

"No, I haven't been imbibing or smoking or anything else," he said impatiently. "It's like this. If I maintain an even keel for six months, prove I can control myself, my business manager *might* take me back and help me rebuild my career. It's like chef rehab," he said, echoing Pete's assessment of the situation.

"Who is this pod person in front of me?" Reggie asked. "I can't believe you're kowtowing to…"

"Pete Chavez."

"Oh." She pressed her lips together. "Gotcha."

Pete was the best in the business, and even Reggie knew it. She shook her head. "What happened to you, Tom?"

It sounded like a question she'd been aching to ask for a long time, and he didn't like the way she was looking at him, as if she felt sorry for him. "I don't know what happened to me!" he snapped, and then he paused and took a deep breath. "Sorry." It was as if everything had caught up to him at once. He really hadn't changed. The way people reacted to him had.

He pushed his hands even deeper into his pockets, gritted his teeth, then came clean. "I have another reason for being here." He indicated her belly with a movement of his chin, and Reggie automatically covered it with her hand. Shutting him out again.

"The baby?" Now she looked defensive.

"I…" Tom closed his mouth, then started again. "We've got to work something out."

Reggie was trying to hide it—trying to look nonchalant, as if they were discussing the most mundane of topics. She swallowed. "Yes," she allowed.

"I don't know much about kids."

"They need stability."

"I think we've been over that," he said

evenly, fighting the instant flare of anger. Who said he couldn't control himself? "I don't know what my role will be...how we'll handle being parents...but this isn't something we can put off. Obviously."

Reggie eyed him for a long silent moment. Her mouth tightened for a second before she again said, "Yes."

A meeting of the minds. That was a start.

"We can work all this out with lawyers, but that's probably not going to be best for the kid," he said. She didn't answer. "I think Pete is right. I need a few months off to rethink some things. I may as well spend it here. In Reno. By the time I get a job, maybe we'll have hammered out some kind of a truce that works for all of us."

Reggie reached down to scoop up that chubby, yellow-eyed cat that was rubbing its head on her ankles, and held it against her chest, stroking its ears. "That makes sense... I guess."

She didn't trust him. Although he wasn't sure why. He'd been thinking about that a lot lately, since he'd never been anything but truthful to her.

Now the next step—to get back into a kitchen. In a way that could help both of them out, but keep him out of the public eye while he reassessed.

"We're both cooks, Reg. The kitchen is where we met, and it's where we can…I don't know…get used to each other again. Figure out some stuff about the baby. Develop a working relationship."

She set the cat down and took a step closer. But not too close. "Only one problem there, Tom. You run kitchens. But this is *my* kitchen."

"I understand."

"Do you? If I wanted things done a certain way, and you didn't agree, would you do them my way?"

"I understand the hierarchy, Reg. Your kitchen, your way."

She put a hand to her forehead as if fighting a headache. "I've got to think about this, Tom. Talk to Eden and Justin."

"I've got to catch a flight back to New York tomorrow morning. Early."

"I'll call you in New York." She shifted her weight, crossed her arms, defensive in a different, more militant way now. "Is your cab still waiting?"

Even though he wanted to press his case, he kept his mouth shut. Instinct told him that more was not better in this case. "Yes," he said simply.

"Great." She walked to the door and put her hand on the knob. "I'll give you a call in a day or two."

CHAPTER FIVE

"You want to hire Tom." Justin leaned against the stainless steel counter and folded his arms over his chest. Not the receptive body language Reggie had hoped for when she'd asked for a council in the pastry room, out of Patty's hearing.

"Damn. Reggie." Eden stared at her as if she'd gone bonkers.

Maybe she had.

"We have to hammer out some kind of working relationship, before the baby is born. This is a way to do it."

"But why does it have to be in our kitchen?" Justin unfolded his arms, picked up the spatula on the counter beside him and began to tap it rhythmically against his palm. "I mean, I'm all for you and Tom working things out. In fact, I'm highly in favor, but—"

Eden reached out to snatch the utensil away from her brother, stopping the incessant tapping. "It'd be on Reggie's home turf," she said. "We're here for backup." But Eden didn't sound all that convinced, either.

"What if it affects the business?" Justin asked, taking the spatula back. "The two of you hammering?"

Reggie forced herself to relax her fingers, release the death grip she had on the counter on either side of her hips. "The second the business is affected, he's out." She couldn't afford to let business be hurt in any way. Not when Tremont Catering had to provide for both her and her child.

"So he'll probably be here for what? One day? Maybe two?" Justin muttered, tapping his palm again. Eden sent him a warning glare and he tossed the spatula into the sink.

"What will he do?" Eden asked. "I mean, a chef of his caliber—"

"Prep work."

Justin's eyebrows rose. "Does he know that?"

"I told him."

"But does he believe you?" her brother asked reasonably.

"If he doesn't now, he soon will."

"And this won't affect business," he said. "Somehow I don't see Tom happily doing prep work. I do see disaster, though."

Reggie shrugged. "There may be a few blips the first day or two, but after that, either he'll leave or we'll settle in."

Justin glanced up at the clock. He was on a close deadline, as always. "If there's trouble, I'm bouncing his ass outta here and you guys will have to work this out in another venue. Like I said, I want you to come to an agreement, but…"

This has failure written all over it. He didn't need to say it out loud.

"Eden?" Reggie asked.

"I'm okay with it."

"I can't believe I'm saying this," Reggie said, not certain she even meant it, "but… thanks."

IT HAD TAKEN TOM TWO WEEKS TO tie up loose ends, sublet his apartment to a friend of a friend and fly back to Reno, during which time he kept hoping for that magical phone call from Pete telling him a great job offer had come in and all was forgiven. No need for penance.

Didn't happen.

Even if it had, he still had a situation with Reggie, but he couldn't help feeling he'd be in a better position to deal with it if he was employed instead of floundering. Floundering was not his normal state of being and he hated it. A lot.

There was one car in the parking lot when Tom arrived at the Tremont Catering kitchen the morning after flying in, and although the interior lights were off, the front door was unlocked. He let himself in.

Reggie had said to show up at eight-thirty, but, still being on eastern standard time, and eaten alive by nerves, he'd been up early and couldn't see hanging around the hotel for hours. He wanted to check out the Tremont kitchen, see where he'd be working.

The instant he stepped into the front reception area, with its cool green walls, bright artwork and granite counter, his stomach knotted. An alien cooking environment for sure. No front of house. No brigade.

He hadn't let himself dwell over the past two weeks on what he was getting himself into, because if he had, he would have spent most of his waking hours raging at the fates. And lately anger didn't feel cathartic. Instead it made him feel as if he was wasting one hell of a lot of energy and accomplishing nothing. Probably because he was.

He was going to be a dad and didn't know the first thing about fatherhood.

All he could do at this point was focus on the game. On what he was good at—cooking. Running a kitchen.

Behind the reception counter was a metal door, propped open with a rubber wedge. Tom walked around the counter and stepped through.

"Hello?"

The kitchen was larger than he'd expected—larger than many he'd worked in—and well designed, with lots of counter space, a walk-in, decent stoves, double convection ovens. In fact, it was almost exactly the kitchen Tom and Reggie had designed together when they'd talked about opening a catering business. Reggie had stuck to the plan.

As she stuck to all plans.

She'd always intended to bring Eden into the business once her sister graduated culinary school, but Justin had been a wild ski bum, freshly dropped out of college. How had he gone from Reggie bailing him out of jail to being a chef? And a pastry chef at that?

Tom didn't do pastry. The thought of concocting desserts in general made him uncomfortable. Give him his knives and a nice piece of meat to butcher. Or pasta. Anything but phyllo dough.

"Hello," he called again, setting his knife case on the nearest counter.

A door opened on the opposite side of the room and a roundish woman with a head of grayish-brown curls came out. She stood taller when she saw him, which brought her height up to about five foot even. Maybe five-one.

"May I help you?" she asked, smoothing the sides of her apron over her sturdy hips.

"Is Reggie here?"

"No, she's not." The woman's gaze traveled over his loose, dark gray cargos and white T-shirt, then settled on the small gym bag he carried. Her eyebrows went up. "Do you have an appointment?"

"I think I'm supposed to start work today. I'm Tom."

"I wasn't informed." She didn't seem to recognize him, which was good. His only concern in this deal was having to explain why he was in a catering kitchen. *I need to build a relationship with my pregnant ex, who wants to see me in hell* would be tabloid fodder for sure. He'd do his best to avoid making that quote.

"Perhaps there was no reason to inform you," he suggested.

The woman's chin snapped up. "Reggie and Eden should be here shortly. Perhaps you'd like to go back out front and wait there. *If* you're starting work today, then you probably have papers to fill out."

"I don't need to fill out papers." Tom opened his knife case.

"W-2 forms are required."

"Perhaps I'm in the country illegally." He heard her rapid intake of breath. A bona fide sniff of indignation.

The back door of the kitchen, hidden behind a half wall, opened and closed. A few seconds later Justin came in, yawning. He stopped when he saw Tom.

"This…man says he starts work today," Patty announced.

"Yeah, I think he does." Justin started moving again. The kid had changed. For one thing, he was no longer a kid. The scrawny towhead was now as tall as Tom and only a few pounds lighter. "Tom." He held out his hand.

"Justin," he replied as they shook. He had the distinct feeling from the strength of Justin's grip that Reggie wasn't the only Tremont he'd be contending with. "I'm looking forward to helping you guys out."

Justin's blue eyes, which Tom remembered as being full of laughter, even when he was in hot water, were nothing short of cold.

"This is Patty, our prep cook," Justin said, nodding at the woman, who appeared to have just swallowed something sour, and was making a mental note to keep an eye on the good china.

"Patty," Tom said. She nodded curtly, and even though she'd been studying him, he still saw no sign of recognition.

"Reggie will be here in a few minutes. She had an early doctor's appointment today." Justin subtly motioned his head toward Patty, and Tom understood that the prep cook didn't know about the pregnancy.

"Great. Do you have a place where I can store my stuff?"

"Lockers in the back beside the door."

Tom picked up his bag and headed through the kitchen toward the door Justin had come in through. He nodded at Patty, who sniffed again and did an about-face. The territorial type. Well, she'd better get used to sharing her territory. As long as she did her job well, he didn't have a problem with jealousy. A normal thing in his world.

Tom found the lone empty locker in the row

of five, and stuffed his bag inside after pulling out an old chef's coat, which he shrugged into and buttoned as he walked back into the kitchen. Justin came out of a side room, where layers of a cake sat on a marble-topped table.

"Why don't you wait in the reception area for Reggie?" he suggested, disappearing inside again and closing the door.

Patty, who was clearly visible in the dry storage area, where she was counting supplies, smiled to herself.

Fine. He'd wait in the reception area. He couldn't really blame Justin for being cold. If the positions were reversed, if Justin had knocked up his sister, he'd probably feel the same.

He left his knives where they lay, went into the reception area and busied himself reading brochures and sample menus.

The menus weren't bad. In fact they were pretty good, but he could see where they could benefit from a few tweaks. A touch of Gerard.

He and Reggie were on an even footing... he'd talk to her about it.

"HE'S HERE," JUSTIN SAID AS soon as Reggie answered her phone, and he proceeded to fill her in. The traffic on 395 was practically at a standstill, so she could talk safely as she inched toward her exit.

"He's early?" Tom was never early. Damn. She'd hoped to get there first and establish ground. "I'm ten minutes away." If she was lucky. She could have walked from the doctor's office faster. Next time she was taking side streets. Today she'd wanted to get there fast, so she'd braved the freeway. Ha!

"I don't think Patty likes him."

"Did she recognize him?" Reggie asked.

"Doesn't appear so, but how she could miss, I don't know. It's like Tabloid Tom in the flesh. Black ponytail, Vandyke. The whole bit." Justin paused before adding, "This is not a humbled man, Reg."

Reggie could so picture him striding in— with his knives, no doubt—looking every inch the master chef. No sign of the damp, slightly desperate guy who'd stood in her living room less than a week ago.

"You know," Justin mused, "I'm thinking of copying that Vandyke. It seems to attract women. Except Patty, of course."

"Good plan, Justin. Why don't you go with that? I'm in traffic. I'll see you in a few."

She hung up and inched the car forward.

Twenty minutes later, Reggie pulled into the alley behind the kitchen and parked next to the Tremont van.

Anticipating this first meeting with Tom while stuck in traffic had not put her in the best of moods, but at least she wasn't nauseous. And her checkup had gone well, which had given her something else to think about while fighting Tom-induced nerves.

She'd heard the heartbeat. The wonderful whispering rhythm of her child's heart. The doctor hadn't expected to pick it up with the Doppler that early, but surprise, surprise—he had, and the child was no longer a shadowy figment in Reggie's mind. It had a heartbeat. She was going to be a mom, and now it was time to come to terms with the dad.

She entered the kitchen through the rear door, quickly scanned the room—no Tom— and then went into the office, hanging her purse on the hook next to her computer and booting up both her machine and Eden's. A second later she turned her sister's computer back off again. Eden had a full schedule out of the kitchen, which was why Justin was working in the morning.

Reggie tucked the medical receipt into a folder in the file cabinet, nearly slamming her fingers in the drawer as she shut it. Then she put on a clean apron, fumbling with the knot. She cursed under her breath.

Since Tom was not in the kitchen, Justin probably had him cooling his heels in the reception area. A good place for them to have a short but meaningful talk before work began. It would be a full day, and Reggie didn't want to waste time with misunderstandings. They were catering an anniversary party the next day and there was still a lot of prep, plus site decorating, which Eden would handle, while Reggie manned the kitchen. Justin would hopefully have the desserts made and in the cooler before he had to drive up to Lake Tahoe for his shift at the hotel.

"Good morning, Patty," Reggie said as the woman stepped out of dry storage, clipboard in hand. Patty liked to do inventory if she wasn't busy with other tasks—or if she came in early, as she always did. Reggie wasn't going to fight her.

"Good morning," she replied, her voice stiffer than usual. "I'll start on the cooler now." Her eyes cut to the door to the reception area and back again.

"You met Tom?"

"Briefly." Her mouth tightened, puckering her lips.

Tom...if you've already upset my prep cook, so help me... Reggie gave her a reassuring smile. "He'll be helping with prep during the next month or two, and it'll free us up to prepare for the Reno Cuisine."

"I see."

Reggie thought not. "As soon as you get done with the cooler, I want you to start a batch of tomato sauce." That should mollify her.

"I'm making the sauce?" Patty's face lit up, even though she tried to appear matter-of-fact.

"We'll work on it together." That evening's dinner was an Italian buffet, and Reggie had to make one more batch of sauce for the manicotti the host had asked for at the last minute. Sometimes she said no to such requests, but whenever possible she said yes. One of the beauties of running a small business was that she could be flexible and creative. If the host had heard great things about the manicotti and she had time to fix it, then she'd oblige.

She had time now because she had an extra pair of hands.

Patty disappeared into the cooler and

Reggie opened the door to the pastry room. "I'm here," she told Justin, who was draping fondant.

"Good luck," he murmured. "Give a yell if you need anything."

"Will do." But she wouldn't. She could handle Tom. She simply liked having Justin there for moral support.

She found Tom reading a menu. He raised his eyes and then held up the brochure. "I have some suggestions."

As Justin had said, this was not a humbled man. The damp, desperate guy was gone. In his place was Tom Gerard. Chef.

"I'm certain you do," Reggie said, wondering how Patty could have failed to recognize him. Maybe she was too short to see the tabloids at the grocery store checkout stand.

"And you don't want to hear them," he said with a half smile that cut through her nerves and reminded her how very much she'd once enjoyed being in his bed.

Reggie took the menu from him and put it back in the display. "We have an Italian buffet tonight and a wedding anniversary party tomorrow, and we both need to get to work. Back-to-back events are rugged."

"Then why book them that way?"

"Money."

Hard to argue with that, and Tom didn't try. "What do you want me to do?"

Reggie turned to face him, glad she was still in her heels so the height difference wasn't so great. "I want you to listen to me for a few minutes." He nodded. "When we agreed to try this you said you wanted to develop a working relationship. For the good of the baby."

"Yes."

"You agreed this was my kitchen."

"I remember," he said patiently.

"I hope so." She had no idea if these helpful reminders of who was in charge were sinking into Tom's head. They'd done well together in the past because she'd never let him push her around, but she'd always had the option of walking away without a backward glance. That option was now severely compromised. From this point on she was going to have to try to manage him.

"So what do you want me to do?" he asked in a polite and professional way as he folded his arms over his chest. She was close enough that she caught his scent, warm and masculine, triggering memories best forgotten.

She stood a little taller. This was something she had to deal with.

"Start chopping veg for eighty chicken potpies."

Tom smiled as if he was humoring her. "You're preparing an Italian meal, which I happen to be rather good at, and you want me to chop veg for potpies."

"Yes."

He nodded. "I understand." And no doubt he did. Reggie was putting him in his place.

She started to fold her own arms over her chest, caught herself and forced them back to her sides.

"And I want you to be nice to Patty. For *some* reason her back is up."

"No problem." This time there was a note of irony in his voice, but Reggie ignored it as she turned and led the way into the kitchen. She stopped next to the counter closest to the storage areas and pulled a list out of her apron pocket.

"Here you go. Veggies are in the cooler and dry storage. I'm sure you can find them as you familiarize yourself with the kitchen. This is your station." She indicated an area of the stainless steel counter with a sweep of her hand. "Let me know when you're done."

She hesitated, then repeated, "And be nice to Patty. I mean it."

"Yes, Chef."

Reggie left him standing next to the counter, and went into the office to change into her kitchen clogs. Patty stepped out of the cooler and handed her the completed inventory on her way by.

"My recommendations are on the bottom," she said.

"Thank you, Patty. Start chopping onions for the sauce. Three should do. It's a small batch." Reggie could have pulled out the frozen tomato sauce, but instinct told her to mollify the prep cook, let her take charge of a project—especially since Reggie wasn't certain how things were going to play out today with Tom.

"Certainly."

When she came back out of the office after taking a call from a prospective client, Tom glanced up, then focused on the veg.

Oh, yeah. This wasn't nerve racking or anything, having him here in the kitchen.

She made herself think of her baby's heartbeat. Of why she was doing this.

Tom was chopping as he'd been told to do, his hand moving so quickly it was a blur.

Reggie knew instinctively he wasn't showing off. He was making a point. Yes, he'd chop veg, but using him that way was a waste. He was probably thinking of how he could revolutionize her kitchen.

He'd lost that chance seven years ago.

Meanwhile Patty methodically chopped away at her onions, in slow motion compared to Tom, whom she was pointedly ignoring.

"Are these all right?" Tom asked when Reggie passed by on the way to her work area.

She inspected the identical cubes. "Perfect. When you get done, store them in the cooler and start deboning the roasted chickens." At this rate, they'd be ahead of the game. Eden could take all the time she needed for setup and for once not have to race back to attend to last-minute details. Having Tom here was going to play hell with Reggie's nerves, but it might not be bad for business.

Tom was in no position to complain, and it was killing him.

He was the one who'd asked for a chance to work in Reggie's kitchen, and she'd graciously complied. Or, rather, she'd seen the potential for a mutually beneficial arrangement. However, not in the way Tom had anticipated. He wanted to get his feet under him concerning fatherhood and his and Reggie's future parenting relationship, and he'd assumed that she'd actually make use of his cooking skills while they did that—skills that other people paid big money for. Or used to.

But no.

Instead she was making him pay for past crimes by asking him to cut up chickens and chop veg, while that dour little woman screwed up tomato sauce. It had been all he could do not to wrestle the knife from her hand and chop the onions and mince the garlic. And then when he'd told her not to add the garlic to the pan until the onions were translucent, she'd given that sniff and dumped the garlic in with the raw onion. The result?

Overcooked, bitter garlic, no doubt. That was always a lovely note to any dish.

Keep chopping.

His stomach was in a knot from trying to control himself.

He'd just finished with the chickens when Reggie started filling manicotti.

"You prep cook is screwing up your sauce," he said matter-of-factly. Patty's shoulders snapped back a fraction of an inch.

"Then I'll use frozen," Reggie said mildly.

Tom set down his knife. "*Frozen* sauce?"

She didn't even look at him as she stirred ricotta filling, which he wanted to taste before she used it. "Yes. You must realize that we can't cook everything from scratch in a catering business. I do as much as possible, but sometimes costs and circumstances are not conducive."

"Frozen?"

She bit the inside of her cheek as she slowly nodded, then met his gaze dead-on, her eyes narrowed dangerously. Tom remembered that expression so well. She used it when she wasn't going to back down.

When she delivered ultimatums that eventually tore them apart.

And that was when he realized he needed to back down. For now, anyway. He was not a patient man, not by any stretch of the imagination, but he did have goals, and one of them was to not get kicked out of this kitchen. Not until he and Reggie had an understanding that didn't threaten her and was acceptable to him.

"I, um, have the chicken deboned," he said, indicating the hotel pan next to him. Reggie's gaze shifted from him to the meat and back again.

"Then I'd appreciate a hand loading the

van. I have a master list. Make sure everything is there before you load."

And so it was that Tom Gerard, James Beard Upcoming Chef nominee, spent the afternoon counting linens and rental glasses, packing coolers, loading a van, while Reggie put together manicotti. Since Patty had scorched the tomato sauce while multitasking, Reggie was topping it with frozen sauce—her own frozen sauce. Apparently, during slow spells, she and Eden put up tomato sauce. It couldn't be as good as fresh, but it had to be better than storebought.

That, at least, made him feel better about her manicotti.

Patty apologized about a hundred times for the sauce not being up to par, and when Reggie told her not to worry, Tom wanted to mention that if she'd simply listened to him in the first place... But he didn't. He would play along.

At least until his head exploded.

CHAPTER SIX

TOM WAS AT TREMONT EARLY AGAIN the next day, prowling around the kitchen when Reggie arrived. She put him to work, and he complied without complaint, taking the prep list and propping it up at his station. All went well, right up until he made Patty cry.

Reggie was in the office, taking a call, when she heard the bathroom door next to the office slam shut, followed by the sound of muffled sobs. As soon as she hung up, Reggie headed out of the office and straight to Tom's station, where he was putting together the potpies, exactly the way she had asked. No twists, no flairs. Just standard Tremont chicken potpies. It had to be killing him.

Reggie pushed up her sleeves as she walked toward him. "What did you do to Patty?"

He glanced up after filling a shell, his expression innocent. Reggie wasn't fooled. "I made an observation."

"What observation did you make, Tom?"

"Look, all I said was that she needed to move faster."

"*How* did you say it? Were those your exact words?"

His dark expression was all the answer she needed.

"She is *not* one of your orangutan kitchen workers," Reggie said tautly. "She is not used to being yelled at or ordered about tactlessly, or...or..."

"I didn't mean to—"

"It doesn't matter what you meant. You did some damage to morale in my kitchen and now I have to fix it." She placed her palms on the counter, one on either side of a potpie, and leaned closer to him, so that they were practically nose to nose. "In six months time, you will be gone, if you haven't left sooner, and Patty, I hope, will still be here. If you make her cry one more time, then our deal is off."

"It's not my fault she's emotional. She wouldn't last a day in a professional kitchen."

"This *is* a professional kitchen and she's doing fine at the job I hired her to do."

"Yeah? Then what happened with the sauce yesterday?"

"Would you stop fixating on sauce?"

"I specialize in Italian food. Tomato sauce is important."

"I let her make it because you were working so fast I would have run out of things for her to do." Not the entire truth. She'd let Patty make it to mollify her. That had backfired.

"Then maybe *she* could have counted linens," Tom said through gritted teeth.

"Oh. You didn't like counting linens?"

"What do you think?"

"I think that for a guy who begged for a chance, you're pushing me." Reggie straightened up, shoving her sleeves even higher. Pretty soon they'd be over her elbows. "When Patty comes out of that bathroom, apologize."

"I—"

"I don't care if you were right or wrong or just trying to help. Apologize. And do *not* upset her again."

Tom's mouth had flattened into a very thin line. For a moment Reggie thought he was going to blow. Or walk out the door. He pulled in a sharp breath, then exhaled, the muscles in his jaw held so tightly that the cords in his neck popped.

"I'm not trying to screw things up, Reggie."

"Then leave Patty alone."

"Fine. But you shouldn't."

"What?"

"Leave her alone. She needs more training."

He was probably right. Patty was good at following orders and she was a quick study, but her kitchen experience wasn't as extensive as it could have been.

"I'll try to remember that," Reggie said stiffly. "Now if Patty ever comes out of the bathroom again—"

"I'll apologize." He pulled another pastry-lined ramekin toward him and started filling it. Reggie stared at the top of his dark head for a moment, realizing she'd been dismissed. Then she turned and went into Justin's pastry room.

Once her adrenaline approached normal levels and her hands stopped shaking, she would put together the puff pastry desserts Justin hadn't had time to finish before going on shift at the lake.

Having Tom around was exhausting.

WHEN PATTY FINALLY EMERGED from the bathroom, her face flushed, her nose red, she walked straight back to her station, ignoring Tom for all she was worth.

"I'm sorry," he called.

She didn't even look at him.

He shrugged and went back to work. A few minutes later, Reggie came out of the pastry room with a phone to her ear.

"Can you make a piecrust?" she asked Tom.

"I think I can handle it," he said drily.

"I need five ten-inch double crusts for apple pies. Pronto."

"Aye, aye, Chef," he said as she walked back to the office without looking at him.

Piecrusts. Right. That was a task he passed off to his sous-chef. He stood for a minute, debating which flour to use, pastry or cake, and which fat.

"Recipes are in the drawer to your right," Patty said frigidly. "The shortening is in the freezer."

That answered the question about butter versus shortening or lard. "Thanks," Tom replied, holding back the sarcasm so she wouldn't cry again. He ignored the drawer and went to the dry storage area for the flour and salt. When he came back out, carrying the containers, Patty gave her pan one final stir and turned off the burner. She was ultra careful about heat since scorching the tomato sauce on his first day.

After removing the pan from the burner,

she pulled a card out of her pocket and checked her next task. The card went back into the pocket and off she headed for the cooler, moving briskly, a woman with a mission.

He had to concede that she was a real workhorse, but she wouldn't have lasted two days in his kitchen. She was methodical but moved at a snail's pace. He liked to have people around that hopped to, moved when spoken to.

People who didn't cry when someone told them they were too slow to cut it in the real world. Honestly. It was just an observation, made when he'd been trying to show her how to cut an onion a little faster, so that maybe they could get that day's prep done before they both grew old. Instantly, her back had gone up. Tom was not used to people fighting him when he gave direction. They either did it or they left the kitchen.

But not here. This kitchen *was* like the school cafeteria that Pete had suggested he work in. And Patty was a lunch lady. There was a push to get the food done, but not like in a nightly service. There was no adrenaline rush. No edge. Tom lived for the edge.

If there wasn't one he created it.

One of his habits that hadn't worked out too well for him lately.

REGGIE PUT THE TRAY OF desserts in the cooler and came out with apples for the pie filling. If this hadn't been a last-minute deal, she would have had Patty peel and cut, but she needed to get this done for one of Justin's steady customers.

When Tom made the piecrusts, he attacked the matter with the single-minded focus with which he always approached cooking. And sex. The guy was a hedonist.

She was having a very hard time keeping her eyes off him.

Patty was sautéing onions, her back as straight as always, and every time she glanced over at Tom, it tightened even more. He didn't appear to know she existed.

This was the kind of single-minded concentration that had ended up driving them apart. He'd been hyperfocused on his career, and even though he'd played with the idea of the catering company, he ultimately hadn't been able to commit. To it or to her.

As she peeled and sliced, she kept glancing up to see what he was doing. The man moved like a panther, smoothly, dangerously. Anyone looking at him would know instinctively not to get in his way. Everyone except Reggie, it seemed.

She had invited the panther into her kitchen.

TOM PUT UP WITH THREE MORE days of chopping, boning, butchering and mindlessly mixing—while doing his best not to make Patty cry—before he took Reggie aside just prior to leaving the kitchen for the afternoon. She was winning on the stubborn front because he had no way to fight back without screwing up his position. Three days and they hadn't once mentioned the baby. His gut told him it wasn't time yet—neither of them was ready. Hell, they were still jockeying for position.

"Are you ever going to use me?" he asked. Because what he'd been doing was a colossal waste of his time.

"I am using you, Tom. You chop better than any prep cook we've ever had."

Tom smirked as he unbuttoned his coat. Interestingly, her eyes followed his fingers for a moment. "You're having fun with this, aren't you?"

She looked up at him, her expression no longer mock-innocent. "No. I'm running my business as I've always run my business. My way. If I go to work for you, then you can tell me what to do. Right now it's the other way around."

"And if I don't like it?" he asked.

She shrugged. "You know where the door is."

"That attitude isn't going to lay a great foundation for co-parenting."

There. He'd brought up The Subject. The one they needed to talk about and weren't. "This is business, not our personal lives, and on the contrary, Tom, I believe it defines our roles perfectly. I'll be the steady one and you'll be heading out the door."

A flash of anger lit his eyes, but didn't flare into a full-fledged blaze. "You don't know that."

Her forehead wrinkled. "Yes. I do. I can't see you staying here. Not unless you can open a restaurant, and with the Nevada economy being what it is, that would be professional and financial suicide."

He was no stranger to professional suicide, but she did have a point. And she was so damned cool about her assessment of their situation, and his shortcomings, that he had to do something about it.

"Then maybe you and the baby could relocate to wherever I get a job, and then *I* could be the steady one," he observed mildly.

SOMEHOW REGGIE MANAGED TO HOLD in the hysterical laughter that rose in her throat, because she knew exactly what he was doing—baiting her. The tension between them hadn't let up one bit since he'd arrived in the kitchen, so she'd been avoiding him. Now Tom was initiating contact in the way most natural to him—by tossing down a gauntlet. Fine. She'd pick it up.

"Go with you so you can get fired, and we'd have to pull up stakes and leave?" she asked.

He raised one eyebrow, a feat that never failed to impress her. "I haven't been fired from every job."

"Name one."

He calmly opened the locker, hung the coat inside. "I've had several. Those didn't make the headlines."

Reggie pressed her palms together and tilted her fingertips toward him. "Let me tell you why I wouldn't go with you, Tom, even if I wanted to—which I don't. Because your career will take precedence. It would always be the deciding factor."

"I'm not going to lie to you, Reggie. My

career is important to me." He closed the locker door. "But that doesn't mean I'm incapable of focusing on other things."

"But for how long?"

"You might be surprised," he said.

She lifted her chin. "I truly hope I am. And for now, I need for you to keep doing exactly what you're doing."

"Fine, Reggie." He shrugged philosophically, but she wasn't fooled. He was stewing beneath his cool facade. "I'll see you tomorrow."

"You knew the deal when you signed on," she said.

He raised a hand in surrender. "I did. I just thought that we'd develop a different kind of relationship."

"Like one where you're in charge?"

"Those are my favorite," he said, just before the door shut behind him.

EDEN SPENT THE NEXT DAY IN THE kitchen with a minimum of four things going at all times, and when she wasn't talking to Reggie, she had the phone to her ear, dealing with clients or purveyors as she worked one-handed. Tom wouldn't mind employing her. In fact, he'd always had a soft spot for Reggie's siblings.

When he and Reggie had been together,

Eden had been in culinary school in California, but every time she got the chance she'd come back to Reno to stay in the house Reggie and Tom shared. And when Justin wasn't in trouble somewhere, he tended to be there, too, since the Tremonts were tight in a way that Tom had never been with his family, such as it was.

His dad had enjoyed great success as a photographer, and since Tom's mother had died when he was barely a year old, his father had married again. Several times. Nice women who disappeared after a few years, tired of being left at home while Tom's dad traveled. Tom had ended up at boarding school between marriages, or with his dad on the road. Some people might say he'd had a terrible childhood, but Tom hadn't minded. He'd simply learned to take care of himself. The Tremonts, on the other hand, stuck together like glue, having practically raised one another. And Patty seemed as if she wanted to become an honorary member of the family.

Leaving Tom as the outsider looking in.

Early in the afternoon Eden and Reggie left the kitchen—Reggie to meet with a vendor, Eden with a bride-to-be—leaving Tom and Patty to man the kitchen. Justin was also there, but he was shut up in his room, which was akin to being in a fortress of solitude. No one ever bothered him, because no one, with the possible exception of Patty, wanted to go anywhere near a superfancy dessert or a nine-foot cake. Some people were born to ice. Others weren't.

Patty rarely talked to Tom, except for the occasional clipped direction or announcement, and she stayed as far away from him as physically possible ever since the ill-fated onion-chopping lesson. And although she was moderately competent, Tom saw a few things he could help with.

But he didn't...until she started working the dough for mini pizzas. Tom knew squat about piecrust, but pizza dough he understood.

"Let the dough rest before you work it," he said when she punched it down and then turned it out of the bowl.

"I have my instructions."

Yeah, yeah, yeah. "It'll be better if you rest it before you work it. Portion it, then cover it with a towel and let it rest for an hour."

"It doesn't say anything about resting it," Patty said primly.

"Did it ever occur to you that I might know what I'm talking about?"

She turned in a huff. "And did it occur to you that I don't care what you know? I work for Reggie. Just like you."

I don't work for her. I'm here for free.

"Fine. Do whatever you want." Damn. He felt as if he were on a playground.

Patty didn't answer and immediately started working the dough, which tore instead of stretching.

Because it wasn't rested....

Tom moved to the other side of his counter station, so that his back was to her and he didn't have to watch her mutilate the dough.

But Patty couldn't leave it at torturing the pizza crusts. No. She apparently complained to Reggie when the boss returned late that afternoon. Tattled on him.

Patty was gone and Tom was changing out of his jacket when Reggie came up to him, the gleam of battle in her eyes.

"Stop trying to direct Patty. It upsets her. As far as she knows you two are on a level playing field."

Oh, yeah. Well, apparently Patty wasn't all that observant. "I'm trying to teach her something."

"That's not your job, Tom."

"All right, all right," he said, putting his

hands up. "I'll keep my mouth shut." Reggie started for the door without a word. "You don't believe me."

"I'm trying to," she said with a sigh.

"What do you think I'm going to do?"

She turned and walked back toward him, her heels clicking on the tile. "I think you're going to do as you please." One corner of her mouth tightened. "I think you can't help trying to take control of the kitchen. All kitchens."

"I'm working on that." He couldn't help trying to set matters right when they were obviously wrong, but on the other hand, he was at the kitchen every day, chopping and doing prep he hadn't done in years. For Reggie. But she didn't seem to see that.

"You're saying you can change?"

He closed the locker and turned, to find her staring at him in disbelief. "I'm saying I *have* to change." It wasn't easy to let those words out.

"Tom...you've built a career and destroyed it...because you refuse to change."

"It's not destroyed," he snapped.

"Well, it's pretty damned close, if you have to hide out for six months."

He made a touché mark in the air with his index finger.

"We are what we are." Reggie folded her arms. It looked as if she was about to start tapping her foot. "I'm not going to pretend to be something else to get what I want. And neither should you, because that's what got us in trouble the last time."

He rubbed his forehead as if trying to massage away a headache before saying with exaggerated patience, "I was not pretending to be something I wasn't. I was figuring out who I was. I was twenty-three years old."

"Did you want to cater?"

"I had my doubts," he admitted.

"Did you talk to me about them?"

"I was working through them."

"Then had a chance to escape, and took it."

"It was an opportunity. And yeah. I took it. Did I miss you? Yes."

"Did you come back? No."

"Well, I'm back now, Reggie. And I'm staying for a while." He could see from her expression that she either didn't believe him or she didn't *want* to believe him. "You honestly have no faith in me at all, do you?"

"You haven't inspired a lot of faith lately. In anyone."

"Why in the hell did you sleep with me all these years later, if I'm such a loser?"

She lifted her eyes and met his gaze. "To prove to myself I was over you. To see if I could walk away with no regrets. Just like you did."

It took him a few seconds to find his voice. "That was the only reason?"

She didn't even flinch. "Yes."

"Did it work?" he growled.

She put a hand to her belly. "Next time I'm coming up with a better plan."

CHAPTER SEVEN

She was a liar. Such a bald-faced liar.

Reggie stopped her car at the intersection of the alley and the street and made a conscious effort to look both ways. Twice.

Yes, she'd slept with Tom to prove a point. No, that wasn't the only reason. Her reasoning had been complicated and flawed, and had involved telling herself a couple big lies. Like that she was over him. She might no longer be in love with him as she'd once been, but it seemed as though she'd never really be free of feeling things for him. Even if she wasn't pregnant.

Now he was here in her kitchen—thanks to those lies she'd told herself—and she was going to have to do something other than make him chop vegetables and do grunt work.

She was losing hope that, after they spent some time together, the tension between them would ease and they would fall into a working relationship. She was wielding control with an iron fist and was afraid to stop, and he was doing as told and resenting every second. She was just as uncomfortable and defensive now as she had been the very first morning he'd showed up for work.

Something had to give, and she was afraid that if she wasn't careful, it would be her.

TOM DROVE HIS RENTAL CAR TO the hotel and searched for the closest parking space. The lot was jammed, being a Saturday night, and he knew from the previous night that it was probably going to be another loud one. Lots of parties and noise in the halls, but he wasn't in a party mood right now.

Running into Reggie in San Francisco had been unexpected and interesting. She'd changed, become more confident, more assertive—although she hadn't been a slouch when they'd been together. She'd invited him for drinks the first night; he'd asked her to dinner the second. And then he'd made the mistake of thinking, when she came on to him that last night, that she'd gotten over their breakup, regretted it as much as he did.

He'd thought when they'd made love that it was an acknowledgment of all the good things they'd once shared. A celebration, if you will. A hot, hot celebration. Instead it had been a vendetta on her part. A screw-you in more ways than one.

Tom yanked the keys out of the ignition.

Cool. Very cool. She'd wanted to stick it to him, and now they were stuck together because of the kid.

Tom got out of the car and walked the half mile to the hotel entrance, keys gripped tightly in one hand. She'd slept with him to prove a bloody point, and he'd been feeling all soft and squishy about it—except for the part where she'd disappeared without a goodbye.

That should have been a hint, but he'd been too thickheaded to read it for what it was.

He bypassed the revolving door for the regular door, which he yanked open. The crowd in the lobby parted as he strode through to the banks of elevators, where about twenty or thirty people were waiting for a ride up. There was some kind of convention in the hotel that involved legions of women. Tom stood and stared at the elevator light.

"Hey," one of the women, dressed in a pink suit, said loudly. "Are you Tom Gerard? *Chef* Tom Gerard?"

He looked into her overly made up eyes and said, "No" in his best conversation-killing voice.

"Are you sure?" Unfazed, she smiled up at him flirtatiously. "Although—" she elbowed her chubby friend "—I could make do with a look-alike."

Everyone was staring at him now. He forced the corners of his mouth into a smile-like grimace and went back to staring at the light.

"Don't be shy," the woman cooed.

I'm not shy, lady. I'm about to destroy you.

Tom pulled a long breath in through his nose, still clutching the keys tightly, willing the elevator to come. Now.

"Here." The woman poked something at him and he automatically took it with his free hand. A business card with a cell-phone number. She smiled, playing to the crowd. "Maybe you could call if you get...*lonely*... tonight?"

Her friend giggled.

Tom folded the card in half with a quick move of his fingers. "Not..." he reached out to tuck the card into the woman's décolletage just above the top button of her pink suit jacket "...interested. Now, bug off." The bell rang and the doors opened.

The woman went even pinker than her suit as Tom pushed by her onto the elevator. A few people got on with him, but not as many as could have fit. Those who did cut him sidelong looks on the ride up.

Great. Just great.

He didn't want word to get out to the general public that he was working for a catering kitchen. He didn't care if Pete knew, but general rumors were not going to do his career any favors. More importantly, though, given a slow news day, the gossip-teers might dig into why he was in such a lowly job…and find out about Reggie's pregnancy. That simply wasn't acceptable. Not yet, anyway.

But he wasn't blowing out of town, as Reggie undoubtedly wanted him to do—not before the issues were settled. He was nothing if not tenacious, and he'd meant it when he'd told her he was in this for the long haul.

For both of those reasons, he needed to get the hell out of this hotel.

TOM HAD INTENDED TO SPEND afternoons after his shifts at Tremont looking at apartments. He ended up looking at houses.

Apartments had parking lots and hallways, and places where he might bump into people who might figure out who he was. Butt into his business. With a house he would have more privacy, and right now, while he sorted through all the unfinished business in his life, privacy was a must. So a house it was.

As he'd suspected, he couldn't find a month-to-month rental, or even a six-month one. It was a year or nothing. But the half year sublease on his New York apartment paid the entire year's lease on the average Reno house. With change.

Pete would have had a cow at his poor business sense, but Tom had no problem signing a lease on a house he was going to abandon once he and Reggie were on terms he could accept. Civil terms conducive to raising a child together. Although right now, he couldn't say that he and Reggie were doing the civil thing well.

He was pissed over the reason she'd slept with him. He felt used. Definitely a first for him.

Trees hung low over the street as Tom cruised toward the address of the third rental on his list. He'd visited two the day before and was squeezing this one in before heading to work.

The neighborhood seemed nice enough— one he wouldn't expect to be robbed in. If he had something worth stealing. A couple houses had toys in the yards and the lawns were all well kept.

He parked in the double drive, and before he could get out of the car, the real estate agent pulled in next to him.

"I see you found the place all right," she chirped.

"I used to live in Reno."

"Are you sure this is the neighborhood you're most interested in? I mean, we do have other options in areas more conducive to say, entertaining."

"I'm not planning on entertaining," he said. The woman's smile ebbed slightly. "I want a quiet area with a small house."

Because he wasn't used to living in many more than four rooms. Five at the most. All he really required was a decent kitchen and a bathroom.

"Well, this is quiet," the woman conceded. She pulled a key out of her blazer pocket. "Shall we take a look?"

"Yes. Let's."

The house was a house. The kitchen was adequate, as he'd suspected from the photos on the real estate website, and the rest of the house livable. It had a small backyard that

Tom stood in for a moment, looking up at the leaves of the one giant tree. Shade. Cool.

The house was on a corner lot with a cinder block wall separating it from the street and a cedar board fence too tall to see over dividing the property from the house next door.

The real estate lady—Sharon somebody—hovered on the steps. He hadn't responded as she'd pointed out various features, and finally she'd quit talking.

"I'll take it," Tom said.

"Wonderful," she gushed. "If you wouldn't mind following me to the office, we can fill out the lease there and...no?" she asked when Tom shook his head.

"I've got to get to work. I'll stop by this afternoon."

"Very well."

Sharon had the look of someone who'd almost made a sale, but hadn't, which prompted Tom to say, "Honest."

She smiled. "I believe you." She went to her car, then before she got inside, she said, "What made you decide to settle in Reno, Chef Gerard?" She'd been studying him as he'd looked at the house, and he'd wondered if she'd recognized him. If she hadn't, then the name he signed on the lease later would have been a dead giveaway.

"I'm taking time out from the rat race. No restaurant. I'll only be in town for a few months." He approached her car, gave her one of his best smiles. "I'd appreciate it if word didn't get out that I'm here."

"Not a problem. And maybe if you decide you like living in Reno and want to trade up, you'll remember me?"

He smiled for real. "It's a deal."

"TOM'S NOT HERE?" REGGIE ASKED as she walked through the kitchen. In the two days since the showdown in the alley, he had been there exactly on time, not more than a minute or two early. He smoldered during the day as he did his prep work, radiating waves of barely contained raw energy, but kept his eyes on the work. And he hadn't spoken, unless checking to see how she wanted something done.

She truly wished she could take back about half of what she'd said. There'd been no need to set the record straight, nothing gained by it.

And while Patty was happier now that Tom left her alone, this new side of him made *her* nervous, too. Reggie could tell from the way

Patty jumped at every unexpected sound, as if Tom were going to attack from over a counter.

"I'd say that's obvious," Eden replied. "Doesn't the kitchen seem kind of empty without him? You know…kind of like an empty tiger cage?"

"He didn't call?"

"Maybe he's had enough. Maybe you won."

"I doubt that. And I haven't even started."

The back door opened then and Tom came in. He went straight to his locker, pulled out his jacket and shrugged into it.

"Sorry I'm late," he said as he walked into the kitchen fastening buttons. "I was looking at a house."

Reggie shot a quick look at her sister, whose mouth had dropped open. "What kind of house?" Reggie asked.

"Walls, roof, doors," Tom said with no trace of humor. "That kind of house."

"A rental?" she pressed.

Tom stopped on the other side of the work counter as he did the last button. "Yes. A rental. Hotels are expensive."

This was no big deal, then. He needed a cheaper place to stay.

Reggie cleared her throat as she reached

into her jacket pocket for the folded paper there.

"Next time you're going to be late, call. Here's your prep list."

When he took it from her, their fingers brushed, and she pulled back a little too quickly, then met Tom's eyes, daring him to make something of it. After deciding that his expression was suitably blank, she turned and caught both Eden and Patty watching her. "You guys have stuff to do, right?"

"Oh, yeah. Right," Eden said. Patty's cheeks grew a little pinker and she went back to her cutting board.

Reggie went to her own station, where she was preparing chili to be served in bread bowls for a search and rescue awards banquet. Rustic food for a local crowd. She concentrated on chopping onions, well aware that her technique, while more than adequate, was nothing like Tom's mastery of the knife.

She didn't give two hoots about knives right now.

A house. He'd rented a house. Not an apartment. Did this house have a yard? A swing set? Room to run and play?

No. He couldn't be setting up for fatherhood. It was a matter of economics.

And why did it bother her so damned much to think of him setting up for fatherhood? He was the father.

Because she didn't trust him to stay. Break her heart, fine. But break the kid's heart? Not an option.

Or maybe she didn't want to share her kid. Be tied to Tom.

She went through the motion of making the chili—browning the meat with a small amount of chili powder, since the order had specifically stated mild chili—then adding the onions, and when that was almost done, the garlic. She measured ingredients into prep bowls, not really thinking about what she was doing, her mind flitting back and forth between Tom's house and having to work out a custody deal.

"Taste," she said to Eden a half hour later when her sister squeezed by behind her.

Eden took the spoon, tasted, then frowned. "A touch more heat. It tastes like bean soup."

"That's what I thought." Eden grabbed the chili container and tapped the side on the edge of the kettle, to coax a small amount out, but the lid fell off and disappeared into the simmering pot, followed by a tumbling cascade.

"Damn it!" Reggie jerked the container upright, spreading chili powder across the counter in a slashing arc of red.

Tom's head came up. "What happened?"

She didn't want to answer, didn't want to admit to such stupidity, so instead she held up the nearly empty chili bottle. Then she set it on the counter and fished the lid out of the chili with the spoon, dumping it on the counter.

Tom took the spoon from her without asking, stirred the mixture, then tasted it.

"Leave it," she snapped.

He gave his head a shake as he lowered the wooden spoon, then set it aside and grabbed a clean spoon. "It's got heat," he said, as if she hadn't spoken. "But I'm pretty sure I can fix it."

"I don't *want* you to fix it," she said through gritted teeth, her voice low and dangerous.

Patty, who'd just taken a cake out of the convection oven, stopped, holding the pan in two gloved hands.

"Reggie…" he said.

She jammed her hands onto her hips. "Go back to your station and do your job."

"Damn it, Reg. I'm only trying to help."

"You're trying to take over."

"Bullshit. You're upset because I rented a house. If I were anyone else, you'd be listening right now."

Reggie snatched up the spoon and shook it at him, spraying tiny red splatters onto his coat. "Get away from my chili."

Tom turned and stalked back to his station, giving Patty and her cake a wide berth, then started chopping with a vengeance. Reggie found that she was shaking. Nerves? Adrenaline? Hormones?

All three, probably. She took two silicone pot holders and pushed the giant kettle to the back of the stove to cool, burning a finger in the process. She barely noticed.

With a clatter she got another stock pot off the rack and started heating oil, went to the walk-in for more hamburger. Yes, this was going to cost her, but she was not serving patched-up chili. Not even chili patched by a master chef.

Tom continued to work as Reggie remade the chili, his anger more than evident in the staccato movements of his knife, his body. Not his usual impatient steaming over the inefficiency of those around him, but rather a cold, quiet anger. He kept his eyes down as he moved quickly, meticulously, finishing everything on his prep list. When he was done, he cleaned his station, took off his coat. Without asking if there was anything else Reggie needed, he gave his counter one final wipe, then headed through the kitchen to the back door, which silently closed behind him.

Patty didn't say a word after he left, didn't announce what she was going to do next. Instead, she disappeared into the pastry room to start a batch of frosting, closing the door behind her. Eden looked up from the cooler she was packing. "He's right. If he'd been anyone else, you would have let him help."

Reggie turned on that one. "I don't think so. I had time to make a new batch and I think that's better than patching."

"Except that you didn't even give him a chance to show you what he could do." She paused, then said, "I have a feeling that Tom wouldn't have offered if he couldn't have done it right."

Reggie didn't answer. She retreated to the office with the real excuse of returning a client's call. Except the line was busy, so she set the phone down just as Eden came into the small room and shut the door behind her. "Look, Reg. I know why Tom is here— the theory at least—but remember how we talked about the possibility of an uncomfortable work environment?"

"Yes." Reggie started shuffling through invoices on her desk.

"We've hit that stage."

Her fingers didn't still. "I apologize for that. It won't happen again. I was just upset about ruining the chili, and I let my emotions get the best of me. Believe it or not, I have a few hormone issues right now."

"It's more than hormones, Reg. You're so tense I'm surprised you haven't shattered. Either you two work it out really, really quickly or one of you has got to leave the kitchen. I vote for Tom."

Reggie stopped going through the invoices and leaned on the desk, staring at her blank computer screen. If Tom left, then they'd be right where they'd started, with nothing worked out. If he wasn't already gone. She had no idea if he was coming back.

Except that he'd rented a house.

A light knock on the door made them turn in unison.

"Excuse me," Patty said. "But I think the chili is burning. I turned it off, but you might want to take a look."

Eden was looking, all right—at Reggie,

who pressed a palm against her forehead. "I'm sorry," she murmured. "I'll get it back together."

"You need to work something out with Tom." Eden sighed deeply. "I'll help in any way I can."

"No. This is all my doing. I'll handle it."

She just had no idea how.

CHAPTER EIGHT

TOM WAS STILL STEAMING WHEN HE checked out of the hotel and drove across town to sign the rental agreement, but he probably would have made it out of the office without being rude if the damned agent hadn't kept blocking his way and chirping about Reno being the perfect buyer's market.

On the third block, he crumpled the signed agreement in his hand and said, "Look, lady, if you don't get out of my way, I'm going to walk overtop of you."

Her mouth dropped open and she took a quick side step. Tom smiled and said pleasantly, "Thank you." He had a feeling that he'd lived up to her image of him.

Glad he could make her day.

Also glad that Reggie wasn't there.

Keys in his pocket, he drove to his new, very empty abode and wondered what the hell he'd just done.

On the way to the real estate office he'd convinced himself that he and Reggie simply couldn't work together under the circumstances and it was stupid to try. Then he'd debated alternatives. There were none. Even if he wasn't trying to redeem himself in this ridiculous way, he needed to hammer out a kid agreement with Reggie, and they hadn't even touched on that.

Both of them seemed to be waiting for some magic moment when it felt comfortable talking about it. That moment wasn't coming. Not in the environment the two of them had created.

So what now?

He'd take a look at his house, figure out what he needed to spend a night there, and think about it later. And if he didn't come up with an answer, then he'd go back to the kitchen tomorrow and he and Reggie could have another fight over matters that had nothing to do with the real issue.

He'd barely pulled his key out of the door and pushed it open when a small dog appeared out of nowhere and shot into the house.

"Wait a minute!"

He followed the dog into the kitchen, where it turned a couple of excited circles in front of the refrigerator.

Tom stared at the mutt. It was golden-brown and about the size of a New York City rat, but with longish hair and ears that stood straight up. It did another circle and then sat, staring back at him. With bright button eyes. Great. Less than a day as a house dweller and he'd picked up a stray.

He went to the back door and opened it. "Come on," he said. "Out." The dog didn't budge.

Tom scooped the dog up and deposited it on the front step. "Go. Home." The dog blinked its bright eyes and Tom closed the door. He was halfway across the kitchen, on his way to inspect his pantry, when it started scratching at the door. With a vengeance.

Wonderful.

Tom tried to shoo it away twice, but after half an hour of industrious scratching at the door and yipping, he gave up. He opened the door, picked up the little animal, who snuggled against him, and started down the driveway. It had to belong to someone. Maybe if he walked around with her, he could find someone who knew where she belonged.

He heard voices as he approached the end of the fence that separated his place from the one next door, and made a beeline to it.

Two older men, one tall, one short, but both with steel-colored hair and nearly identical features, were standing on either side of a barrel cooker. "It was your turn to clean it out," the taller man said, as the other one shook his head adamantly.

"Hi," Tom said, lifting the little dog into view above the fence. "I just rented this place and was wondering if you know who owns this dog?"

"Yeah," the taller guy said. "The people who had the place before you."

What? "They left it?" Tom asked, making no attempt to squelch his sense of outrage.

"I think it's a her," the shorter man offered helpfully.

"Well, what should I do with *her?*"

Tall man shrugged. "Either keep her or call animal control."

"You guys wouldn't want to…?" Tom lifted the dog hopefully. He didn't know much about animal shelters, but he was pretty sure they had to put unclaimed animals to sleep. He might not want a dog, but he didn't want to be responsible for murdering one, either.

The taller man shook his head. "My brother would take her, but I have allergies. Cats are bad. Dogs are worse. If you don't want to keep her, you really should call the Humane Society. Otherwise she might get hit by a car."

Tom looked past the men at the very large shop building next to their house. It seemed to him that the dog could easily live there...perhaps something he could suggest in the future if the dog kept hanging around. "Thanks, guys."

"I'm Frank," the taller guy said. "This is my brother Bernie."

"I'm Tom," he stated. *Who doesn't want to get involved with his neighbors.*

"Welcome to the neighborhood, Tom."

"Thanks. See you around."

He walked back across the yard and into the house through the back door, still carrying the dog. Once inside, he set her on the floor, where she plopped her butt down and stared up at him, her tail slowly brushing the floor behind in a gentle swishing motion.

Where had the little beast been when he and the real estate agent had toured the place? On the run from the dog catcher?

The tail continued to swish back and forth as she watched him. Then she cocked her head. Crap.

He was in no position to keep a dog.

He reached for his phone, then dropped it

again, feeling the weight as it hit the bottom of his pocket. He could call animal control at any time. Maybe someone at Tremont knew of someone who wanted a dog.

It wouldn't hurt to have her spend the night. Unless...

"You don't pee on the floor, do you?"

Swish. Swish.

Tom exhaled. "I don't have any dog food."

But someone had to have been feeding her, because she wasn't skinny. Maybe the short brother next door? He'd looked shifty when the tall one said they couldn't have a dog.

Tom walked back into the empty bedroom where he'd be sleeping on the floor tonight, and opened his suitcase. Without any clothes hangers, he was pretty much at a standstill. He had a few important purchases to make if he didn't want to sleep on bare carpet. With a rat dog.

TOM'S PHONE RANG WHILE HE WAS in Walmart shopping for all the stuff the hotel had provided and he'd taken for granted. Plus dog food—just enough for a couple days, while he decided what to do with the little beast.

Reggie's number.

He answered with a curt, "I'll call you back when I get out of this store." If she was going to fire him or reprimand him for insolence, it wasn't going to be while he was buying toilet paper. He had standards.

A sudden thought struck him before he ended the call. "Unless it's an emergency."

"No emergency," Reggie said.

"Right." As if she'd contact him in an emergency. She wouldn't even let him help her with a food crisis. "I'll call back in about ten minutes."

Tom loaded bag after bag into the car's trunk. Linens for the bed he didn't own, a couple towels, soap, waste cans, dish rack, paper products, a floor lamp, since his bedroom lacked an overhead light. Every aisle he went down revealed something he needed. Finally, he stopped, because of space issues. And he still hadn't gotten any cooking stuff. He'd go to a restaurant supply store for that.

When he did leave this town, he was going to have a great donation for some charity thrift store, but he didn't regret getting out of the hotel and into a house for a while.

He loaded the last bag and wheeled the cart to the overfilled cart corral. It was a warm evening, so he leaned back against the side of his rented Honda Civic instead of getting inside as he punched redial and Reggie's phone rang.

"Are you calling to fire me?" he asked when she answered.

"It's rather hard to fire someone you aren't paying," Reggie replied.

"True," he said in a low voice, "but you could lock me out of your kitchen."

"Can I meet you somewhere?"

"Now?" He looked at his watch.

"Yes."

"Neutral ground?"

"How about your place?" she asked.

"Curious?" he suggested sarcastically.

"I want to speak in private." She didn't have to tell him that if they met at her place, she wouldn't have the option of leaving. Instead she'd have to kick him out. "And I'm slightly curious."

"Fine. It's at 5567 Maylark Street. Do you know the area?"

"I have GPS."

REGGIE PULLED INTO TOM'S driveway shortly after he finished unloading the last of his purchases. He went to meet her as she stepped out of a small, low-to-the-ground Neon, her heels making the job more difficult than it had to be.

"Nice neighborhood," she said after shutting the car door. *Small talk. All right*. Tom was willing to engage in some small talk until she got to the point. He led the way to the front door.

"Why a house, Tom? Why not an apartment?"

"I didn't want to be recognized."

"Cut your hair." Reggie moistened her lips, telling him that she was nervous.

He reached up to touch his shortish ponytail. He'd grown it by accident during a time when he was too busy to get to the barber, and found that pulling his hair back was actually comfortable while he was working and sweating in the kitchen. And then it had become a kind of trademark. The hair. The five o'clock shadow that had eventually become his Vandyke beard.

Was he ready to cut it? It was so handy.

"Let me show you the place," he said. The tour took almost thirty seconds as he gestured and said, "One bedroom, one bath, one office, one living room and—" he led the way into the last room, where there was a frantic scratching at the back door "—one kitchen."

Tom opened the door and the dog shot out.

"What is *that?*" Startled, Reggie looked from the dog to Tom.

"Rat dog. Came with the house."

"And you're keeping it?"

"As opposed to turning her over to the pound to get—" He made a slicing motion across his throat.

"I see." But from the way she was staring at him, Tom didn't think she did.

"I'm going to find it a home." He went to the counter, leaving Reggie staring at the dog with a dubious expression.

"You wanted to talk," he said as he took a can of dog food out of the bag, only then realizing that he'd forgotten to buy a can opener. The dog danced in circles and Tom had a feeling if he didn't get this can open, there'd be hell to pay. Why hadn't he bought the pop-tops?

"Having you in the kitchen isn't working."

He'd expected her to say something along those lines, but his stomach still tightened in response. He really didn't want her to fire him, or dismiss him or whatever one did to volunteer staff, but he looked up at her from where he was rummaging through his shopping bags. "Maybe because you're more intent on punishing me than taking full advantage of me?"

"I'm not punishing you."

"Yes. You are." He came out with a new screwdriver and tore it out of the packaging, dropping the garbage into one of his two new waste cans without bothering to open the box of garbage bags.

Reggie watched him with a slight frown. "I'm not letting you steamroll over me. There's a difference between that and punishing you."

"When…" Tom asked in a reasonable tone, as he set the can squarely on the counter, took aim and stabbed the screwdriver into the top, making Reggie wince "…have I ever managed to steamroll over you? I'm not saying I didn't try, but when did I succeed?" He wrestled the screwdriver out and stabbed again.

"When you left."

"That wasn't steamrolling. That was making a pretty damned hard choice that I had to make because someone backed me into a corner."

"You pretended you wanted to start the catering business with me."

"Unless something else came along more suited to my abilities."

"You didn't say that part."

Tom aimed and stabbed again. "I did, but you weren't hearing me."

Reggie pushed a hand into the front of her hair, pressed on her forehead. "Regardless of what happened then, it's different now, Tom. Before it was just me. I could afford to make mistakes. Now we have a kid to think about."

"Do you think I'm going to be a bad father?" Another stab. Then another. He was doing a pretty good job of circumnavigating the can with holes.

"I think you'll put your career ahead of the kid."

"For real? Or is that a handy excuse? Because you slip it in every chance you get."

"I'm judging by your track record."

He pushed the screwdriver into one of the holes and started prying upward. "So Uncle Justin should be his only father figure?" Tom could see from her expression that had been exactly what she'd hoped. "Do you want to work this out with lawyers?"

The can lid bent up and, with a satisfied exhalation, he used the screwdriver to dish food into a cheap bowl he'd bought in the cereal aisle. The dog turned a quick circle then dove into the food as soon as the bowl was on the floor.

"I'd hoped to avoid that," Reggie said. He cocked an eyebrow. "All right, I planned on having a signed custody agreement after the baby is born, but I hoped we could work it out ahead of time. Amicably."

"With you having the lion's share of the custody? If not all of it?" He shook his head. "Talk about steamrolling, Reggie. I'd say you're guilty, too."

He put the screwdriver on the counter, then closed the distance between them and settled his hands on her slender shoulders. Her muscles instantly tensed.

"How do you feel about me, Reggie?" he asked softly. "Other than angry?"

"Angry." She stepped back and he dropped his hands. "We'll work out the baby truce, but it won't be in the kitchen. Not the way things now stand."

"I think you need me there."

"I know you do," she said. "It's one of the symptoms of your megalomania."

"You're short-handed," he said, refusing to rise to such obvious bait. She didn't answer and he said, "I tried my damnedest to do as you said. I peeled, chopped, counted. I didn't use my brain. I made your prep cook cry only once and I apologized."

"But I'm not loving coming to work, Tom," she said tightly. "And I used to."

"But it's not all about you anymore, is it? Or me?"

Where had those words come from? He had no idea, but the instant he said them, he knew they were true. "Believe it or not," he confirmed, "I wasn't trying to take over when I offered to help with the chili."

"And believe it or not, I'm not used to having to fight my prep cooks to handle matters my way."

"I am who I am, Reg. But I wasn't taking over." She didn't answer, so he asked the big question. "Do you want me to come back?"

"The way things are right now...no. I don't."

"Ever?"

She pulled in a breath. "I don't know."

"I'm not leaving town. Not until we settle a deal, or we have a kid, whichever comes first."

"Is that a threat?" Reggie asked quietly.

"Just a fact, Reggie. You know where to find me when you want to work something out."

REGGIE'S DOCTOR STARTED SEEING patients at seven-thirty each morning, which was one reason she'd chosen his clinic. She could work early morning appointments into her schedule and had actually booked tentative visits for the duration of her pregnancy. Which was one strange feeling—having a fully booked pregnancy.

There were only two other women in the waiting room, unlike the first visit, when the place had been packed. And both were deep into baby magazines.

Reggie was alone with her dark thoughts.

She'd fired Tom.

Now the stress she felt in her kitchen would be the good kind, the beat-the-clock kind, not the why-can't-I-stop-thinking-about-that-guy-and-what-is-he-going-to-do-next kind.

If only it was that easy to fire him from her life.

But regardless of what happened, her life had changed forever. It would have been great to blame Tom, but she couldn't.

She might, however, consider filing suit against the condom company.

Yes, she resented the pregnancy, resented what it represented and how her life was entangled with Tom's. But on the other hand, since she'd heard the heartbeat, she wasn't unhappy to be having a baby.

Which made no sense at all, but that was the way of it.

"Ms. Tremont?" Reggie looked up at the nurse. "Time for your weigh-in...."

IN A WAY, TOM WAS SURPRISED he'd lasted as long as he had in Reggie's kitchen. She might not want him back, but that didn't mean he was leaving town. And if he was staying, he needed something to sit on. His first idea was renting furniture, but one brief phone call had immediately nixed that idea. Oddly, it was cheaper to buy. One futon, recliner and kitchen table later, he realized he was in need of a truck, since he'd saved a boatload of money by purchasing at a warehouse store. No delivery.

So what now? Rent a truck? Borrow a truck? Any chance that Patty might have a truck? Surely she'd be willing to help out a fellow prep cook.

Justin.

During the short amount of time he'd been at the kitchen, Justin remained cold, stand-offish. Protective of Reggie. They'd once gotten along quite well. Now he looked as if he wanted to beat the crap out of Tom.

But maybe, since he was no longer invading Justin's turf, they might be able to at least work out a civil relationship. Which might be helpful in the future. And what better way for two guys to bond than over a truck?

That evening, Tom drove by the kitchen. Justin's car was in the lot, so he pulled in. He didn't have a key to the building, so he rang the buzzer. Several times. Finally Justin pulled the back door open, a scowl on his face. "Did you forget something?"

"I wanted to talk to you and I don't have your phone number."

"You could have called the kitchen."

"I did. Maybe you couldn't hear it over the music?" Green Day's "American Idiot" was blaring from the pastry room.

"That's possible," Justin conceded. "What do you want?"

"To ask you if you had a truck I could borrow to move some new furniture to my house."

"The place doesn't deliver?"

"I found what I wanted in WareCo, but they don't deliver." Justin didn't reply immediately and Tom added, "I can rent a truck. I just thought—"

"I can get a truck." Justin pulled his head

back inside. "I'm on a tight deadline. Come on in."

Tom followed him to the pastry room and stood staring at the three-layer cake on the table in front of him.

"How did you ever get involved with specialty cakes?" he asked.

"Totally by accident," Justin said, taking up his spatula and carefully moving a perfect confectionary orchid to a butter-cream—covered layer. "I did one in a wedding emergency after a bakery had an electrical fire and got closed down. Word spread."

He bit his lip as he placed the flower and then stood back to make an assessment. Putting down the spatula, he picked up his piping bag.

"So, what's the deal with you and my sister?"

"I thought you knew the deal."

"Not the part where she's pregnant." Justin removed the ring and then the tip of the pastry bag. "The part where she said you wouldn't be returning and I should cut back on the cake orders until we hire someone to take up the slack. Now you're buying furniture."

"Why do you have to cut back on cake orders?" Tom asked.

"Because with you here, Patty has time to do more for me, so I took more orders."

"Sorry to screw things up for you."

"Yeah. So what's the deal with you and Reg?" Justin asked, refusing to be sidetracked.

Tom rubbed his cheekbone with a knuckle. "We're having trouble communicating, I guess."

"Do you want to communicate?"

"In the worst way."

"Good answer," Justin muttered as he choked up the bag and finessed an intricate swirl of pale gold icing next to an orchid. Tom found himself holding his breath as Justin leaned in for a tricky bit of piping. "Do you really mean it?"

"You ever have anything like this happen to you?" Tom asked when Justin straightened to reassess. He cut Tom a sidelong look. Apparently not. "Well, I can tell you this… it's unreal. I have no other experience I can use to judge how to handle this, so I've been hanging around a kitchen peeling carrots and counting inventory while I try to figure it out."

"And here I thought you were proving to the cooking world you can stay out of trouble." Justin adjusted the pastry tip.

"I'm here because I want to do what's right. For her. And the kid. Which means we've got to communicate at some point." He hooked a thumb in the front pocket of his cargos. "I kind of thought being in the kitchen would help." He shifted his weight as he shook his head. "It hasn't."

"No kidding." Justin gave him a second long look, then lowered the pastry bag. "So what now?"

"I wait, I guess."

"In your new house."

"I need something to sit on while I wait."

Justin set his jaw. "This situation sucks, Tom. And now you guys are bringing a baby into it."

"Not on purpose." Which was no excuse.

"But you are." Justin paused for a moment, then continued in a lower voice. "If you hurt my sister again…"

How in the hell could her hurt her? She'd made it clear she no longer cared about him, that she'd slept with him for closure. To prove something to herself.

Tom drew in a breath, told himself to hold

it together. "Reggie has all the power, Justin. I'm just trying to figure out what my role is. I'm not going to try to steal the kid away from her. I just want what's fair." He reached up to rub his temple as he rapidly approached his frustration max-out point. "If you'd ever been in this situation, then you'd understand. I'm doing the best I can. Hell, I feel like I'm juggling chainsaws."

Justin still said nothing.

"Do you know what?" Tom finally said. "I'm so far out of the loop, I don't know the kid's due date." Because he hadn't asked. He'd been waiting for the "right time."

Well, the right time was never coming. He had to man up and ask those questions he'd been avoiding because it made the situation too real.

"I guess there's stuff you guys need to talk about," Justin agreed. He squeezed a small amount of icing onto his finger, testing to see if it had dried inside the tip. Then he looked up at Tom, his voice flat as he said, "Let me know when you need the truck and I'll see what I can work out."

CHAPTER NINE

REGGIE ARRIVED AT WORK A HALF hour late because of another traffic snarl. She'd gained a couple more pounds and was looking forward to sharing the news, but she was so late that Eden had already left to do last-minute shopping for her family meals.

They were all rushing around like crazy people, since the kitchen had been swamped with business after she'd told Tom not to come back almost a week ago.

Fate's way of spanking her?

And then she found out that Justin had actually taken time away from a cake to help Tom haul furniture. Next, Eden would be doing his laundry. But Reggie didn't say a word. Justin could do as he pleased.

Patty met her at the door with a notepad. She was so happy in the kitchen now that she was an only child, and the frantic pace didn't seem to faze her. She still worked slowly and meticulously.

"Eden left a sketch for the Reno Cuisine

event," she announced, pulling a paper off the top of the notepad and handing it to Reggie. "Mrs. Maddox called about the possibility of having extra guests."

"I'm so glad she called," Reggie said. It was next to impossible to stretch a lamb chop dinner. "Anything else?" The words were barely out of her mouth when the phone rang.

"Probably Mrs. Maddox," the prep cook said. "Would you like me to get it?"

"Thank you." Patty would undoubtedly have been the kid in class who always raised her hand first.

Reggie held up Eden's sketch and studied it as Patty hurried to the office. A French bistro was a little pedestrian, but it was doable in the amount of time they had to throw it together—if they could find a carpenter. She'd discovered through the professional grapevine that Tremont had gotten into the event late because Sutter's Catering had failed to pay the entry fee on time. But in was in and she was happy.

"Tremont Catering. How may I assist you?" There was a brief silence and then Patty gasped, "Oh my goodness! Is she all right?"

Reggie set the sketch on the counter and

hurried to the office. There was only one other "she" involved with Tremont Catering.

"Yes, let me get her sister." Patty held the phone toward Reggie, who snatched it up.

"Hello?" The word stuck in her throat.

"This is Mike Maynard. Reno Fire Department Paramedic. Are you Eden Tremont's sister?"

"Yes." Reggie swallowed drily.

"She's been in a pedestrian-automobile accident."

"A what?" Reggie struggled to get her frozen brain to translate. "She got hit by a car?"

"Yes. In the Super Saver parking lot. The only apparent injury is a broken or badly sprained ankle. However, she did hit her head on the pavement and we'll be transporting her to Washoe Med for further evaluation."

"Reggie!" An angry female voice cut in as soon as the paramedic stopped talking.

"Uh, is that my sister yelling in the background?" Reggie asked.

"Yeah. That would be your sister."

Reggie felt a huge rush of relief at the sound of Eden's very irritated voice. "Can I talk to her?"

"We really need to transport her. We're blocking traffic."

"I don't want to pay for an ambulance!" Eden shouted.

"Is this life threatening?" Reggie asked the paramedic. Because if it was, then Eden was getting in that ambulance.

"Whenever a head hits pavement—"

"Reggie! Get over here. Take me to Urgent Care!"

"I'll be right over," she told the paramedic. "Do *not* transport her."

"I'll drive," Patty said as soon as Reggie hung up. "You are in no condition."

Startled, Reggie looked at her, then realized Patty was talking about the shock of the accident. "I'm fine. I can't tell you how many times I went through this with Justin." Which was why Eden knew enough not to get into the ambulance and pay for one hell of an expensive short ride.

"If you're certain…"

Reggie set a firm hand on Patty's round shoulder. "I need you here to hold down the fort. My cell number is on the business cards there." She pointed to the holder next to the computer. "Call if you have any difficulties at all."

"What shall I do while you're gone?"

"Mini quiches," Reggie said as she snatched up her keys and purse.

"Mushroom or broccoli?" Patty called as Reggie maneuvered around the counter and opened the door.

"Your choice. I've got to go."

THE AMBULANCE WAS STILL PARKED in the Super Saver lot when Reggie arrived, and Eden was sitting on the pavement with a good-looking paramedic crouched next to her. He helped her to her feet and into the passenger side of Reggie's car.

"Thank you." Eden spoke stiffly, her face as white as Reggie had ever seen it.

"She's in shock," the paramedic said. "Take her to the hospital. Do not mess around with this."

"I am familiar with the procedure," Reggie said shortly, getting behind the wheel.

Reggie was no fan of emergency rooms and urgent care, having spent a great deal of time over the years waiting for Justin to get patched up. It had been particularly tricky the two times their father had been away and Reggie had had to call him to get verbal clearance for Justin to be treated. That had pissed her off. Her father should have been there with them, but he was always chasing the open road. Promising that this long haul was the last and then he'd go short route only. As far as she knew he was still on the road. None of them had heard from him in months. He'd eased out of his children's lives after a bad blowup concerning Justin in high school.

She glanced sideways at Eden as she pulled into an urgent care parking spot. Her sister was overly pale and her ankle was huge and turning bluish-black. Fortunately, the paramedics had removed her shoe, so that trauma was over.

"I'll get someone to help you in."

Eden shook her head, but Reggie ignored her. A few minutes later a nurse followed her out with a wheelchair. Thankfully, it was a relatively slow day at the clinic.

Eden was treated and released within an hour. Reggie helped her back to the car, clutching concussion instructions in her free hand as Eden made the painful journey. They weren't yet sure if the ankle was broken, but she'd hit the pavement hard and was feeling the effects.

"Oh damn, Reggie," Eden said miserably once they were both in the car. "I'm sorry."

"Not your fault." As Reggie understood it,

the teenage driver had rounded the corner too fast and hadn't been able to stop in time to avoid bumping Eden, who'd stepped out from between two cars without looking. She'd been knocked sideways into another car. Technically, his insurance should have paid for the ambulance Eden was so worried about, but Reggie was glad they weren't dealing with the emergency room.

"How am I going to get food to my families?" Today was Eden's cooking day. Tomorrow morning was delivery.

"Patty will help. We'll do fine."

"The luncheon...the wedding..." Eden let out a growl of frustration.

"I can handle it, Eden." *Just let me drive. And think. And try to avoid the obvious solution.*

The phone rang before they reached Eden's street. She answered, nodding as she spoke. "Yes, I'm fine... Kind of... No plan yet.... All right. I will. Here."

Eden held out the phone and Reggie took it, keeping her eyes on the road. "Justin?" she guessed.

"Call Tom," he said, almost before she got the phone to her ear.

"I—"

"Call him, Reg."

She exhaled heavily as she turned the corner into Eden's driveway. "I'd already planned on doing that. What if he tells me to go to hell?"

"Then maybe in some small way you deserve it. Do you think that'll happen?"

"Yeah," Reggie said with a sigh. "I think there's a good possibility."

SMOKE FROM THE BARBECUE NEXT door was rolling over Tom's fence when he pulled into his driveway after an hour in Whole Foods. The rat dog was happily working over a stick near the fence and the old guys on the other side were arguing about something. The wonderful aroma of barbecue beef wafted over on the breeze, giving Tom a sudden hankering for ribs.

He was putting groceries away when he heard a strange noise on the back steps—a thumping, as if something was being dragged to the top. He opened the door to see the little rat dog standing proudly with one end of a giant raw beef rib in her mouth and the rest of it between her legs.

"Where did you get that?" Tom asked, reaching down to take the meat-and-fat-laden bone away from her. The rat dog reluctantly relinquished her find to the alpha male—Tom—and then sent him a reproachful look.

"Hey, I'm sorry, but I'm only thinking about you. It isn't like I want to eat this." They'd been together for only two weeks, but during that time Tom had learned that table scraps, or even changing food, had a detrimental effect on the dog's digestive system. And the carpet.

Time to make a neighborly visit. He popped the dog into the house, took the bone and headed for the driveway, to walk around to his neighbor's front gate.

Smoke nearly choked him when he approached the cedar fence and looked over. Frank and Bernie, the neighbors he'd met the first day he'd moved in, were staring at the cooker.

"Too much mesquite!" Bernie yelled at Frank.

"You're the one that put it in there."

Tom cleared his throat. Frank instantly turned, while Bernie continued to glare at the cooker. Frank, Tom could see, was wearing hearing aids. Bernie was not.

"Hi," Frank said. "Need something?"

"Uh, yeah." Tom held up the rib. "I think the dog got one of your ribs somehow."

"I didn't give your dog a rib. Bern? Did you give one of the ribs to the dog?"

Tom was still working on the "your dog" part of the comment. She wasn't his dog.

"Well, you know…" the shorter man said.

Frank turned back to Tom. "I'll try to control my brother's bad habits."

"I'd appreciate it." He stood on tip-toe to get a better look at the barbecue setup. "Smells good," he said.

"Smells like too much mesquite," the man answered, directing the remark at his brother.

"Is there such a thing?" Tom asked.

The old guy's eyes cut back to him. "Do you know anything about cooking?"

"A little," Tom allowed.

"Here," he said, shoving a sauce stained paper plate with a few individual ribs on it over the fence toward Tom. "Tell me what you think."

Tom obediently picked up a rib, held it up to inspect the glaze.

"They're storebought ribs—not as good as the ones we get from the packing plant."

"I'll keep that in mind." Tom bit in. The texture was perfect, the glaze almost there. The flavor… "A little heavy on the chipotle, but the smoke is perfect. I don't think you have too much mesquite."

"I told you," Bernie said.

"This is the first year we've tried the chipotle."

"All in all, not bad."

"We're aiming for perfect. We compete in the rib cook-off every year and we want to win while we're still vertical."

"Good start."

Frank nodded, his cheeks reddening. "I thought they were pretty good."

"Oh, they are. Just not perfect." Tom shrugged. "But what is?"

Frank frowned at him. "I know you."

He waited, wondering if his neighbor would make the connection. Finally Frank shook his head. "Maybe not. You just remind me of somebody."

"I get that every now and then. One of those faces. I look like a bartender." Reggie was right—he'd have to cut his hair. He'd gotten rid of the beard a few days ago and figured that would be enough. Apparently not.

Frank laughed. "Actually, that was what I was thinking, but since I only go to one bar anymore and you don't work there, I don't think that's it."

"Excuse me."

All three of them turned at the unexpected sound of a woman's voice. Reggie stood at the side gate, looking as if she was about to walk the long green mile.

"I have company," Tom said, although judging from her expression, this was not a social call. "I'll see you guys later."

"What does he know about sauce?" he heard Frank mutter to Bernie as he walked away.

REGGIE'S FIRST THOUGHT, ridiculous under the circumstances, was that Tom had shaved and she wasn't sure she liked it—because he looked so much more like the man she'd once fallen for. He crossed the distance between them in a matter of seconds, his expression one that had probably struck fear in more than a few sous-chefs.

"Eden's been hurt," she said abruptly.

Tom's hand stilled on top of the gate latch and his eyes shot up to hers. "Hurt? How?"

"Hit by a car in a parking lot." And then she ran out of words. Couldn't bring herself to say, "Can you help me?"

"Let's talk inside," he said as he unlatched the gate and walked through, shooting a quick glance back at his neighbors, who were watching them closely. She followed him to the back door of his house, having no clue how she was going to ask him to help...or if she was.

The little dog turned a circle when Reggie and Tom entered the kitchen.

"You kept her," Reggie said. There were matching ceramic dog bowls next to the fridge and a bed filled with dog toys under the kitchen table.

Tom shrugged as the dog sat on his shoe and leaned against his leg. "Until I find her a home. Tell me what happened," he said. "Is Eden all right?"

"She stepped out in front of a teenager driving through a parking lot. You know how she is—going a hundred miles an hour, her mind on the next thing she has to do." Reggie had witnessed a couple near misses while shopping with Eden. "She has a concussion and a broken ankle."

"And the kid who hit her?"

"Scared to death," Reggie said, surprised he'd asked. "They were treating him for shock when I got there." He'd been getting almost as much attention as Eden. "Thankfully, he wasn't going fast, but a bump by a car going ten miles per hour still does some damage."

She tugged briefly at her ring, then said, "I need help from someone I trust in the kitchen. We can't handle the workload without Eden, and the temps we're familiar with are all booked."

"So I rate after the temps?"

"Of course not. But I didn't know if you'd come back after…" she made a frustrated gesture "…you know…so I checked in with the temp agency."

She fell silent then. She'd said her piece. Asked for help. Now all she needed was a quick answer. Hopefully not "Go to hell."

"What do you need me to do?"

"Eden cooks as a private chef for three families. The food needs to remain up to par and we can't trust it to just anyone."

"What if it gets a whole lot better?"

CHAPTER TEN

RELIEF FLOODED THROUGH REGGIE. Maybe this week wouldn't be a wreck—for the kitchen anyway.

"Then Eden's going to have to work harder when she gets back on her feet."

"I'll help you out," Tom said. "On one condition."

"What?" Reggie asked, at that moment ready to agree to almost anything.

"I get some say in what goes on...and some answers about the baby."

"What kind of answers?" Reggie worked to keep the defensive edge out of her voice. They had to have this discussion. It wasn't exactly the perfect time, but she could understand Tom's position—which she'd been trying hard to ignore.

"I know nothing about the baby," he said.

Which was wrong. She could admit that. Reggie drew in a deep breath. "It's too early to tell if it's a boy or girl."

"There's one answer," he said.

"It's due in mid-November."

"I guessed at that one. Do we have a day?"

"The fifteenth."

"Do you *want* to find out if it's a boy or girl?" he asked.

Reggie smoothed her hair from the sides of her face with both hands. "It'd help me get ready. The doctor said he should be able to tell in about four weeks."

Tom nodded slowly, as if thinking of new questions now that he had this free pass. "Okay. So...you see the doctor, what? Once a week?"

She smiled slightly. "Once a month for now. Visits get more frequent later."

"And you take vitamins. Eat right. All that."

"All that," she agreed.

He seemed to have run out of questions. He studied the floor for a moment, then looked up at her. "What do you see as my role in this, Reggie?"

That's it. Smack her with a question like that when she needed his help.

"I, uh, think time will tell on that."

"What do you want it to be?"

"Supportive," she said. As in let her take the lead in this. Let her decide what was best for her and the kid. Let her be the primary caretaker.

"Do you think we should try to, you know? Raise the kid together?"

Reggie's eyes widened. "No."

"Just asking, Reggie. I wasn't offering."

"And I'm not trying to be insulting, Tom. It's just that with your career and mine, and the way things are…"

"I get it, Reg." He let out a breath. "Enough baby questions for now."

"You didn't get many answers," Reggie pointed out.

"I'll ask the occasional question while we're working together. That was, after all, the plan when I came to work out here in the first place. Right?"

"Yes. But I never thought it would work."

"And it didn't." His lips curved. "Maybe it'll work better this time."

"Damn, I hope so," Reggie said.

"So Tom is really going to take my place," Eden said groggily. The pain meds were doing their job, but she was fighting to remain conscious.

Reggie exchanged glances with Justin, who'd gotten off shift at the hotel early. "Yes. And he's going to follow your recipes."

"You won't let him get all fancy?"

"For the twelfth time, no."

"All right." Her eyelids started to close. Reggie had made up a bed on the sofa, where it was easier to elevate Eden's ankle so the swelling would go down and it could be cast.

"I need something to do if I'm stuck here," she murmured.

"You can work on invoices and billing." A job that could be done on a laptop in a horizontal position. "Plan the Reno Cuisine."

"Make prank phone calls to Candy's Catering Classique," Justin added helpfully.

Eden started to answer, but the words came out as a slurred whisper and then her jaw went slack.

"Finally," Justin said. "Where does she keep the liquor?"

Reggie closed her tired eyes. She wouldn't have minded a belt if circumstances had been different. "Cabinet next to the fridge."

Justin went into the kitchen and came back a few minutes later with a whiskey for him and a glass of cranberry juice for Reggie. He sat in the easy chair next to Reggie and the two of them sipped as they watched their sister sleep.

"You know," Justin mused, "I've done a lot of things, but I never got hit by a car."

"Not for lack of trying."

He lifted his glass in a salute and she smiled back at him, letting her head rest against the cushion behind her. "You never got pregnant, either."

"No…funny thing that." He looked at his glass instead of at her, and Reggie had a feeling he was going to say more, but he only took a healthy gulp of whiskey. "Are you and Tom any closer to working out an equitable arrangement?"

"I, uh, answered some questions."

"That's a start."

"It's hard to make decisions and choices when I have no idea what he's going to do in the future. Where he's going to be."

"Maybe the baby will affect that decision."

Reggie frowned over her glass. "Oh, I don't think so."

Justin raised his eyebrows.

"I believe he wants to do the right thing. But if he ever gets past this roadblock in his career… I don't know, Justin."

"So you trust him in your kitchen, but not in your life."

"He wasn't very dependable in my life."

She got the feeling Justin had more to say on the matter. "What?" she asked.

Her brother swirled his drink, but made no response.

Reggie decided to follow suit. She didn't want to talk about this. Not when she had a sister lying out on the sofa drugged out of her mind on pain meds, and a backbreaking week ahead of her.

"I'll stay here with Ed," Justin said. "You need to get a decent night's sleep."

"But—"

"Which of us is more adept at getting by on next to no sleep, and which of us is sleeping for two?"

Reggie couldn't argue with that. She finished the juice and set the glass on the table. "I will need my strength tomorrow." *In more ways than one.* "Thanks, Justin."

Tom AROSE EARLY THE NEXT morning, showered, fed the rat dog and put her in the fenced backyard with a rawhide chew for entertainment. The dog had taken to sleeping with him, curled up in a ball on the end of the bed until he fell asleep, at which point she would burrow under the covers, more like a gopher than a rat. Scared the hell out of Tom the first time he'd woken up with something warm and furry pressed against his ankles. Last night, though, he hadn't minded the companionship as he tried to make sense of his life, which had once been so focused, so freaking on track.

His cell phone rang as he headed out the door.

"Hi, Tom," said a familiar female voice. Eden. "Reggie gave me your number so we could coordinate."

"How're you feeling?" Tom asked, opening the car door. There was a hesitation at the other end. Was he such a bastard that being polite threw people into confusion?

"Sore. I appreciate you helping out."

"No problem. Do you want to wait to talk until I get to the kitchen to discuss the meals?" He'd have access to her recipes there.

"I didn't call about the meals. I called about Reggie."

"What about Reggie?" he asked, his pulse bumping up.

"If you don't play nice in the kitchen, I'm coming after you."

"I'll be nice, Eden," he said, relieved she was only calling to threaten him.

"She's got a lot going on, Tom, and hormones on top of it. Plus…she's still angry about the way you left her."

No kidding. "Get well. Soon you'll be back in the kitchen to referee." He clicked off and got into the car.

Why did everyone assume that Reggie was the only one who'd been demolished by the way their previous relationship ended? She was the one who'd drawn the line in the sand. All he'd done was step over it.

THE KITCHEN WAS QUIET. Reggie set her purse next to the computer and then stood in the office doorway, looking out over the kitchen that, despite all the drama of putting on catered events, always provided her with a sense of peace. It was her place. Where she belonged, doing what she loved.

Then Tom had arrived, and the peace had disappeared. Now he was coming back. The disturbing part was that she was beginning to suspect the shattered peace was more her fault than his.

That wasn't going to happen again. She had too much to do to let Tom get to her. Besides, last night things had changed a little. They'd take an important step and she didn't want to screw things up.

Reggie stepped back into the office, tied

on her apron and changed her loafers for the clogs. This was a pivotal day.

The back door opened behind her and Reggie jumped. But it was Patty, not Tom, who came in, shrugging out of her yellow sweater as she walked toward the lockers. She beamed at Reggie over her shoulder.

"I'm here early since I knew you'd need me to fill in for Eden. I took the liberty of going through her menu cards and I'm ready."

"I, uh…" Reggie rubbed the side of her face as Patty tied on her apron.

"Justin and I finished all of yesterday's prep while you were gone."

"Yes, I know. I came back. Remember?" Right after she'd talked to Tom. She and Justin had made a loose game plan for the next day, but she'd never dreamed that Patty had assumed she was taking over. Patty was a wonderful prep cook, but…Eden's families were used to flair.

"Patty, we have someone filling in for Eden for the next week."

"Someone else?" Her mouth didn't quite close.

"Yes. We still need you to do your regular job."

"Of course," she said stiffly. "I wouldn't

have gotten up so early, had I known. I had hoped to use this opportunity to become a more integral part of the operation." She straightened her apron. "Who?" she asked with a slight tilt of her chin.

"Tom."

Her mouth fell open. "But I thought—"

"He's got a lot of experience." Reggie wished she could sugarcoat it, but the truth was Eden wouldn't trust Patty to cook the way she did.

"Of course." Patty busied herself straightening her coat, which didn't need straightening. "What would you like me to do?"

"I made a prep list," Reggie said, pulling a card out of her apron pocket. Patty took it from her, held it out as she read, then nodded once and walked to her station as the back door opened again.

Crisis averted. Reggie rubbed a hand over the back or her neck, feeling utterly exhausted. And the day hadn't even begun.

Tom headed straight for his locker, pulled his coat out of his bag, which he dumped inside, then shut the metal door.

Patty pointedly ignored him as he came into the kitchen.

"Ready," he said, adjusting the collar. "Where are Eden's recipes?"

And once again the kitchen seemed too small.

"I'll show you." Reggie started for the office. "Come with me."

"Patty's really happy to see me back," he said once the door was closed.

Reggie reached for Eden's notebook on the high shelf above the computer. "She, uh, thought she'd be filling in for Eden. Showed up early, ready to go."

"That had to be a blow." Reggie looked over her shoulder, surprised. "I *am* capable of putting myself into other's people shoes, you know," he added.

She turned, cradling the notebook loosely in her arms. "I didn't mean to imply you couldn't, but you aren't exactly known for compassion in the kitchen."

"Touché."

She handed him the notebook. "Eden is totally anal about her families. There are three of them, and she makes evening meals for Monday through Thursday for two. Monday through Friday for the third. She has all the recipes, menus and portions under the appropriate tabs, and if you have any questions…

any questions at all," she repeated, as Eden had earlier that morning, "call her."

Reggie looked out the closed glass door to where Patty was making filling for one of Justin's cake projects, her movements jerky. "I'm a little surprised Eden hasn't called you."

"We talked," Tom said. "Early this morning."

"A *good* talk?" she asked cautiously, bringing her attention back to him.

"No complaints."

Reggie left it at that. "We also have the Reno Cuisine coming up."

"Which is?"

"A charity fund-raiser and competition. Catering companies, as well as restaurants that cater, set up in the park along the river in late June. Invitation only. It's the first year we've made it in."

"Is there a payoff?"

"Bragging rights. A feature in a couple of regional magazines. A lot of publicity even if we don't place in the competition."

"Will I be helping out with that?" Tom asked.

"Uh, yeah. I think you'll be a real asset." She smiled ironically. "But you probably don't want to be at the actual competition."

"Why?"

"I don't think it's wise to be in a place with tons of food-loving people. Not unless you want to answer a lot of questions about why Chef Gerard is catering in the park."

He reached up to touch his jaw. "Shaving didn't help?"

"Not that much." Reggie tilted her head, studying his face as if gauging the recognition factor, when she was actually trying to get a read on him—not very successfully. Tom was better at covering his feelings than he used to be. Probably because in his world, feelings were not an asset.

He lifted the notebook. "I'd better get busy."

"Me, too." But neither of them moved. Reggie shifted her weight as she ran a hand up her arm to the elbow. She wanted him to know that things weren't going to be like they were before...which hadn't worked well. "Um...we *will* talk more about the baby."

"I know."

"I just wanted to throw that out there so it isn't lurking under the surface, like it was last time."

"I appreciate that." He hooked his thumbs

in the pockets of his chef's jacket. "Anything else?"

"Don't make Patty cry?"

"Got it." He touched Reggie's waist as he moved past on his way to the door. "I'll give a yell if I have any questions about the meals."

A second later he was gone, but Reggie could still feel the exact place where his fingers had been.

TOM OPENED EDEN'S NOTEBOOK and flipped through the pages. Eden, for being such a whirlwind, had notes that would have made an engineer proud. Meticulous. She'd made tiny adjustments to ingredients, amounts. Had a rotating set of menus, shopping lists for each one.

Okay. Tom set the book down and went to the cooler. He had a full day's work ahead of him and he was looking forward to it. He'd been throwing food together in his kitchen the past few days, but he missed cooking for others. Even people getting dinners in plastic containers because they were too busy to cook.

He put the pasta water on to boil, the Italian sausage on the burner, whistling under his breath.

And thinking about how Reggie's body had

practically vibrated under his fingertips. He'd touched her without thinking, as he'd touched her a hundred times in the past, but he hadn't expected to feel a response, and it had jolted him.

REGGIE STAYED IN THE OFFICE and concentrated on orders and schedules, assuring herself that now that Tom was here, they'd pull off the wedding and the dinner just fine. The only problem was that Eden knew the routine and she and Reggie worked together smoothly, with their own separate duties. Tom, not being familiar with wedding preparation, needed to be directed. As did Patty.

But, Reggie thought, abandoning the computer mouse and leaning back in her chair to take the kink out of her spine, Tom needed only minor direction, and Patty...Patty was steady and would do whatever she was told. With only a couple dozen questions. A lot of this stress eating at Reggie was self-generated, and she needed to relax. This tension couldn't be doing the baby any good.

Relaxation proved elusive, however, with another minor emergency—no twenty to twenty-five shrimp available until Friday morning—and the florist calling to say she was still having trouble with the small orchids. Seems there'd been a run on them.

The orchids Reggie could work around. If the shrimp didn't come in on schedule…well, Reggie didn't want to think about how she was going to make shrimp cocktail without them.

Then, to add to her joy, Eden called four times before noon, checking and double-checking on Tom and the schedule for the week. Reggie suggested that, since she was injured and on pain medications, she might want to take it easy, but Eden was having none of that.

"Listen," Reggie finally said, "I'll email you a list that can be done from the sofa."

"Excellent. How are things with Tom?"

"If you mean is he following your recipes, for the twentieth time, yes, he is."

"No…I meant how are *things* with Tom? Is it tense in the kitchen?"

Reggie debated for a moment. How were they? "Better," she finally said. "I unleashed him and he's cooking away."

"How's Patty?"

"Good question." Reggie glanced up at the carrot-shaped office wall clock, a gift from a client, and grimaced. "Eden, I've got to go.

I'll send the email, then no more communication. Okay?"

She hung up and rubbed the back of her neck. Stress. But for once Tom wasn't the source.

CHAPTER ELEVEN

TOM WAS MORE THAN READY FOR A beer when he got home after a long-ass day, made longer by the fact that Reggie was stressing over both Eden and a big wedding scheduled at the end of the week. She'd tried to hide it, as she hid all major stress in her life, but he recognized the signs. He kept his mouth shut and let her work. The last thing Reggie needed was to be told that everything would be all right, because, obviously, until the Wednesday business dinner and the Saturday afternoon wedding were over, everything wouldn't be all right.

Platitudes never helped and his platitudes were rarely well received, since they usually ran along the lines of "get over it."

So as Reggie made and destroyed lists and schedules, Tom did her a favor and kept his head down, cooking. But every now and then he noticed her watching him, when she didn't think he was looking.

So what did that mean?

Damned if he knew. But in spite of Reggie's tension, they'd had their best day ever in the kitchen together—probably because she wasn't trying to control him and he wasn't seething at wasting his skills.

Tom dumped his keys on the counter on his way to the back door to let the rat dog inside. She scrambled in, dancing around his feet as he opened the fridge, not yet understanding that beer came first. He was reaching for the bottle opener when she suddenly went on alert, hair standing on end, and started making a hellacious yipping. A few seconds later, there was a knock on the back door.

It was Frank, without his brother, and carrying a tinfoil-covered bowl. Tom opened the door and as soon as the dog recognized her neighbor she dropped her intimidation stance and trotted over to greet him, making Tom smile.

"Hey," he said. "Come on in. Want a beer?"

"No beer," Frank said, stepping inside. He held up the bowl. "I was wondering if you'd give me an opinion."

Tom closed the door. "Sure." Was this the Western equivalent of dropping by the neighbor's to borrow a cup of sugar?

Frank stepped inside, glanced around at

the nearly bare interior. All Tom had in the kitchen was a table with two chairs, a stockpot sitting on the stove, a French press coffeepot on the counter and a bunch of dog toys in the bed his dog didn't use. Because she had his bed.

"Nice place." The man placed the bowl on the counter and took off the foil. Tom eyed it critically, sniffed, then tasted the sauce. "Okay," he said, a few seconds after he'd swallowed. "This is better. The finish is superb."

"Who are you?" Frank asked abruptly.

Tom lowered the spoon. "Meaning?"

"Are you a cook? A rib expert? A talented amateur? Or what?"

"I'm a cook," Tom said. "Just not at the moment."

"So you are Tom Gerard?" When he didn't answer, Frank said, "Bernie told me you were. I didn't believe him. He watches all those gossip shows. He said he recognized you. I told him he was nuts."

"Maybe he is."

Frank shook his head. "No. I think he's right. So…why are you here? In Reno?"

Tom set the spoon in the sink and put the foil back over the bowl. Better to meet this head-on than to let the boys spread rumors. "I used to live here. I decided to come back and enjoy some peace and quiet." He emphasized the last words, hoping Frank would take the hint.

"Why? Too much good food and too many beautiful women?"

"It gets wearing after a while," Tom replied.

"I should have problems like that."

A sudden flash of orange in the backyard caught Tom's attention. He stepped to the window, frowning, then dropped the sauce spoon.

"What's wrong?" Frank asked as Tom bolted to the door.

"Your fence is on fire!"

The fire was taking hold by the time Tom got to the door. He raced through the back gate and was halfway down the driveway to the gate leading to Frank's property when the old man passed him at a dead run. Tom decided he would give the matter of a sixty-something-year-old guy outrunning him some thought later. Right now he wanted to make sure they still had a fence dividing the properties and no big red trucks rolling into the drives.

"What in the hell—" Frank's question was

drowned out by the hiss of the fire extinguisher as Bernie sprayed down the Weber kettle that stood beside the smoker.

Within a matter of seconds the fire was doused and the barbecue was covered in white foam.

"This is going to be a bitch to clean," Frank said. "What happened?"

"Too much lighter fluid," Bernie yelled. "I didn't realize how close to the fence I was. The wind came up and…"

"How long have we been doing this?" Frank demanded. "How long?"

"Don't talk to me like I'm some kind of a fool!"

Frank gestured at the charred fence.

"Could have happened to anyone." He glanced over at Tom and then back at his brother. "Well, is he?"

Frank rolled his eyes. "You almost burn down the fence and you're on celebrity watch?"

"Are you Tom Gerard?" Bernie asked point-blank.

Tom put his hands on his thighs as he caught his breath. "I'm Tom. Your next-door neighbor. Can we leave it at that?"

"And also our sauce and rib consultant?" Frank asked shrewdly.

"Sure," Tom agreed. "I'll consult." *And you keep quiet.*

"How's Eden?" Tom asked when Reggie parked next to his car in the alley Monday morning. He'd gotten there early only to find himself locked out. He'd gone for a coffee but still had had to wait another ten minutes for her to arrive.

"Fighting to come to work, but the doctor hasn't released her." Reggie got out the keys. "And won't until the swelling in her ankle goes down enough to put it in a cast."

So far the Johnson's wedding was going according to plan, except that Reggie also had the Wednesday luncheon for a business-woman's sorority group, which she'd booked before the wedding and before she'd had any idea she'd be working without Eden. The luncheon was cutting into her wedding prep.

"I hope she's learned a lesson about look-ing both ways before crossing," Tom said.

"I wish she *had* looked both ways." Reggie glanced up at him as she turned the key. "My sister isn't the most patient patient, and it was my turn to stay with her last night." She left it at that, since the phone started ringing the second the door was unlocked. Tom pulled it open and Reggie ran for the call, dropping her tote bag on the chair.

Because of a shipping issue, the florist

couldn't get the Lady Slipper orchids she wanted for the wedding display. Reggie pushed her hair off her forehead and told the woman to keep trying. If she couldn't get fresh Lady Slippers, as the bride had requested, then they might have to go with silk. Which the bride had not wanted.

Reggie made a note: "Talk to bride about flowers."

"Everything okay?" Tom asked from the door.

"Yeah. Just a flower problem."

"You do the flowers, too?"

"For the cake table and the buffet." She started her computer and kicked off her shoes, nudging them under her desk with the side of her foot. "I have to do the site check at the Masonic hall for the dinner and make a preliminary delivery today. Patty's nervous about being left alone with you."

"Why?" he asked mildly. "No chaperone?"

"She's afraid of you."

Tom snorted. "She is not. She just wants me gone."

"Be nice to her. I don't want her to quit. Not on top of everything else." Reggie reached for her apron, pausing when she saw the way he was looking at her. "What?"

"I promised myself not to indulge in platitudes, because I don't do that kind of stuff, but..."

There was genuine concern in his eyes. For a moment Reggie simply stared, feeling unexpectedly touched by that concern, and then she pulled the apron off the hook. "Everything will be okay?"

"Relax a little, all right?"

Reggie tied the apron, then made an effort to smile. Sure. She'd relax. Just as soon as this week was over.

REGGIE LEFT ABOUT AN HOUR after Patty came in, leaving Patty with an extensive prep list and simply telling Tom what she needed him to do—brie-stuffed chicken breasts, a gourmet version of scalloped potatoes, poached Bosc pears in a cabernet sauce.

Tom cubed the brie and then sliced pockets into the chicken breasts, stuffing a few cubes of cheese in each one before sautéing them and then placing them on a baking sheet.

Patty was baking the sheet cake and cutting crudités. Slowly cutting crudités. It was almost as if she was doing it on purpose to drive him insane, but this wasn't his kitchen. He didn't need to fix the problem. And if he turned his back to her, he could almost believe it.

And if he couldn't believe it, he'd fake it.

Once the chicken was stored, Tom disinfected his area then started on the potatoes. Regardless of what Reggie wanted, he had to do a few fixes to this sauce. While he was making the white sauce, he started to smell the distinct scent of burned vanilla and glanced over his shoulder at Patty, who was arranging carrot sticks and radishes.

"Patty?"

Her chin jerked up.

"Cake?"

She gave him a haughty look, then glanced at the timer next to her crudités plate. Her eyes bulged and then she whirled around to the oven.

"Oh, no. Oh, no," she repeated over and over as she jerked the pan out, dropped it on the rack waiting on the counter. Tom was surprised she'd slowed down long enough to put on an oven mitt. *Forget to set the timer, Patty?*

"Ruined," she moaned. "Look at it. Look at it!"

Tom could see the black edges from where he was finishing the white sauce. "Don't cry!"

If Reggie came back and this woman was bawling, there'd be hell to pay.

Her eyes suggested his command came too late.

"No," he said, as firmly as he could without raising his voice. He was tethered to the white sauce that had yet to thicken, so he called, "We'll fix it. Just. Don't. Cry!"

Had he ever said those words in his kitchens?

Never. And now he'd just said them twice.

"How will we fix it?" Patty practically shrieked. "This is for an event!"

"I know." Tom's sauce had thickened to the point that he could take it from the burner. He set it aside and crossed over to where Patty stood wringing her hands next to the cake.

"Everyone makes mistakes," he said.

She glared at him. Platitudes really didn't sound convincing coming out of his mouth.

"You have time to make another cake."

Patty gestured dramatically at her prep list. "When? Reggie is depending on me to do all of this."

Tom scooped up the paper and quickly read through it. Child's play. He set the list down on the counter and put his hand on top it. "I'm good at this kind of thing. I'll handle your list and mine while you make another cake."

"But Reggie—"

"Doesn't need to know."

Come on, woman. He was offering the easiest fix, the quickest fix, and yet she was dithering… But he hadn't taken her head off. *Good, Tom. Very good.*

"All right," she said with a sniff. "But I will have to tell Reggie."

"Patty…Reggie considers herself lucky to have you." For reasons Tom didn't quite get. "She'll be all right with this."

The prep cook gave another slight sniff. "Then we'd best get going."

Finally.

"Yes."

By the time Reggie returned, both prep lists were done and a perfect cake sat cooling on the rack.

"Wow, Patty," Reggie said. "This is beautiful. Justin will have to watch out."

Patty blushed, hesitated, started to speak, then glanced over at Tom. He shook his head and her mouth closed again. A second later she simply said, "Thank you."

THERE WAS A CAKE IN THE TRASH. A yellow sheet cake, parchment still attached to the almost black underside, doubled over and lying beneath a few eggshells and vegetable peelings.

Both Tom and Patty had left, so Reggie had no one to ask about it. But whatever had happened, Patty hadn't been in tears and Tom hadn't been raging—which made Reggie wonder if he even knew.

No. If Patty burned a cake, he'd know. He had an extraordinary nose.

Strange… And perhaps best to let the cake go out with the trash and ask no questions. Even if she was dying of curiosity.

She touched her belly after closing the lid of the garbage can. "Your father's going soft."

Your father.

It still gave her pause when she thought of Tom as the father of her baby.

He was biding his time now, waiting out the aftermath of his professional faux pas, but he didn't belong in a catering kitchen. He'd actually made the right choice seven years ago, and so had she. She wouldn't have been happy globe-trotting from restaurant to restaurant, trying to roll with the punches when he'd gotten fired more than once, trying to put down the roots she would have needed so badly in such a fluctuating environment.

So, yes, they were having a baby together.

But she didn't see how they could possibly make a life.

WHEN TOM PARKED HIS CAR IN THE driveway that evening, an awful high-pitched mechanical squeal came from his neighbors' oversize shop, followed by muffled shouts.

Ah, suburbia. What were Frank and Bernie up to now? Hopefully, this wasn't part of their new sauce-making procedure.

The rat dog was waiting on the back porch and shot into the kitchen when Tom opened the door, skittering across the floor as she tried to stop her momentum.

"Did you have a good day?" he asked, getting the food out of the fridge and scooping some into the ceramic dish next to the table.

Tom poured a half glass of wine, then stood swirling it as he watched the dog dig into her food. He should probably give her a name, because there was no sense pretending he was going to turn the little beast over to animal control. As he'd told Reggie, he was no dog murderer, and he wasn't going to take the chance that she wouldn't get adopted before zero hour. Besides, she kept his feet warm.

He'd find her a home—a real home—when he left. Maybe with Eden. She looked like the rat dog type. Reggie had that spoiled cat he'd seen the night he was there, who'd probably hog all the dog's food and knock it around when Reggie wasn't looking.

The dog looked up at him, cocked her head, then went back to eating. She'd undoubtedly once had a name, given to her by those bastards who'd abandoned her. He'd ask the boys next door.

As Tom approached Frank and Bernie's shop, the metallic squeal started again. He knocked on the door, but no one answered—probably because they couldn't hear over the racket—so he let himself inside.

The brothers were at the far end of the cavernous building, next to a screaming saw Bernie was feeding wood through. Both men were wearing hearing protection, and Tom wished he was, too.

He clapped his hands over his ears until the noise stopped, and Bernie popped Frank on the chest, then pointed at Tom.

"Hey," Frank said.

"I see you guys do more than cook ribs."

"You gotta fill your hours after retirement," Frank said.

"What are you retired from?" Tom had

wondered what they'd done before moving in together and cooking ribs.

"Construction. We built a lot of the houses in this neighborhood."

"Home boys, then."

"I guess," Frank said dubiously, obviously not one for puns. "We're building a picnic table now."

"I've never built anything in my life," Tom said.

"You never had shop class?"

"I didn't go to a regular high school. Got stuck in boarding school a lot."

"Oh. I see."

Frank seemed at a loss as to whether or not he should offer sympathy, so Tom said, "I was wondering…did that dog that came with my house have a name?"

"Muffin."

He made a face. "Those people abandoned a dog named Muffin?"

"You never know about people," Frank said. "Hey, you need a picnic table? We're making a prototype, but it's not quite right."

"Why don't you guys keep it?"

"We have three picnic tables. Hobby of Bernie's. Making picnic tables. Pretty soon we won't have room for grass in the back-yard." Frank laughed.

"I'm not going to be here for long, unless something radically changes."

"After this, then what?"

"I hope to have a new job," Tom said simply. "How's the sauce coming?"

"Made some adjustments. We'll be grilling tomorrow if you want to try it."

"I might not be here," he said.

"Well, anytime you see smoke rising, come on over. We're always happy to have people by."

It probably did get lonely, just the two of them. Tom wondered if they'd once had separate lives, wives and such, or if they'd always been together. Kind of like Reggie and her siblings.

"Well, I gotta go," Tom said. He raised a hand to Bernie, who was measuring a board. Bernie waved back.

"That's a nice dog," Frank said before Tom turned back to the door. "I'm glad you're giving her a chance."

"Yeah," he agreed. "I'm becoming a be-liever in second chances." And so, even though they had to part company eventually, the dog was getting a name, and it wouldn't be Muffin.

As soon as he walked into the house, she trotted over, cocking her head. He picked her up and held her out at arm's length, studying the little animal for inspiration. She stared back with her bright eyes. Small and brown. Warm and comforting. Muffin was appropriate in some ways, but Tom wasn't a muffin kind of guy.

Petite Brioche.

Perfect.

"Come on, Brioche. Let's go surf the net." He tucked her under his arm and headed for his laptop, where he found a ton of junk in his email in-box, plus one very unexpected message from Lowell. Tom hadn't heard from the guy since their "you're screwed" conversation six weeks ago.

The message was short: How's your French?

He wrote back Bon. Lowell was well aware that his French was adequate in most places, fluent in the kitchen. Tom knew all the curse words.

He leaned back in his chair, a sense of excitement building in him. Lowell wouldn't ask unless there was a reason, but he worked in his own way. Tom knew better than to ask questions, which tended to make Lowell react in a contrary manner. Tom began to feel a faint hope, though, that maybe he wouldn't be unemployed or face underemployment for much longer.

Maybe he could work in a decent kitchen again—where he didn't need to worry about making people cry. Make a decent salary so he could provide for his child's care.

And maybe he'd be smart enough to keep his mouth shut and cook.

But if it involved speaking French... Canada? Or France?

CHAPTER TWELVE

CATERING A WEDDING, Tom discovered, was very much like preparing to fight a battle. Plans, details, to-the-minute time schedules.

There were also other less militaristic aspects. Florists, displays, rentals, temps... multiple details to juggle.

If one also had to create a business dinner a mere three days before the wedding, the tension and potential for disaster increased exponentially. Very much like a busy professional kitchen of any sort.

Reggie took it all in stride, despite Eden's return to the kitchen being delayed by two days because of the swelling in her foot and ankle. Tom kept in the background as much as possible, doing whatever Reggie asked of him without argument, trying to take some of the pressure off her. Patty tried to outdo him, finishing tasks in record time, reinforcing his belief that professional rivalry was a fine thing when used for the forces of good.

And through it all, deveining shrimp, chopping crudités, making biscotti and roasting chicken breasts, he thought about Lowell's email.

Lowell was a contrary bastard. He was also one of Tom's closest friends and wouldn't screw with him for too long. Tom hoped. Even this hint of possibility had lifted his mood...and also made him well aware that if he was offered a job, he had more to consider than he used to.

"Hey, Tom." Justin came out of his pastry room, the white cotton stocking cap he wore smeared with blue icing. "I'm starting to get into the juice here. Could you give me a hand?"

"Sure." Half afraid of what he was going to have to do, Tom followed Justin into his lair, where the cake was taking form. Fortunately, no frosting was involved. Just frou-frou desserts. Justin explained how to make the éclair filling and then pipe it into the shells he'd made earlier that day.

"You'll do the final touches with the piping bag?" Tom asked, thinking that Justin probably didn't want his reputation riding on Tom's decorative skills.

Tom made the filling, cooking custard and then, after it had cooled, mixing it with whipped cream. He started piping filling into the éclairs, while Justin continued to work on his cake. Big piping he could handle. Leaves and flowers? Forget it.

Classic rock played through the speakers mounted on the ceiling, and Justin moved his head in time with the beat as his hands remained steady, creating petal after petal.

"Anything else?" Tom asked forty minutes later.

Justin looked up as if he'd forgotten Tom was there. He shifted the pastry bag to his left hand and flexed his right. "We just need to get them in the cooler, so I can spread out here."

"Will do," Tom said. He wrapped the pans and made a couple trips to the walk-in, making room on one of the shelves for the wrapped trays. When he was done, Reggie was nowhere to be found and he needed another assignment, so he headed for the office.

The door was open a crack, and since Tom didn't hear Reggie talking on the phone, he knocked and then pushed it open without waiting for a response.

Reggie was sound asleep, her head resting on her folded arms on her desk.

REGGIE WOKE WITH A GUILTY start, wondering where she was and why there was a warm hand on her back. Tom. She sat bolt upright.

She'd laid her head down for a minute and that was the last thing she remembered.

"Are you all right?" he asked.

"Fine. Yes. Just resting my eyes."

"How much sleep did you get last night?"

She rose to her feet, straightened her apron, then looked Tom in the eye. "Plenty of sleep. Sleep is important, which is why pregnant woman fall asleep at odd times. Like now."

"I see."

"Are you finished with the chicken breasts?" she asked, cocking her head.

"As a matter of fact, I am." Over an hour ago.

"Good." She reached for her clipboard with the battle plan attached. "I have a million things that need to be done."

TOM ARRIVED AT THE KITCHEN early the next morning, but Reggie was already there, deep in preparations.

How much sleep could she have gotten?

She greeted him with a smile, then turned back to her work, leaving him with a strong desire to go over and put his arms around her from behind. Like he used to do. Back when they were in love.

Patty came into the kitchen within moments of his arrival, calling a cheery hello to Reggie and giving Tom a curt nod. They may have made an uneasy peace during the burned cake incident, but she was by no means a fan. Justin showed up next and the kitchen seemed almost crowded.

Or maybe Tom had simply wanted a few minutes alone with Reggie.

It wasn't to be. Everyone worked steadily, cooking, packing, wrapping and loading, right up until midafternoon when Reggie and Patty took off to finish cooking at the Masonic lodge hall where the dinner was being held.

Justin rolled his shoulders as the van pulled away.

"More time on the cake?" Tom asked.

"Nope. I'm going home, having exactly two beers and then sleeping until it's time to come back and help Reggie and Patty unload the van. Tomorrow is going to be a killer." He opened the door to the kitchen. "I prescribe the same for you."

Tom did indeed go home, leaving Justin to lock up. He was determined to beat Reggie there the next morning. It still bothered him that he'd found her asleep the day before— to the point that after feeding Brioche and making himself a salami sandwich, he settled on the futon with his laptop and punched "pregnancy" into a search engine.

What he found was hair-raising.

The stages of pregnancy themselves were matter-of-fact. But on the various websites he'd explored, he not only saw photos of the fetus—which was not a handsome creature by any stretch of the imagination—he also read about the many things that could go wrong with a pregnancy.

And then the birth…

He finally had to force himself to turn off the computer.

How on earth could Reggie be so calm when faced with so much potential for disaster?

THE LIGHTS WERE ON IN THE kitchen when Reggie pulled the van to a stop near the rear entrance. Justin was here as planned. Or not. The rear door opened and Tom, not her brother, stepped out into the alley. What the heck?

"Is something wrong?" Patty asked from the passenger seat. Instead of answering, Reggie got out of the van, as did Patty and Jenna, the temp for the evening, and went around back to where Tom already had the doors open.

"You're still here," Reggie said in surprise, pushing a few loose tendrils back from her forehead.

"I borrowed the key from Justin so I could help you unload."

"Why?" She reached in for the first thing she could get her hands on, anxious to get the unloading done so she could go home, go to bed. It was going to be a long day tomorrow.

Instead of answering, Tom took the box she'd just lifted from the van, and handed it to the temp, who carried it inside. And then another. And another. For a few minutes it was like a bucket brigade. Reggie would grab a box or cooler and either he or Patty, not to be outdone by Tom, would take it away from her. "Why are you doing this?" she finally asked.

"Are you getting enough sleep?"

It sounded more like an accusation than a question. "Yes," she snapped. "Are you?"

"I'm not pregnant," he snapped back, close to her ear, so no one else would hear.

Reggie stared at him.

"Okay," he admitted. "Maybe I didn't do that well. I'm worried about you overworking yourself while Eden's out."

"You're worried about me," she stated flatly, as she took hold of another container.

"Yeah."

Making a face at him, she lifted it and walked around him. He grabbed a cooler and followed. The van was almost empty, and Patty and Jenna could handle it while she put stuff away.

Within twenty minutes, everything was stowed, and the two women left.

"Let's go grab something to eat," Tom said after the door finally swung shut behind them. "Then you can go home and get some sleep."

Reggie regarded him warily. "Would you believe that the last thing I want is food?"

"You need to eat," he said. "Either I take you out or I cook something here."

She shook her head wearily. "I need some sleep." The perfect argument.

Tom's shoulders slumped in defeat. "A peanut butter sandwich?"

They'd practically lived on peanut butter for a time, while they were still in California, before moving to Reno. Cooking school was expensive and time consuming. PB and J was fast and cheap. She actually had very warm memories about peanut butter and jelly.

"I don't have the good jelly here."

The good jelly was a plum-and-ginger chutneylike concoction. Sweet but with a bite. Reggie had to special order it now from a company in California. She always had at least two jars in her pantry at home—although it had been a while before she could eat it after Tom went to Spain.

"We'll make do."

Tom took her by the shoulders and steered her over to a high stool and sat her down. "Stay," he said. "I mean that nicely."

Reggie couldn't help smiling as he backed away, keeping an eye on her as if she was going to jump to her feet and bolt for the door. He disappeared into the pantry, returning with peanut butter. "No bread," he said. "What kind of a catering place has no bread?"

"Delivery tomorrow."

"This makes it difficult for me to feed you tonight."

"Bring me a spoon."

He smiled, a wonderful sensual curving of his nearly perfect lips, then went to a utensils drawer and took out two spoons.

Reggie lifted her eyebrows as he positioned a stool next to hers. "Having dinner with me?"

"I am." He went to the fridge and pulled out a gallon of milk, poured Reggie a tall glass, then brought it to her.

She already had the top off the jar and had dipped in. "Food tastes better when you're pregnant," she said, pulling the spoon out of her mouth and closing her eyes for a moment, savoring the taste and texture. The peanut butter was freshly ground and tasted of roasted peanuts. Good stuff.

"I may never know about that," Tom said, taking a scoop of his own.

"After the nausea disappears, that is."

"It's gone?"

"Yes. It just—" she shrugged "—went away. I'm starting to feel surges of energy." She reached across her body with her free hand to rub her shoulder. "Or I was."

"How was service?"

"Flawless. Patty relaxed and moved a little faster, and she got a stain out of a guest's blouse." Reggie put the spoon into her mouth again, slowly drew it out. Tom never took his eyes off her, which made her feel warm. Exhaustion. Nothing to do with a hot chef on the stool opposite her.

"Are you sure peanut butter is enough?"

"I've been noshing all day."

"But you need actual meals, from all the food groups," Tom said with a frown.

"Trust me. I ate from all the groups today, including the ice cream group at lunch." She took a drink of the milk. "Are you going to be my pregnancy sheriff now? Because if you are, you need to know that it's going to drive me crazy."

"I did some internet research on fetal development," Tom said. "Learned a few things."

"You have?" Reggie asked. "Like what?"

Tom met her eyes. "At this point, our kid is really, *really* homely."

Reggie almost choked on the peanut butter. Tom automatically reached out to pat her back a couple times.

"I mean," he continued, when she'd finally got control of herself, "it looks like an alien—all head, with little black eyes and a tadpole body."

"Rumor has it they get cuter as time passes."

"Man, I hope so."

Reggie drank her milk, licked the spoon, then got up to rinse it in the sink.

"Done already?"

"Honestly, I am tired, and tomorrow is another long day." And the unexpected intimacy between her and Tom was throwing her off. It was pleasant at the moment, but she didn't trust him, or herself, enough to encourage it.

"Call me when you get home?" She opened her mouth to protest and he added, "Just so I know. Okay?"

"Okay." She went into the office to get her purse. When she came out again, she said, "Thanks for dinner."

"Someday maybe we can have a real dinner."

In the old days, real dinner would be followed by...

She drew in a deep breath. "Yes. Maybe. But probably not anytime soon."

Tom walked to the door with her and held it open. "But...maybe someday?"

"No promises, Tom." She reached up to touch his cheek, because she didn't seem to be able to stop herself. "But...thanks for dinner."

As JUSTIN HAD PREDICTED, wedding preparations consumed Friday, when most of the food had to be prepped and then stored, to be transported and finished on site the next day.

Tom took over the kitchen, since Reggie had a herd of temps to manage, all of whom she knew by name. She rehired the same people over and over, and they appeared to like working for her. More importantly, they knew their jobs.

Eden showed up that morning, hobbling in with her foot in a compression boot. She would not be much help in the kitchen at the event, slow and awkward as she was with the contraption on her foot, so Tom offered to go along, take up slack.

Reggie shook her head. "It's the bride's day. If anyone recognizes you, it would shift the attention."

"I don't think that's much of a possibility," he said. Especially if he was in the kitchen. But Reggie held firm and he agreed to stay at Tremont, answer the phone and tweak some of the dishes Eden had come up with for the Reno Cuisine competition. Which he also didn't get to attend. But he was hoping by that time Lowell might have come up with something for him. So far, he hadn't heard another word from his alleged friend.

Eden cornered Tom shortly after Reggie told him he couldn't go to the wedding. "Thank you for taking my place this week." Since there was no belligerent gleam in her eye, Tom deduced that he hadn't screwed up her food. Or made her sister unhappy.

"Are you guys going to need me next week?" Not that he wasn't coming in, but it would be easier with Eden's blessing.

Eden snorted. "Uh, yes. Reno Cuisine prep starts next week."

That was news. He was working on dishes as per Reggie's suggestion, but...three week lead time on the prep? "I thought that wasn't until the end of June."

"We have to come up with a theme. Build the display."

"You guys build displays?"

"We'll hire a carpenter."

"How big is this display?"

Eden shrugged. "That's what we'll figure out next week. Plus we have two weddings coming up."

Tom was aware of that. Both were smaller, more intimate affairs, but with higher-end food, so again careful prep was involved.

"And," she added as her sister came out of the office, clipboard in hand, "Reggie seems more relaxed with you around."

"We've...talked."

"So things are going okay?"

"I'd say so," he said cautiously, wondering if she was leading him into a trap of some sort.

Eden leaned her forearms on the counter. "How long you going to be here?"

"I can honestly say that I don't know." Tom was very familiar with Tremont protectiveness and knew the easiest path was to simply accept it.

"Any job leads?"

"Nothing concrete. Just some wishful thinking."

"What are you wishing for, Tom?"

"Something that allows me to provide for my child and still build a career."

"Building hasn't been your forte lately."

Tom pursed his lips. "You're a lot like your sister, you know?"

Eden shrugged.

"All right. Rebuild. Anything else?"

"No," she said, pushing herself off the counter. "Just getting an update, since Reggie won't tell me a damned thing." She smiled up at him, then hobbled toward the office.

THE CREW LEFT THE KITCHEN IN waves the morning of the wedding. Justin and the cake went first, followed by the rented refrigerator van with Patty at the wheel. Eden and Reggie were to follow in the Tremont van.

"I wouldn't mind having you there today," Reggie said to Tom after changing into her black dress. "But I don't want to chance it." He saw her point, since even his elderly neighbors had put a name to his face.

"Don't trust me in the kitchen alone?"

"Well, there is a potential for disaster." She smiled up at him. "Fire. Sharp things."

"I'll try to follow all the safety rules," he said in a low voice, then watched as her color rose. There'd been a definite change in her since the night he'd fed her peanut butter. He couldn't help but wonder what would have happened had he been able to get his hands on bread and the good jelly.

"Yes, you can see where following safety rules has gotten us," she said. Then, before Tom could answer, she added, "You don't have to meet us tonight. We have plenty of people to put things away."

"Tomorrow?"

"We'll see," was all she said before Eden called her from the doorway. Reggie took two backward steps, always a risk on a rubber-matted surface, and said sternly, "Behave."

"Yes, Chef."

CHAPTER THIRTEEN

IT WAS EERILY QUIET IN THE kitchen after everyone had left, and Tom found that quiet wasn't necessarily his friend. He was used to movement, noise and controlled chaos while he cooked.

Since he hadn't heard a peep from Lowell, he'd taken to perusing professional journals online, looking for opportunities. Not a lot of luck so far, but he still had time. He was well-off financially, but not so well-off that he could live without working—fiscally or mentally.

He needed to get back into a real kitchen. Real to him, anyway. If anyone ever found out that he'd practically begged someone not to cry in this kitchen...well...Pete would probably be proud of him, but Tom would have lost the respect of everyone else he'd ever worked with.

So how to get back into a kitchen without being underemployed, yet be able to watch his kid grow up?

Conundrum city.

Start his own place with the backers he didn't have? For some reason that didn't seem like the solution—even if he had backers. In fact, the thought made his gut twist. Never a good sign.

Tom had just finished a veal dish that he thought might do well at the Cuisine competition when a buzzer went off. Someone had come into the reception area. He wiped his hands on a towel as he walked across the kitchen.

A middle-aged woman, masquerading as a thirty-year-old, stood on the other side of the counter, her expression one of barely suppressed outrage.

"I'd like to speak to Reggie," she said loudly, her large hoop earrings quivering as she spoke.

"Not here." Tom continued to wipe his hands.

The woman's chin jerked up. "When will she be back?"

"Tomorrow morning. Can I help you?"

"Are you familiar with the invoicing?"

"Yeah," he said. Why not? Reggie didn't need to deal with this if he could take care of it.

The woman slapped a paper down on the counter in front of him. "I paid the bill in full *before* the dinner."

Tom took the sheet and read it over. It was for a sit-down dinner almost a month ago. Twelve people paid for in advance. The invoice was for an additional four.

"Apparently you didn't pay for the extra four guests," he said matter-of-factly, noting when he glanced up that the woman was now studying him.

"Why would I pay for the extra guests? You served pasta and smaller pieces of dessert, cut the rolls in half and refused to leave the leftover pasta."

"It doesn't look like you were charged extra for dessert." Eden had actually broken it down into extra charges for drink, salad and dinner. She'd probably had to run out and get more food to stretch the meal for the extra guests.

The woman slapped her hand down on the counter. "I am not paying this bill. It's outrageous. And I will tell my friends to avoid this caterer."

Tom placed his palms on the counter on either side of her hand and she snatched it back. "How fair is it to hire someone to serve twelve people, then spring an extra four on them? Do you have any understanding of the amount of planning that goes into putting on a decent dinner?" He spoke in what he believed was a reasonable tone, and there was no reason for her eyes to glaze over like that.

"I *understand* that I hired this firm to cater my dinner. They did nothing more than stretch the food—which I paid for!"

"You contracted twelve people. Did Tremont let the other four *uncontracted* people go hungry? No. They rolled with the punches and fed your guests. Probably ran to the store to get more food." She started to answer, but he cut her off, saying, "Now you have the gall to flounce in here and say you aren't going to pay for services rendered and food consumed?"

The woman's hand went up to her chest and she pressed it against the oversize pendant necklace she wore. "They didn't leave the leftovers."

Tom leaned farther across the counter, his voice dropping as he said, "I bet that if I went and pulled this contract, it clearly states twelve people, no leftovers. Am I right?" The woman glared at him. "So it comes down to you wanting something for nothing after throwing a giant damned monkey wrench into the evening." He pushed the invoice toward her.

"I'll take this to small claims court."

"You'd better damned well check your contract first." *Reggie was going to kill him.* He reached out and took the invoice back. "But you know what? I'll pay this fricking bill and you can get your ass out of here." He was so proud that he didn't say "bony ass."

"You really are him, aren't you?" the woman said. "That...that...rude chef."

"I don't know what you're talking about."

She gave a couple slow nods as she backed to the door. "You're going to regret talking to me that way."

"Lady, as I see it, you don't have an invoice and this conversation never happened."

Tom watched through the window as the bitch got into her pricey car and drove away.

He was so not cut out for this business.

And he was going to have to confess, so Reggie wouldn't be blindsided by this—he glanced down at the invoice—Mrs. Bremerton. He crumpled the invoice.

Was he going to have to join a twelve-step program to learn to stop triggering like that? Reggie was right. When he saw a fool, he pointed and cried fool, and it was doing nothing but getting his ass into trouble.

Justified or not, he was going to have to rethink this strategy.

FRANK SHOWED UP AT THE BACK door with a bowl of sauce shortly after Tom got home. When he'd agreed to be a sauce consultant, he hadn't realized it would be a full-time job.

He tasted it, then shook his head. "The other recipe was better."

"That's what I thought. Want to come eat with us tomorrow? Bernie's all agog at the prospect of cooking for a top chef."

"Some people get intimidated by that."

"Not Bernie. Not much sense, but loads of confidence." Frank bent to pet the dog.

"Yeah. I'm free. Should I bring anything?" Isn't that what neighbors did? Bring a dish? He'd seen stuff like that in movies.

"Dessert?" Frank asked.

Tom grimaced. "Not my forte, but I'll see what I can do."

Frank grinned. "Bring something frozen. We don't care. You're the guest."

Tom went to check his email. The wedding reception would last into the night. Reggie thought they might get back to the kitchen around one in the morning. Not the best time for confessions.

Maybe the next morning. Or even Sunday, after Reggie had had some time to rest. Whenever it was, he had to make certain that he gave Reggie a heads-up before Mrs. Bremerton attacked.

CHAPTER FOURTEEN

REGGIE SLEPT IN LATE Saturday morning, since Eden and Justin had insisted they could handle the after-wedding breakdown and inventory. And Reggie was too exhausted to argue. The wedding reception had gone off perfectly, a rare turn of events she believed was well-deserved payback for a high-stress week.

Justin's cake, finished a good hour ahead of time—thus allowing him to help in the kitchen—featured a spectacular cascade of confectionary daisies down one side. The florist had managed to find Shasta daisies at the last minute for the buffet display, so Reggie had used the silk daisies as accent pieces at the end of each banquet table, tying bouquets with white ribbon and attaching them to the tablecloths.

As Patty gained confidence, she started to become more vocal. And a bit bossy with the temps. Reggie would address the issue if it continued, but for right now she was satisfied with the result of a long week's work. And she and Tom had done all right. They had managed to enact a workable truce.

But for how long?

She finally got out of bed at eight, when Mims walked over her for the sixth or seventh time, demanding breakfast. Now.

Reggie slipped into her robe, scooped cat food into Mims's bowl and started water for herbal tea. The smell of coffee didn't bother her as much as it had when she'd first discovered she was pregnant, so she thought about investing in some decaf. Perhaps today.

And maybe she'd stop by the Home Depot and look at paint chips for the baby's room. She didn't want to make hard-and-fast color choices until she knew if she was having a boy or a girl, but now that she could barely button her pants, some planning was in order.

She walked into the living room, opening blinds as she went, letting the sun in, then stopped and backed up a few steps to take another look out the front window. She knew that car.

And the dark-haired man sitting inside.

What the heck?

The teakettle whistled, since she'd barely filled it, and she went back into the kitchen, grabbing her cell phone off the end table on the way. She punched in Tom's number after turning off the burner. He answered on the first ring.

"Are you sitting in a car in front of my house?" she asked, dropping a tea bag into a cup.

"If you're asking that question, then you probably know that I am."

"Why?"

"Can I come in?"

"Yes. I think you better," Reggie said, her heart beating harder. This had to be bad news. What had happened? Did he have a job? Had there been a mishap in the kitchen?

She went to the door after quickly pouring water over the tea bag. She had a feeling she'd need a drink of some kind after talking to Tom.

"Why are you here?" she asked after letting him in and closing the door again.

"I made an error in judgment yesterday."

Just as Reggie had thought. Disaster after the perfect service. "What kind of error?"

"This woman—a Mrs. Bremerton—showed up with an invoice."

Instant bad feeling.

"Did you argue with her?" Reggie guessed.

Tom shrugged. "I told her what I thought of people who tried to weasel out of paying what they owed."

The sinking feeling reached *Titanic* depths.

"How did she respond?" Reggie asked flatly.

"Well, she threatened me. But you don't need to worry about the invoice. It's paid. In cash."

"You didn't extort money from her?"

"No. *I* paid the invoice—"

"You paid!"

"Someone had to. Then I told her the conversation never happened, and sent her on her way."

"Politely."

"Under the circumstances."

Reggie held in a rant. "Good customer relations, Tom."

"I'm sorry," he said. "She was…aggravating."

"Do you want some tea?" Reggie asked, hoping to get a few more details so she knew what she was up against.

"No. I drank about a gallon of coffee waiting for you."

"How long have you been here?"

"Since six. I wanted to talk to you before you went to the kitchen. And I couldn't sleep."

"Because of Mrs. Bremerton?"

"Because of a lot of stuff."

For some reason, the thought of Tom not sleeping bothered Reggie—probably because nothing ever bothered him. If he wasn't sleeping, then...well, she didn't know what. She'd never known him not to sleep.

"My tea will oversteep if I don't get to it," she said, leading him to the kitchen. She pulled the bag out and dumped it in the trash. "Have a seat."

Tom took the chair she indicated, tapping his fingers on the table as she situated herself opposite.

"Tell me what happened."

He gave her a recap, which didn't include much more data than she already had, so when he was done, she asked, "Do I send flowers?"

"Hell, no. You're better off without her business."

"Reno's a little smaller than New York City."

"Even if you do, I think her beef is with me." His mouth tightened momentarily before he said, "She recognized me as 'that rude chef.'"

Reggie laughed. Rude chef. She couldn't help but love the description. And while she'd lost a customer, the curiosity factor of having the rude chef in her kitchen would quite possibly mitigate any damages Tom may have done. "You denied it?"

"She didn't believe me."

"I'm never leaving you in charge again."

"Thank you," he said. "I don't think I'm ready for public relations."

Reggie stretched her feet out under the table, her toes brushing the side of his canvas shoe. She shouldn't feel this relaxed about his confession, but what was she going to do?

All she *could* do was keep it from happening again.

"Am I forgiven?" Tom asked, not moving his foot away from hers.

Reggie nodded slowly, picking up her tea and taking the first slow sip. Somehow lemongrass flowing into her system wasn't quite the same as caffeine, but it tasted good.

"Thank you." He leaned back, settled his eyes on her face, raised his eyebrows. "When are you going to the kitchen?"

"I'm not. Eden's orders."

"Good for Eden."

"No. Good for me for following them."

He smiled. "So what are you doing today?"

"I, uh…"

He held up a hand. "Never mind. I didn't mean to pry."

"Paint. I'm going to look at paint." She had to stop shutting him out.

"You're painting?" He looked around at her cheery red walls, then a look of dawning comprehension crossed his face. "Nursery?"

"Yeah."

"Wow."

Reggie laughed again. She couldn't help it.

"What?"

"Nothing. It's just that…I know the feeling. This has been a life changer."

"Yes." He reached out to take her free hand, and she didn't pull back. His hand was big and warm and safe feeling. "I should pay for at least half of that paint."

She allowed her fingers to curl around his. "You should."

"What color?"

"I'm not making a decision until I know if it's a boy or girl."

"Maybe we could get a neutral color."

She bit back the "we?" that formed on her

lips. "You're right. Traditional pink and blue is kind of…"

"Traditional?"

"Well put." Reggie slipped her hand free and clasped her cup in her palms. "You want to come?"

His eyebrows lifted. "Yeah. I do. But I have to be done by two."

"What's at two?"

"Barbecue with my neighbors."

Reggie almost dropped her cup. "You're going to a neighborhood barbecue?"

"With the old guys next door. They blackmailed me into being their sauce consultant. Want to come?"

"Why don't we see how the morning goes? If we haven't killed each other, then maybe I will."

CHAPTER FIFTEEN

TOM WAS EXPERIENCING A MAJOR disconnect. Reggie was definitely pregnant; his child was growing inside her. Over the past few weeks, she'd gone from being upset about the pregnancy to, well, nesting. Seeing her so excited about paint drove home the point that they had very different perspectives on this pregnancy.

Why did the kid still seem so surreal to him? Why wasn't his paternal instinct kicking in?

Maybe getting involved with painting—preparing the baby's room—would spark some paternal instincts and he'd know what he needed to do to be a decent father, because right now, he hadn't a clue.

Reggie didn't talk much on the drive to the home-improvement store, but once they hit the paint section, she lit up. And for a person who had a bright red wall in her kitchen, Reggie seemed hopelessly drawn to pale pastels. Tom favored the bright and the bold.

"I'm thinking peaceful, restful colors," she said, holding up a pale lavender chip.

"I'm thinking stimulation." Tom grimaced at the color. "I read babies need a lot of stimulation."

"They also need sleep."

Tom continued on down the long row of paint cards, pulling whatever happened to catch his eye, until he had a handful. Then he turned and propped the cards against the gallons of paint on the opposite side of the aisle.

"How about this green?" he asked. "I know you said you didn't want green, but this one is kind of peaceful and at the same time kind of stimulating."

She cocked her head, studied the color. "Put it in the pile." So far they had a muted blue, an apricot, a pale yellow that Tom hated, and the green.

Reggie looked at the back of a paint card. "Which of these are the really nontoxic paints?"

A store associate in a red vest walked by within seconds of her asking, and Tom called him over. "Which of these paint brands are nontoxic?"

"All of them," the associate said proudly, rocking back on his heels.

"So, I can eat this paint and nothing would happen to me?"

The man's eyes bugged. "What exactly are you planning to do with it, sir?"

Reggie laughed. "We're painting a baby's room."

"Ah." He smiled with exaggerated relief, ready to play along and make a sale. "Well, I can understand your concern. These paints are all nontoxic, but I still don't recommend eating them." He led the way to a special display. "These are the least toxic and also, unfortunately, the most expensive."

"The colors we picked aren't this brand... except for the yellow," Reggie added with a note of triumph, holding up the color chip.

"Oh, we can create the tones with any base paint," the associate assured them in a conspiratorial voice.

"Great," Tom said, suspecting Reggie already knew that from the look on her face. "Thanks for your help."

"Wait until you see the yellow in the room," Reggie said as they headed for the exit twenty minutes later, each with a handful of favorite colors. "It'll be great."

"Kids fight more in yellow rooms."

Reggie stopped walking and stared at him. "How do you know that?"

"I read a lot." And he did. Every night, with his laptop balanced on his legs and Brioche curled up beside him. What else was he going to do during the evenings? He'd learned a lot, but it ate at him that he couldn't visualize his kid—even after searching in vain for the perfect nursery paint color. Did all guys experience this? Was he destined to be a failure as a father because he had no paternal instinct? Is that why his dad was able to spend so much time away from him?

Tom shoved the matter out of his mind. Or tried to.

They'd driven to the store in Tom's rental car, so after he got behind the wheel he said, "Let's get something to eat."

"I thought you had a barbecue at two."

"Part of going to a barbecue, done properly, is sitting and smelling the meat cooking for three or four hours."

"You're right. We need to eat."

"Now all we have to do is find a good peanut butter joint."

Reggie laughed and Tom felt a deep sense of satisfaction. It felt so damned good not to be at odds with her. He was beginning to believe that hanging out in her kitchen really had been a good idea. The baby would benefit.

Tom pulled into a breakfast place in a small mall.

"Internet?" Reggie asked.

"Yep."

The food was good. Not stellar, but satisfying. When the server brought the check, she asked, "How was it?" with a perfunctory smile as she set the slip on the table.

"The eggs were good. The bacon overdone and, frankly, the home fries would have benefited from a little hot paprika." He held up his thumb and forefinger. "Just enough to color them, but not overpower the potato flavor."

The server nodded blankly and said, "I'll, uh, tell the cook," before she hurried away.

"I think that was more of a rhetorical question," Reggie said with a laugh, reaching for one of his leftover fries.

"If you don't want to know, don't ask."

It felt so much like old times that Tom had to remind himself it wasn't.

"Do you want the ham bone for your dog?" Reggie pushed the ring of bone across her plate with her fork.

Tom shook his head and reached for the check. "I try to regulate her diet."

Reggie gave him a who-the-hell-are-you stare. "The dog you aren't going to keep."

"Right now she's good company. I'll find her a home when I leave. I'm working on the old guys."

"Will you miss her?" Reggie asked, an odd note in her voice.

"Of course I will. A lot, actually. But...if I end up in a city, I won't be able to care for her."

"Does she have a name yet?"

"Brioche."

Reggie's eyebrows shot upward. "You named your dog Brioche?"

"You saw her. She's got many briochelike qualities."

Reggie nodded slowly. "I guess." But she continued to look at him as if he were some kind of alien.

"Let's go," he said.

When Tom parked in front of Reggie's house, she turned in her seat and said, "If you don't mind, I'll take a rain check on the barbecue."

"You don't want to come?" Or maybe she didn't want to spend more time with him.

"I plead exhaustion." She was tired. Tom could see it in her face.

"All right. I'll go alone." He walked her to the door, feeling like a high school kid delivering his date home...although he'd never done that, having been away at boarding school.

When they reached the porch, she asked, "Do you want to come in and see the baby's room?"

In an odd way, the idea seemed intimidating. "I'd like that," Tom said, manning up. Why should a room be threatening?

Reggie unlocked the front door and led the way through her living room to a hallway. The first room they came to was obviously her bedroom. He recognized the purple afghan lying across the foot of the bed—a present from her mother many years ago.

Reggie opened the next door and stood back, allowing Tom to go in first. The room, empty and smallish, had a closet and a window looking out over the flower garden in the backyard.

"It used to be my office," Reggie said, "but now that I do everything on a laptop, I prefer to be out in the living room when I work."

"It's nice." Tom had a hard time visualizing

his child living here, in this room. He glanced down at Reggie and asked the question that had been on his mind as he'd watched her debate about paint and plow through two lunches.

"Can you feel it?" A perplexed expression crossed her face. "The baby," he said softly. "Can you feel it move yet?"

She shook her head. "Soon, the doctor tells me."

He nodded. Looked out the window again. She couldn't feel the baby yet, but still had a parental instinct. Maybe it was just him. "Nice view."

"Stimulating," Reggie agreed. She took in a deep, audible breath.

"Do you get lonely, Reg? Living here alone?"

A shadow crossed her features. "Sometimes. But everyone gets lonely. And I spend a lot of time at the kitchen."

"No friends?"

"I have friends. Just…not a lot of time, you know?" She jutted out her chin. "But I'll have time for my baby."

"I know you will." He'd never doubted that. Reggie was a caregiver.

She turned off the light. His signal to leave.

He didn't want to. He wanted to go back to the past. Have things between them be the same as they used to be.

But they couldn't, because he and Reggie hadn't yet discovered where they belonged in the world back then. The equation hadn't been complete.

When they reached the living room, Tom went for the door, even though he didn't particularly want to leave. She followed him out onto the porch.

"Reggie...are you still angry with me?"

She contemplated the question for a moment as she dug the toe of her shoe into the porch planks. "You are who you are, Tom."

"That's not an answer."

"It is," she said. "You have this ambition that overrides everything else."

He didn't want to admit it, but there was more than a grain of truth to that. What was wrong with wanting to be the best?

"I'm sorry, Tom." Though he wasn't sure why. She rose up on her toes and planted a chaste kiss on his jaw. "See you tomorrow."

"Yeah. Tomorrow."

She turned and went into the house, leaving him on the porch.

As he walked back to the car, he touched his jaw, wishing that he'd really kissed her. There on her porch, for the entire world to see.

THE FIRST ORDER OF BUSINESS ON Sunday morning, before Eden started cooking for her families, was a meeting on the Reno Cuisine competition. Eden had made good use of her downtime, designing both a menu—which Tom had also worked on while the rest of the crew was at the wedding—and a set based on a French bistro theme. She had lists of supplies, building materials and costume necessities, which she distributed to Tom and Justin. Reggie already had a copy. As near as Tom could tell, the purpose of the meeting was to bring a yawning Justin up to speed.

"I assume you've taken that weekend off from the hotel, right?" Eden asked her brother.

"I haven't heard back, but yeah, I requested it."

"You'd better hear back soon."

"Tom will take my place if I have trouble getting off."

"If I'm here," he said. Reggie cut him a quick glance, but said nothing.

"We'll wear white shirts, black pants and suspenders," Eden said.

"Suspenders?" Justin echoed with a grimace. "Why?"

"I like them."

"Fine. Sissy shoes?"

"Anything black and comfortable."

"Gotcha."

"Not Vans," Eden said. "No skateboard shoes."

"I no longer own Vans."

"Someone raid your closet?" Eden asked sweetly.

"My *concern*," Reggie said, "is the set. We need to find a cheap carpenter. I don't want to pour a lot of money into this, since we have no place to store it."

"So we break it down," Justin said.

"And no doubt try to store the pieces in my garage with all the rest of your stuff," Eden said.

Tom reached out and turned the design so he could see it. A simple storefront with a wide window that acted as a serving surface. A door. An awning. He looked up. "Do you want me to ask my neighbors for an estimate? They have time on their hands."

"Can they build a set?" Justin asked.

"They built the house I live in. And they have a big shop."

"If they were agreeable, and affordable," Eden said, "then maybe one of us could be present during construction. Kind of okay it as they go. Tweak it as necessary."

"I'll ask," Tom said.

"Yeah. Do that," Eden replied. Reggie nodded in agreement.

"And I'll get a couple estimates from legit carpenters," Justin added. "I just need a copy of the plans."

The meeting broke up and Tom went to help Eden cook, since she had trouble moving around the kitchen in the compression boot for her broken ankle, which kept hanging up on the rubber floor matting. Reggie disappeared into the office and shut the door. Tom wondered if it was just business, or if she was erecting another wall. She'd barely said two words to him since he'd arrived at the kitchen.

"What do you want me to do?" he asked Eden.

"Well, Chef Gerard, how do you feel about chopping? Reggie tells me you're the best."

"She should know," Tom said. "Onions?"

She beamed up at him. "For a start."

REGGIE SPENT MOST OF SUNDAY IN the office, catching up on what little paperwork Eden hadn't done, and hiding from Tom. It was the safest tactic until she got a few things straight in her head—like convincing herself it was possible to enjoy Tom's company and not get herself into trouble.

She was so damned afraid of being hurt again.

You have the power to stop that from happening.

And maybe if she kept repeating that to herself, she'd believe it. It didn't help that when she'd given him the we're-just-friends kiss yesterday, all she could think about was how his stubble-roughened skin had felt beneath her lips. And about all the other places she wouldn't mind putting her lips.

Tom left early on Sunday and came in late on Monday. Reggie was once again holed up in the office, and she did her best to stay there, letting Eden run the kitchen. The schedule was light, a welcome relief after the previous week, so Reggie called vendors, dealt with clients, and basically did what she could to stay out of sight.

As part of her prep work for Reno Cuisine, she'd driven by the riverside park that morning, even though it was miles out of her way. She'd attended every competition since its inception as a spectator, getting ready for the year they got in. She'd been sure they would as their reputation grew.

Now that Tremont *was* in, she wanted to make a damned fine showing. Who was she kidding? She wanted to win. And she wouldn't mind seeing Candy Catering Classique go down in flames.

Ah, fantasy.

When Reggie finally emerged from the office, it was to see Tom at his locker, changing out of his coat.

"Pasta mishap." He spread his arms wide to show her the red-splattered front.

"You look like you've been shot."

"Just winged." He shrugged out of the coat and rolled it into a ball.

"We can wash that here if you don't have a washing machine."

"Actually, I do. Came with the place."

"Like the dog."

"It's a very well equipped house." He stuffed the coat into his gym bag.

"You want to borrow an apron?"

"Eden already gave me one." He closed the locker and took a couple steps closer. "Why are you avoiding me?"

Reggie reached up to rub her earlobe, fiddling with the gold stud she wore. "Honestly? Because I'm tempted not to ignore you."

That got his attention. "Not ignore me how?"

"Not ignore you in the way that got me into trouble." There. It was out. Now she could deal with it. It was no secret there was chemistry between them. Now she'd made an open commitment to not acting on that chemistry.

"*Us* into trouble."

"Exactly."

"Well," he said in that low voice that made her nerves tingle, "it isn't like we can get into more trouble."

"Speak for yourself, Tom."

Reggie started for the kitchen. She needed to put a little distance between them, she was banking on him not wanting to continue the conversation in front of Eden. Justin was, of course, locked in the pastry room, music blaring through the door.

Tom caught up with her. "We had a great time on Saturday."

"And that's the problem, Tom." Why couldn't he see that?

Because he was a man and didn't think logically.

She stopped and turned toward him. "We had too great of a time. It was like a date."

Eden was trying not to look at them as she stood at the stove stirring a pot, but she was listening for all she was worth. Patty, thank goodness, was nowhere in sight. Maybe she'd taken out the trash.

"I'm not date worthy?" Tom demanded, making no effort to keep his voice down.

Reggie did an abrupt about-face and went into the office, pushing the door shut. It opened again immediately.

She turned and attempted her professional voice. "Could we please discuss this later?"

He came to stand within inches of her, staring down at her, daring her to stay put. Reggie, heaven help her, met his dare and didn't step back.

"I don't get what's happening," he said fiercely. "I'm trying to make a workable relationship with you."

"I know."

"This is my kid, too, but I feel like a freaking sperm donor."

Reggie's lips parted as she stared up at him. "You're not a sperm donor," she said softly.

"I feel like one."

"You're not," she repeated, so low she doubted he heard her.

Reggie slowly let her head fall forward until it rested on his chest. She felt the tension in his body as his hands settled on her hips.

"I'm not getting involved with you," she said without raising her head. She could feel his heart beating. Feel the solid warmth radiating from him. He used to make her feel safe.

Not anymore.

"I know." He spoke with utter sincerity. Break-your-heart sincerity.

She slowly raised her head.

"I won't," she repeated, looking into his dark eyes.

He would destroy her again. He wasn't part of her kitchen. He was here, but he didn't fit. And though it killed her to admit it, he'd been correct in not staying with the catering company they'd planned to start. They hadn't had a hope back then.

"I believe you," he said softly, bringing his hand up to rub the back of his fingers over her cheek before cupping her neck and lowering his mouth to hers.

Reggie didn't back away from the kiss. A

person had instincts for a reason, and she was following hers.

Tom kissed her as he used to before a long trip...and after he came back. A deep, deep, soul-melding kiss. Her arms ended up around his neck, as they always had, her body firmly against his. His hand was on her ass, pressing her into him.

And then, when the kiss ended, and he slowly lifted his head, meeting her eyes with that electric gaze, she knew why she hadn't backed away. Because if she put up barriers, he would try to scale them. But this way they met on even ground. No chase, no pursuit. Just a whole lot of conflicting signals shooting in all directions through her mind and body.

The door creaked behind them.

"Oh, sorry," Patty said. "I didn't realize—"

"Have you heard of knocking?" Tom growled.

"Tom..." Reggie stepped away from him, smoothing the front of her blouse.

"I didn't know anyone was in here," Patty said stiffly, her cheeks bright red. "I'll just leave you two."

"Is something wrong?" Reggie asked.

"I wanted to discuss what hours you needed me next Saturday. For the wedding."

"I thought you didn't think there was anyone in here," Tom muttered.

Reggie delivered a subtle warning nudge. "Just give us another minute and I'll be right with you."

A red-faced Patty turned and marched out, closing the door behind her with a brisk click.

"I meant what I said, Tom."

He stared down at the floor. Then he nodded without looking at her. "Yeah. I don't want you sleeping with me to prove something."

"I wish I'd never said that."

He looked at her. "But that's why you did it." They stared at each other for a moment, then he deftly buttoned the top button of her blouse with one hand. "Now you're Patty worthy."

"Thank you."

He forced a smile that didn't reach his eyes. "I bet if I open the door fast, she'd tumble into the room."

"Then make a lot of noise," Reggie said, taking the out Tom was offering her. "Because I don't want a workman's comp claim."

CHAPTER SIXTEEN

FRANK AND BERNIE WERE SO enthusiastic about being part of the Reno Cuisine set building crew that Tom was a little afraid. It was difficult to believe a man who accidentally set a fence on fire could be a master carpenter competent with power tools. But Tom counted and Bernie had all his fingers. So did Frank.

The guys had only two questions. When would the lumber be delivered to their shop and when could they begin?

"How difficult will this be?" Tom asked, gesturing at the plans he'd brought.

Bernie gave a dismissive snort. "Piece of cake."

"It's a lot like the theater-in-the-park sets we built back in the eighties," Frank said, as if Tom would remember theater in the park. But that was way before his time. He'd landed in Reno a decade ago, following Reggie here from California after she'd graduated from culinary school. During his stint in a Reno hotel kitchen, they'd made preliminary plans for their catering business, and then Lowell had called and Tom had gone to Spain.

And now Tom was once again waiting for word from Lowell. Something was brewing, but since his old friend hadn't answered Tom's terse email, Tom had no idea what it was.

"THEY'LL BUILD THE SET FOR the cost of the lumber," Tom said, crossing the kitchen to where Reggie was standing at the stove, making adjustments to a filling.

"We can't let them do that. We need to pay them." She dropped in the slightest pinch of salt, then added a healthy grinding of black pepper.

"I'll let you negotiate with them," he said. "They were pretty adamant."

"I can be adamant, too." She frowned as she considered the flavors she'd just sampled. Then she held out the spoon. "Taste."

He opened his mouth and tasted. "Not bad."

"Suggestions?" she asked.

"Go with that."

She seemed surprised. "All right. I will."

He settled his hand lightly on the upper curve of her hip, bringing her attention back to him. She didn't try to escape, but was miles away from relaxed.

"You're a hell of a cook, Reggie."

"I know," she said simply, "but you're better." And she seemed fine with that. She'd always held her own with him. In the kitchen, in the bedroom. Nothing intimidated her... except the thought of trusting him. He'd screwed the pooch there, but he'd never been anything but honest with her. It wasn't as if he'd crept away in the night.

And she was so damned tense, despite an obvious effort on her part to appear nonchalant. Her entire body was like the proverbial coiled spring.

Which, in his opinion, needed to be sprung.

The kitchen was empty. Patty was undoubtedly lurking somewhere, ready to jump out and surprise them, but Tom took a chance and settled both hands on her shoulders from behind. He started a slow massage with his thumbs, feeling the tension flow from her body into his hands. He decided Patty must not be anywhere near the kitchen or Reggie wouldn't allow herself to relax like this.

He caressed the delicate skin over her collarbones and her shoulders dropped. He massaged the tight muscles at the back of her neck with his thumbs. She let out a soft sigh.

And she didn't move away.

THOSE MAGICAL FINGERS WORKED their way up from her shoulders to her temples, gently stroking. She lifted her chin. The fingers of his one hand brushed over her lips, over her chin, trailed down her throat between her breasts to her stomach, where his large, warm hand curved around to settle on her negligible baby bump.

Reggie's lips parted. His holding her stomach shouldn't feel this erotic, but it did.

She could feel his breath on her temple, wanted in the worst way to turn her head and kiss him. His lips pressed against the side of her head and lust shot through her as she let herself lean back against his hard body.

"You were right about the green for the baby's room," he whispered against her hair. "It looked awful in natural light." The tension she'd felt coiled so tightly within her dissipated.

"Chef Gerard is conceding a point? Alert the media."

He touched her chin and she turned her head to look over her shoulder at him. He kissed her very lightly on her lips. She wanted more.

More was a bad idea.

She stepped away.

"I need to get back to work."

He smiled crookedly at her, but it wasn't the who-gives-a-damn smile he was so famous for. His eyes weren't involved. He was as cautious as she right now.

"I have a list for you, if you're here to work."

"Hand it over," he said.

She reached into her pocket, pulled out a card and handed it to him.

"Some fancy food here," he said.

"Small expensive dinner party," Reggie replied. "I figured I may as well take advantage of your talents while you're here."

"I have lots of talents, Reggie."

"Go to work, Tom."

Heaven help her.

TOM DIDN'T SEE A LOT OF REGGIE that day, but he had one of his best days ever in the kitchen. No Patty and no insistence that he stick to Tremont recipes.

Traffic was light after he left the kitchen, and it continued to be a good day right up until he got home.

Brioche was not at the back door, scratching madly as usual. Strange. Maybe Bernie had broken the rule and tossed her a really big bone. Tom walked out into the backyard and his heart stopped. The yard was empty. No rat dog.

"Bree!" The name ripped out of his throat and a split second later her small head appeared from under the fence.

Brioche wiggled through the hole that led to Frank and Bernie's yard, and raced over to him, turning a circle when she got there. He scooped her up with one hand and held her against his chest, brushing dirt off her head with his other hand as he walked back to the house.

"You scared the piss out of me," he told the dog, who snuggled up against him. He fed her, then went back to the yard and filled the hole, stomping the dirt to pack it down. He didn't want to leave her in the house while he was gone, but he would if he had to. It was good that the fence on the street side had a thick cement base. The cedar plank fence she'd burrowed under led into Frank and Bernie's yard, so even if she dug under again, she'd be in their yard—where she'd undoubtedly be distracted by bones and forbidden food, probably hand-fed to her by Bernie.

Tom would have to tell the guys to keep an eye out for her.

Losing his dog, even for a few seconds, had not been a pleasant experience.

Tom poured a glass of wine and went to sit on the futon. It wasn't so much that he was attached to Brioche as that he was worried about her safety. He'd learned his lesson about becoming attached to animals as a kid. He'd had two dogs, both excellent, loyal animals. One had gone to his grandparents when he'd started boarding school the first time, and the other he'd had to give away when he and his father moved from the United States to Great Britain.

Both times he'd felt as if his heart had been ripped out. And even though decades had passed, he wasn't going through that again. No way.

And in that regard he was very much like Reggie. He let his head fall back against the cushions and stared up at the ceiling. She would kiss him, consider sleeping with him, but wasn't going to let herself fall for him again.

Probably a wise move on her part.

But what about the baby? That was attachment incarnate.

He closed his eyes. He was scared. Scared spitless.

What was the right thing to do here? Disappear? Or try to be part of the kid's life and fail, as Reggie thought he'd failed her? Would fail her again.

Tons of other guys went through this. But Tom had a feeling that a lot of them were better prepared, not having been raised a vagabond by a sometimes single parent. Although…thinking back on that, too, Tom realized his father may have married, but his mind-set had always been single. Solitary.

Was he the same?

Brioche jumped up on his lap, nearly knocking his wine out of his hand. She settled and he stroked her ears as she laid her chin on his thigh. He couldn't remember another time in his life when he'd felt less sure of himself, or of his abilities.

Reggie didn't trust him.

He didn't trust himself.

"I LIKE THE GREEN," EDEN SAID, picking the paint sample out of the dozen scattered across Reggie's kitchen table.

"Tom and I decided against the green."

"Then why did you show it to me?" she asked, shuffling through the chips. Then she gave Reggie a sideways glance. "The *two* of you decided against green?"

"We went paint shopping. The green was Tom's favorite until he saw it in natural light."

"Get out."

"It was a nice day. We can have fun doing superficial stuff. Enjoy each other's company."

"I think you did okay in the serious stuff, too."

Reggie shrugged. "We did."

"Any chance Tom could stay here?"

"And do what?" Reggie held up the blue chip, her favorite.

"Work at a hotel restaurant and not get fired?" Eden suggested.

"He could try," Reggie conceded. "He could possibly work his way through several hotels here." She dropped the card on the table. "He's not a corporate guy, Eden. A hotel kitchen would be rough on him and he'd be rough on it." Her mouth tightened ruefully. "Want to hazard a guess as to who would be the loser?"

"Maybe he could run his own place?"

Reggie shrugged before settling her elbows on the table. "He's never said one word about doing that."

"Maybe..." Eden said slowly "...he's afraid of failing?"

"And maybe Tom was never meant to settle."

"You guys haven't talked custody yet?"

Reggie closed her eyes and shook her head. "I think the kid is just now becoming real to both of us."

REGGIE HAD COME TO AN agreement over the phone with Frank and Bernie, and planned to meet them the next morning before work. The lumber, which the brothers had already ordered, even though Tom told them not to, had been delivered that morning. The truck had frightened Brioche and woke Tom out of a dead, wine-induced sleep.

And now he was yawning as he worked on the appetizers for a luncheon the next day.

"Tom?"

He looked up as Eden came into the kitchen from the reception area.

"There's a large Scottish bear here to see you."

Tom knew only one man who fit that description. How in the hell had Lowell found him at the Tremont kitchen?

"Tom!" Lowell called from the outer office. "Can I come back?"

"Could I stop you?" he asked.

"Probably not." Lowell came through

the kitchen door, tall and broad with bushy auburn hair, and enveloped Tom in a brief hug. Eden leaned her upper body out of range when Lowell turned his attention toward her.

"Why are you in Reno?" Tom asked, trying to redirect Lowell's attention.

"Simone and I are getting married again."

"But…did you ever finish getting divorced?" *And don't you have to be a citizen?*

Lowell waved his hands as if Tom was talking about a minor detail. "And I wanted to talk to you."

"Have you heard of phones?"

"Newfangled tools of the devil."

Tom jerked his head at his station. "You caught me at a busy time."

Lowell frowned. "You're a catering cook now?"

"Something wrong with that?" Eden asked.

"Uh, no," Lowell replied as she gave him the evil eye. "Just…" he leaned closer to say sotto voce "…just not what I thought you'd end up doing. I think it's a good thing I came." He turned and smiled placidly at Eden.

"Where's Simone?"

"At the hotel," Lowell said, as if surprised by the question. "They have a bang-up spa and she's getting something done. Or a lot of somethings. No matter what, it's going to cost me."

"I have to finish getting ready for this wedding. Could we get together tonight for a drink or something?" Tom winced as he made the suggestion. He'd yet to be in a situation with Lowell and alcohol that had ended well.

"Give me a call when you're done here."

"So now you believe in phones?" Eden said.

Lowell shrugged a shoulder.

"It'll be late," Tom warned. As if that was a deterrent.

"I'll be up," Lowell said confidently. "I'll see you tonight." He checked his watch. "Another couple hours and Simone should be done. Maybe I'll just check out the bar at the pool."

"Good plan." Tom picked up his spoon again.

"Who's he?" Eden asked as soon as Lowell had lumbered out.

"Lowell Hislop. An old friend."

"Huh." Eden balanced on her good foot. "Why's he here? Other than getting married?"

Tom hoped he didn't look guilty as he said, "I guess I'll find out tonight."

"ORDER GUINNESS," LOWELL SAID many hours later as they sat at a table close to the hotel bar.

"I don't want a…" Tom knew he was going to lose. He looked up at the server. "Like he said."

"They have the most amazing method of pouring it here."

"There's more ways than good and bad?" Tom asked.

"Yes. Watch."

The kid, who was barely old enough to pour beer legally, and knew nothing about Guinness, shoved the glass under the tap and pulled the handle. He didn't pause halfway through the pour to let the beer rest, but instead filled the entire glass, then slammed it down onto the bar with a loud thunk. Tom watched in amazement as millions of tiny bubbles developed throughout the brew and rose to the top to form a creamy froth.

"Go figure," he said.

Lowell laughed. "I was affronted the first time I watched, but I am now officially entertained." He indicated his glass. "My third, and if Simone is going to be happy tonight, my last."

Tom couldn't say he wasn't relieved.

"What I want to talk to you about is a partnership," Lowell said after the bar server had placed the glass of beer in front of Tom.

Tom settled his forearms on the table and waited for him to continue.

"Simone and I are opening a restaurant and we want you to run the kitchen. It'd be like old times except that I can't get fired!" Lowell laughed and took a long swig of beer. "But you can."

Tom realized that his heart was beating faster. "France?"

"Simone inherited property from her grandmother. A small house that can be converted into a restaurant. It's something we've both wanted to do for a long time, but we need someone we can trust to run things during the times when Simone and I are..." His voice trailed off as he sought an adequate description of their rather unusual yet long-lived relationship.

"Working things out?" Tom saw no reason to beat around the bush. He'd witnessed the fireworks more than once. However, never at a restaurant. They might pout, ignore each other whenever possible, but they never allowed it to affect service. The fireworks happened, as all good fireworks do, after-hours.

"Exactly."

Tom felt as if he'd been turned inside out. "I don't know if I can go to France."

"Why ever not?" Lowell asked, his eyes bugging slightly. "You love France. And you need a job."

"I do." He took a swallow of the Guinness. He hadn't wanted it, but it tasted pretty damned bracing now. "Reggie is pregnant."

"Reggie?" It took a moment for the name to register. "You don't mean the woman who dumped you way back when?"

"The same. She owns the catering business."

"You knocked up the boss?"

"She wasn't my boss when I...knocked her up. That's why I'm here. I'm between jobs, we need to work a few things out."

Lowell leaned on the table, which creaked slightly under his weight. "So are you going to get married or what?"

"She won't have me," Tom said matter-of-factly.

"Smart girl." He studied Tom, his expression too shrewd for someone who'd downed nearly three pints of beer. "Bugs you, don't it?"

"I can't say I'm ready to offer marriage, but I wish things were more...normal."

"There is no such thing as normal. You know that. Let me serve as an example." He raised his beer and gestured at Tom. "So tell me, Chef Gerard, what events are you catering next?"

Tom didn't answer. He picked up his Guinness and took a long, long drink before setting it down again. "You may as well tell me about this restaurant."

"Are you hungover?" Reggie asked the instant she set eyes on Tom the next morning. He knew he was looking beyond rough when she opened the side door of Frank and Bernie's oversize barn of a garage and stepped inside. But at least he was there, instead of passed out on his futon, as he'd been a mere twenty minutes ago.

He attempted a smile. It cost him. "Why do you ask?"

"First, you look like I used to feel in the morning not that long ago, and second, Eden told me Lowell stopped by to see you."

Tom scratched his ear. "Yeah. He did, and I probably do feel like you did not that long ago."

She set her bag on a workbench and pulled the rolled plans out of it. "Kind of odd. Lowell. Here." Reggie didn't know Lowell, but she'd had one very bad experience with him—when he'd buzzed through Reno years ago with the offer for the job in Spain, at a restaurant owned by his uncle. Lowell was probably not on Reggie's favorite-person list.

"He was passing through town. Getting married, in fact."

"Wasn't he married before?" Reggie asked with a slight frown. But there was something bubbling beneath her calm exterior. "And doesn't he need to be a citizen to get married here?"

"I'm not certain of the legalities," Tom muttered. When should he tackle this? Now? During a candlelit dinner?

Frank came into the shop, followed by Bernie. "Hey, you two. Ready to rock and roll?"

"Always," Tom said.

Reggie smiled at the brothers. "Shall we go over the sketches and I'll tell you exactly what I want?"

"You bet," Frank said. The three looked over the hand-drawn plans and Reggie answered their questions. Less than five minutes later she was done.

She waved to the two men as she headed to the door, which Tom opened for her. "Frank.

Bernie. See you guys later, and thanks." The second she was outside her smile faded. She walked toward her car, Tom following, but before she got there she stopped so quickly he almost tripped over her. "Is there a job offer involved in Lowell's swing through town?"

Just like last time?

Tom squinted into the sun. "As a matter of fact, there is."

Her eyebrows lifted. "Where?"

"France."

"France?" No anger. No angst. Not much of anything by way of a response. A far cry from his announcement of a possible job in the north of Spain seven years ago.

"Nothing carved in stone," he added.

Reggie's expression remained calm. Almost serene. Ridiculously accepting. They might as well have been discussing the weather.

"It would be a good career move for you." She walked to the car, but didn't open the door.

"Is that a dig?" Tom asked flatly, stopping by the hood of her car.

"An observation, Tom."

Was she trying to get rid of him?

Reverse psychology, maybe?

"Here it is, Tom. Spelled out. You had a

career that many people would give their right hand for. Something like that involves sacrifices, which I didn't really understand seven years ago. But I do now."

"What do you mean?"

She gave him a weary look. "You aren't done yet."

"Aren't done with what?"

"You aren't done doing the work you have to do. The work you need to accomplish before you can settle."

"How do you know that?" he asked, with more of a sneer than he intended. The headache was bringing out the worst in him. And Reggie wasn't helping.

She just shook her head and opened the car door. The sunlight glinted off her dark hair as she got inside, bringing out the red.

"I'll see you at the kitchen."

Where he was supposed to make chicken cordon bleu this morning for an old-school dinner party, and where Patty would make conversation impossible.

As Reggie backed out of the driveway, Tom stalked to Frank and Bernie's garage and jerked the door open with too much force. It got away from him and slammed into the side of the metal building, the reverberating crash making the pain in his head spike.

"You all right?" Bernie yelled.

"Fine," Tom lied, as he tried not to wince. Damn Lowell and his Guinness. "Are the plans clear?"

"Yep," Frank said. "Piece of cake."

"And you can definitely be done by the weekend, so we have time to paint."

"Without breaking a sweat," Frank stated.

Tom wished he could say the same thing. Kitchens were hot and today he'd be sweating. And thinking. Not his favorite combination.

TOM WORKED LIKE A MACHINE FOR most of the day, silent and withdrawn. Patty stayed far away from him. So did Reggie.

She wasn't going to bring more drama into her kitchen. They both knew Tom wasn't going to settle for spending his days working as a prep cook here. He had dragons to slay. He was leaving, and before he went, they would make a preliminary agreement about the baby, since actual legal custody couldn't be settled until the child was born.

She wasn't looking forward to the discussion, because she had no idea what Tom was going to counterpropose to her full custody proposal. Summers in France, perhaps?

Justin swung into the kitchen around three o'clock with the happy news that the bistro was ahead of schedule. And it was spectacular. His only concern was transport and setup, since the piece was large and heavy and required hefty supports to avoid squishing the general public.

"Are you sure it's sturdy?" Reggie asked.

"Once it's bolted together, an elephant will be able to lean on it," Justin said, his eyes cutting over to Tom, who'd barely looked up. "I'm going to get Donovan to help transport it."

"Great." Reggie went back to rolling out potpie crusts.

Justin looked from one to the other, then back again. "All right then. I guess I'll just start in on those desserts."

He stood there for another few seconds, then shook his head and disappeared into the pastry room. Patty looked as if she wanted to follow him.

A second later Tom's hand closed over Reggie's upper arm. He motioned with his head to the alley and she gave up and went.

When they got outside, Tom didn't immediately say anything. Instead, he glared at her, as if it was her fault they were in this situation...which it was. So Reggie took the initiative.

"What do you want from me, Tom? I didn't offer an ultimatum. I accepted that you may be going to France."

"If I go," he said, "it doesn't mean that I'm out of your life. Out of the baby's life."

She only nodded, because he was deluding himself. Of course it would take him out of their lives. How could it not? And she knew the frantic pace of a restaurant, especially with a start-up. He'd be consumed.

"This isn't like Spain," he said.

"How so? The job in Spain catapulted you into the limelight. You need this job in France to jump-start your career."

"That doesn't mean the career comes first. I...just need to make a living in a way that doesn't eat my soul."

"I know, Tom. You have tough choices to make here." She leaned back against the brick wall. "When would you go...if you did take it?"

"The end of the month. The restaurant opens in September. Lowell needs an answer soon."

CHAPTER SEVENTEEN

TOM SHOWED UP FOR WORK EVERY day after dropping the France bombshell, and Reggie kept contact to a minimum—until she went over to Frank and Bernie's garage to help Eden paint the bistro front. Tom was there, too, with the little dog prancing around him.

The five of them painted the set, then Frank and Bernie attached the hardware and showed Eden and Reggie the awning they'd devised.

"Now it's just a matter of getting it there," Tom said, standing back, hands on his hips.

"Shouldn't be a problem. We're lending Justin our flat trailer. All we'll have to do is attach the side braces on site."

Reggie and Eden exchanged glances.

"You want us there, right?" Frank asked. "For technical assistance?"

"Of course," Eden said. She leaned down to scratch a spot of paint off her compression boot with her fingernail, but Reggie could see her smiling.

Tom left with Reggie and Eden, carrying

the little dog in one hand, calling good-night to the brothers, who were still inspecting their handiwork. Once outside, he said, "I want to go."

"Why?"

"Because I want to be there, and I can't be trusted alone in the kitchen to answer the phone. Remember what happened last time?"

Eden took her cue and limped away from them to the car. Tom didn't seem to notice.

"I thought you wanted to avoid recognition."

"No one cares anymore, Reggie. I'm yesterday's news. So I show up at a catering competition. Helping out a friend."

"I don't know that *I* want you to be recognized."

"Embarrassed to be seen with a washed-up chef?"

Reggie massaged her forehead. "I'm not sure your reputation jibes with ours."

He put his hands on her shoulders. "No one will recognize me behind the scenes." One corner of his mouth tilted up. "I'll cut my hair." And then he smiled that predatory smile of his. "Or better yet, you can cut my hair."

"I haven't cut hair since…well…since I

used to cut yours." Back in their peanut butter eating days. She'd honed her skills on Justin over the years—until he was sixteen and no longer let her touch his hair, preferring to shave it himself into a rebel skater do.

"I have scissors," Tom said.

"Decent ones?"

"Hopefully."

"Because I'm not cutting your hair with kitchen shears."

Tom laughed and touched the side of her face. "Let's get Eden. She can give technical advice."

"I don't need technical advice." Reggie started for the car. "I've done this a time or two." She waved her sister out as they approached.

Eden rolled down the window. "What?"

Tom settled a hand on Reggie's shoulder. "Reggie's cutting my hair if you don't mind waiting."

Eden's jaw dropped. "Why?"

"Tom wants to help out at the competition."

Eden petted Brioche, shaking her head and obviously not saying whatever it was she was thinking. "Fine by me as long as it's fine by you."

Reggie had no idea what was and wasn't

fine anymore, but she was glad Eden was there when Tom sat in the kitchen chair and she stood behind him, scissors in hand. And they weren't kitchen shears. They were the same scissors she'd used back when they'd been together, and still very, very sharp. Chefs had a thing for sharp cutting utensils, which made this job all the more easy.

She pulled the band out of his thick locks and combed through them with her fingers. His hair was wavy when it was shorter, which it soon would be. She held out her hand for the comb. Eden slapped it into her palm like a surgical nurse.

"Make it into a mullet," she whispered before Reggie took the first big snip. Tom winced.

She held out the hank of black hair before opening her fingers and dropping it on the floor. "Chef Gerard no more."

Tom tilted his head back to look at her. "Maybe we could change that to the new Chef Gerard?"

"One can only hope," Reggie muttered, pressing her belly into the back of the chair as she pulled sections of hair up and started snipping.

And as she worked she kept thanking her

lucky stars that her sister was here, because standing behind Tom, letting his hair slide through her fingers, was damned heady stuff. Throw elevated hormones into the mix and... oh, yeah. She was surprised her hands weren't shaking.

When she was done, she stepped back and cocked her head. "What do you think?" she asked Eden.

"He still looks like a rogue chef to me. You should have gone with the mullet. And you need to take a little more off on the left side. See?"

"You're right." Reggie did some touch-up snipping, then the sisters stood side by side regarding the results.

"How do I look?" Tom asked drily.

Like the guy she'd been in love with.

EVERY YEAR THAT REGGIE HAD made an application to the Reno Cuisine, she'd assumed eventually Tremont would get in—but she'd never dreamed she'd be pregnant and have a vanquished celebrity chef with a new haircut working behind the scenes at her booth.

Their designated area was three spaces down from Candy's Catering Classique, which had a display that had made Reggie stop and stare.

A papier-mâché tree trunk, wonderfully gnarled, with a squirrel hole in the center, stood at one side of her booth space, its branches somehow supporting the canopy. Jeweled fruit hung amid the paper leaves and were also scattered over the display tables as if they'd fallen there from the branches.

The risers were sheets of jewel-tone glass, supported on mosaic cylinders. Candy herself was dressed in a lovely gold dress with a simple white organza apron tied over the front. When she saw Reggie staring, she gave her a smug look that clearly said, "I have this all sewed up."

Meanwhile, Justin, Tom, Frank and Bernie were struggling to put together the bistro display on the Tremont site. They had the front and supporting side wings in place when Reggie and Eden arrived.

"It looks great," Reggie said as she pulled open the van doors.

"Thanks." Justin continued fastening screws, while Patty stood at a distance, eyeing the structure critically.

"It looks a little crooked to me," she called.

"Don't worry about it," Justin said.

"No, really." Patty walked closer to inspect

the supporting wing on the side closest to the van.

"It's fine," Tom said.

"No," Patty said adamantly. "The serving counter is at an angle. This side needs to be lowered." She attempted to nudge the supporting wedge farther out from under the side wing. Instead of shifting, though, the support shot out from under the unsecured wall, which instantly dropped two inches.

Patty shrieked, trying desperately to hold the wing in place, but the entire structure leaned heavily toward her, twisting under its own weight.

Tom rushed to help her hold it up, putting his shoulder to the structure as a wooden support piece broke free and raked up his side. He gritted his teeth and held up the heavy pressboard, with Bernie's and Frank's belated assistance, while Justin shoved wedging under it.

"Don't let go," Justin said, grabbing for his drill and sinking several screws, then reattaching the 2x2 that had ripped up Tom's side. Finally, Justin decreed the piece sturdy, and Frank, Bernie and Tom all carefully released their grips. Justin turned to a red-faced

Patty. "I think we'll let it be a little bit uneven. *All right?*"

Patty turned even redder. "I'm sorry...I—I..." She swallowed convulsively, then turned and walked quickly toward the van.

"Damn it, she'd better not quit," Justin muttered. "Frank, Bernie...can you help me get the other side of this thing screwed together so we don't crush any bystanders—shit, Tom. You're bleeding."

"It's not that big a deal," he said. "I'll go clean up."

"Let me see it," Reggie said. Tom obediently hoisted his jacket and she grimaced. The wound didn't need stitches, but was slowly oozing blood. Not a good look for a food server.

"I'll take care of it," he assured her. "You should be setting up."

"I have to wash my hands, anyway," Reggie said, "and I don't know how you're going to reach your back." The deep scratch started on his side and twisted around almost to his shoulder blade.

Please do not let this be a harbinger of the day to come. One prep cook bleeding, the other probably crying.

Reggie got a small first aid kit from under

the seat of the van, then gestured with her head to the office building that served as headquarters for the event.

"Your jacket is ruined," she said as they walked the short distance. "I have another in the car."

They went into the family rest facilities and Reggie put the first aid kit on the sink and raised his jacket again. Tom stood as if at attention as she turned on the water and let it run until it was warm. Then she took a gauze pad and dampened it. His muscles contracted as she started wiping the blood away.

"I'm sorry if it stings," she said without looking up at him. She took gauze and adhesive tape out of the kit.

"I'll tear tape," Tom said, taking the roll from her. She stretched gauze over the wound while he tore off a chunk of tape with his teeth. "This is the first time I've gotten a back wound while cooking."

"Considering your temper in the kitchen, that's surprising." The muscles of his back contracted again as he laughed.

"A sous-chef did chase me with a knife once. Around and around the counter."

Reggie looked up to see if he was kidding. He wasn't, and there was something in the way he looked at her that made her mouth go dry. She quickly went back to taping the gauze in place.

Had he made a decision about France?

Just ask him. Get it over with.

No. She wanted him to tell her.

"Well," she said after patting the last piece of tape over the dressing, "it's a bit primitive, but you won't be bleeding through your jacket."

"The booth looks good when it's not attacking me," Tom said as they crossed the grass toward it. Indeed, the bistro front, with the elegantly lettered Tremont sign, looked authentic and thankfully sturdy, the awning a clever touch. Lace-edged linens covered the tables in front of the windows, and Eden was starting to arrange plates. The vendors to the left of them had just finished setting up a saloon front and the people on the other side were struggling to get an inflated palm tree for their luau themed display to stay put.

"I can't find Patty," Eden said as soon as Reggie got into earshot.

"Great. Do you think she quit?" Reggie asked.

"I'll go find her," Tom said.

"No. Start finishing the hors d'oeuvres. I'll—"

"I'll find her," Bernie interrupted as he walked by with his portable drill and toolbox. "I saw her head toward her car."

"I hope she's still here," Reggie muttered. "I don't want to find another prep cook after you're..." Her voice trailed off.

"Gone?"

"Exactly."

Tom made a gesture with his chin and Reggie turned to follow his gaze. Patty was on the opposite side of Bernie and Frank's truck, and Bernie was talking to her, his hands on her shoulders. Her eyes were down, but she nodded as he spoke.

"Bernie saves the day," Tom muttered.

At ten o'clock the general public was allowed into the cordoned off area of the park, and from that point on it was a steady stream of work. Tom stayed in the background, out of sight, replenishing trays of food, stacking napoleons, piping fillings into various hors d'oeuvres. He worked on a long portable table hidden behind the display, made level on the grass by a wooden wedge jammed under one leg. Justin worked the hot station in the wide lace-edged storefront window to the left of the false bistro door. Eden served the cold food out of the window to the right. Reggie circulated, lending a hand where needed, greeting people and explaining dishes whenever she had a free moment.

Patty, also in black pants and a white shirt, her curls pulled away from her face with a black fabric headband, worked the back with Tom. She took care not to make eye contact, focusing on the food with a laserlike intensity.

"Damn it, Patty," he finally growled.

"What?" she asked, snapping to attention at his tone.

"I'm not going to eat you."

She swallowed, raising her chin. "I've never injured anyone before."

"You barely scratched me. You made a mistake. We all make mistakes. Wallowing in guilt doesn't help." He narrowed his eyes. "Haven't we had this conversation before?"

"Yes," she allowed. Her mouth puckered tighter for a moment, then she said, "Sometimes I wonder why they keep me when they have you."

Tom stared at her, frowning deeply. "Because I'm not staying."

"Really?"

"Reggie did me a favor. I needed some time

to reevaluate some aspects of my life. I asked for a job and she gave me one. Temporarily." Pouring his guts out to Patty. Had hell frozen over? "We'd better get back to work."

Tom loaded a plate of napoleons out of the cooler, then came around the counter to set them on a marble board. When a young red-headed woman dressed in jeans and a khaki blazer touched his arm, he glanced at her, impatient to get back to his work area.

"I have some questions if you have a minute, Chef Gerard."

Well, shit. He frowned at her and shouldered his way back behind the set.

"I don't think the general public is allowed in here," he said when she followed him.

"Just a couple questions. I was surprised to see you, of all people here, with a catering company. This is a bit of a step down from your usual gig."

"Who are you?" Tom demanded, as Reggie came around the other side of the booth.

"Christine Miles. *Reno Standard.*" She handed him a card, which Tom looked at, then dropped on the ground. He felt Reggie's hand on his back and resisted the urge to grind the card into the grass with his shoe.

"I'm sorry, Ms. Miles. I'm busy."

"But a catering competition...for someone with your background—"

"How do you know my background?"

"I read the tabloids."

"And how do you know I'm Tom Gerard?" So much for the fricking haircut and people forgetting.

She lifted her phone and snapped a picture. "Well. If I'm not certain now, I will be shortly."

"Look. I'm busy and you need to—"

"Tom." He felt Reggie's hand tense on his back.

"I'm fine," he said over his shoulder. "And busy. If you'll excuse me?"

He moved past the reporter and started working, head down, seething. He wasn't so much worried about his career as privacy, which was a first for him. He didn't want anyone bugging Reggie.

"No spectators back here," Reggie told the woman.

"It really is him, isn't it?" the reporter answered. "My aunt's friend told me she had an encounter with him in your office, but I thought she was confused. Apparently not."

Mrs. Bremerton, no doubt. Bitch.

The reporter cocked her head at Reggie. "How on earth did he end up here?"

"He's not who you think he is," Reggie said evenly, "and if you don't leave this area, I will call security."

REGGIE AND PATTY SPENT THE remainder of the competition transporting food Tom prepared behind the booth. They didn't talk, but their fingers touched as he handed her dishes and trays, and she liked the casual contact. She wanted to thank him for not telling the reporter to go to hell, as he'd no doubt wanted to. He'd done well. For Tremont. For her.

Tremont didn't win the Reno Cuisine, but they placed first in People's Choice, right after Candy won the big trophy for the fourth time in a row.

"We've won the congeniality award," Justin said with an air of satisfaction when he returned with their plaque.

Tom leaned close to Reggie. "How in the hell did we lose?" Smoke was practically rolling out his ears.

Reggie put her palm on his chest. "It's about more than the food. The display is a big part of the scoring."

"Our display is great."

Reggie motioned toward the bejeweled fruit

tree, where Candy stood beaming in her fairy-godmother dress. "But not a Hollywood set."

"This bites," Tom said in disgust.

"Hey. We handed out tons of business cards and brochures."

Reggie had to hand it to the reporter, though—she hadn't started any rumors. People had not flocked to their site to see if they had a master chef on the premises.

"I don't trust her," Tom said when Reggie mentioned that to him later as they packed up the food. Justin, Bernie and Frank were breaking down the display—which they did with no injuries, although Reggie had had her heart in her throat as she'd watched the heavy front get lowered to the ground.

"You don't trust any reporters," she replied.

"With good cause."

The breeze ruffled the hair that had escaped her French twist as she gazed up at him, and she pushed it out of her face with one hand. He reached out to get a few strands she'd missed, tucking them behind her ear. "Well, it wasn't like I was going to punch her or anything," he said with a half smile.

"Are you worried that she'll write something that'll hurt your career?"

"You mean how the mighty have fallen?"

He shook his dark head, a protective expression in his eyes that she hadn't seen in a long time. "No," he said quietly. "I just don't want anyone bothering you to find out about me."

Reggie's lips parted as she digested what he'd said. Good point. "Well, I'll try to work a publicity angle if that happens."

"The reporters I attract won't give you the kind of publicity you want." He reached out and put a hand on the curve of her waist. She didn't move any closer, but the connection between them was palpable.

"Are you coming over to Frank and Bernie's for a celebratory drink?"

"Hard not to when they're storing the set for us until next year."

"Yeah." Tom pulled her a step closer, still looking down at her, his head dipping lower until he lightly touched her lips. "You let me know if anyone harasses you. Right?"

Reggie felt an electric jolt when his lips made contact. "Yeah," she said on a husky note. "I'll do that."

Reggie, Eden and Patty drove to the kitchen to store the food and clean out the van, while Tom and Justin helped Bernie and Frank haul the set. By the time the sisters and a hesitant Patty arrived at the house, the four guys were sitting in lawn chairs around the cold barrel cooker, holding beers.

Reggie popped the top of an orange soda and sat in a chair across the circle from Tom. Eden settled on the grass and held Brioche. Patty sat next to Bernie, who smiled warmly at her. She smiled back, albeit stiffly. Frank pushed a beer into her hand without asking, and after a moment's hesitation, she opened it and poured it into the plastic glass Bernie offered her.

"If you think this year was good," Frank told Reggie, "just wait until next. Justin thinks we should turn the set into a Western saloon and perhaps offer some barbecue...."

Reggie smiled, sipped her orange soda and listened to Frank expound on what a team they made.

Patty loosened up after finishing her beer, giggling at Bernie's jokes and going so far as to accept another. Justin told story after story about working in the hotel kitchen, until he had the brothers choking with laughter. As the celebration flowed on Reggie caught Tom studying her. He was going to France soon. And he was concerned about her.

When she and Eden said goodbye to the group, Tom went with them. Eden didn't slow down on her way to her car. "I'll see you guys later," she said.

She knew, too.

Reggie looked up at Tom. "Do you want me to change the bandage on your back before I go? You're soaking through."

He pulled the shirt around to the side to see the dots of blood. The cut had to hurt like crazy, especially earlier today, when he was hot and sweat had probably been seeping into it.

"I don't have first aid supplies except for Band-aids."

"I do," Reggie said. She never went anywhere without a way to deal with a knife slice.

Tom relented without further argument, wincing when she pulled the gauze free several minutes later in his bathroom, which didn't even have towels on the racks. "Sorry," she said. "I should have soaked it longer." She cleaned the long cut, then applied another dressing. When she was done, she pulled down his T-shirt to cover his back.

Tom adjusted the shirt as he turned toward her. His bathroom was not small, but somehow the walls seemed to be closing in now that she could see his face. "I should be going." Liar. She wasn't going anywhere.

Tom settled his hands on her waist and pulled her a few steps forward, until she was between his thighs as he leaned back against the bathroom vanity. Oh, those thighs. Long and muscular.

"Why are you here, Reggie? Was it really to change the bandage?"

She shook her head. "No…it was more along the lines of kissing you and making it better." His eyes darkened and she brought her hand up to his face, running her forefinger over his lower lip. "And not because I have anything to prove."

She leaned in to trace her lips over the trail her finger had made, and Tom wrapped his arms around her and kissed her. But not gently or reverently. He pulled her to him and ravaged her mouth. Reggie, ever up for a challenge, gave back as good as she got.

When he finally raised his head, she could feel his erection pressing into her. It made her even more urgent as she started undoing his shirt buttons, but he put his hands over hers, stopping her.

Her gaze shot up and he planted a soft kiss on her lips, then took her arm and led her out of the bathroom and into his stark bedroom. Once there he put her hands back up onto his buttons, and her fingers went to work.

"What's wrong with the bathroom?" she whispered, finally breaking the silence. "It used to be one of our favorite rooms." The bathtub. The shower. Any available surface.

He peeled her shirt up over her head. "The counter doesn't allow for a long…" he kissed the crook of her neck, making her shiver "…long…" he reached around to release her bra "…leisurely…" he sucked his breath in as her hand dipped down into the top of his pants "…exploration."

"I see your point," she murmured against his skin. She loved how he smelled. It made her want to eat him alive.

They undressed each other with the practiced moves of old lovers, but this didn't feel like old times to Reggie. Just as when they'd made love in San Francisco, she felt she was exploring uncharted territory—with a vengeance. She could not get enough of this man.

Once naked, Tom backed her up again, his thighs bumping hers, until her legs made contact with the futon, and he slowly lowered her down. Then he lay beside her, pulling her against him and kissing her as her palms played over his skin, rediscovering all the places she'd once known.

"You're sure about this." He rolled her onto her back, his lips tracing the sensitive skin at the side of her neck, then along her jawline. She shifted her head on the pillow to give him better access.

"I'm sure."

"No regrets in the morning?" He placed the flat of his hand on her belly, frowning slightly as he caressed the swelling there, then met her eyes again. "You'll *be here* in the morning."

"No regrets. I'll be here."

"But you're not getting involved with me?"

"This is our involvement, Tom." Her voice took on a softly pleading tone. "I can deal with this part of it. I need this part. Please?"

She slid her fingers into his hair and pulled his mouth to hers before he could answer. He gathered her to him, stretching her body against his before rolling onto his back, tugging her on top of him. His muscles were long and hard, his erection even harder as it pressed against her abdomen, making her ache with the need to feel him inside her. Somehow the world was right when he was there, joined with her.

But instead, his finger slipped inside and she gave an involuntary gasp at the delicious sensation.

"That's it," he murmured as she moved against him, almost without conscious thought. One finger, then two. He knew exactly what she liked, exactly how to drive her to the edge.

And she could return the favor. In a minute or two...

When she sighed against his chest, Tom laughed softly, the first sign that he'd let his guard totally drop. "Like that, do you?"

"You know I do." She bit her lip, then put her hand down to stop him before it was too late.

"Are you sure?"

"I never eat dessert first," she said, rising up slightly so that she could slide down his chest. He folded the pillow behind his head and watched through half-closed eyes as she took him in her mouth. It wasn't long before his hand fisted in her hair, and then he gently eased her back. She gave him a roguish smile and one last long lick.

He pulled her up his body once more and rolled over her, kissing her deeply as he nudged her thighs apart and moved in between them. When he pushed into her, she closed her eyes at the sensation, so glad, so very glad she'd come to his house this evening. He was heavy. Hot. She raised her hips to draw him in to the hilt.

"Oh, yeah," he breathed into her ear.

And then they stopped talking, communicating instead through the response of their bodies as they moved against one another. Reggie had never made love to anyone else who could bring her to the brink and then back off, holding her there. It was maddening. It was delicious.

It was Tom.

But good things last for only so long, and even though she fought it, she could finally hold off no longer. Tom had more self-control—about a minute more. When he finally emptied into her, Reggie cradled his head, brushing the dampness from his forehead.

"You okay?" she asked, and he laughed against her shoulder.

REGGIE WOKE UP WITH TOM HALF sprawled over her, like old times. She lay there awake, secure in his embrace, feeling the even rise and fall of his chest as he slept. Her gaze fastened on the open suitcase, its top leaning against the wall opposite the bed. Reality. She felt him shift, and then his lips pressed into the crook of her neck.

"You're going, aren't you?"

He rolled off her and propped himself on one elbow. "I have to."

She understood. Sadly. And she told him so.

"It's a site visit. I'll see the kitchen, meet the other guys he's hiring."

Reggie curled into Tom instead of pushing him away, as instinct demanded. She closed her eyes for a moment.

His hand settled on the side of her head, holding it against his shoulder. Reggie sucked in a breath. Slowly exhaled.

"I'm using this as a stepping stone, Reggie. I'll put in time until I can get something back here in the States."

She pulled away from him, brushing the hair from her face. There were many things she wanted to say, but settled on, "When?"

"Lowell is booking the ticket. Sometime soon. I'd planned on telling you after we were done with this competition."

"I knew this was coming," she said simply, but there was nothing simple about her emotions. "That's why I told you I wouldn't get involved."

"It's not forever," Tom said.

She nodded, stunned at how, now that his leaving was official, it hurt. No, she'd never gotten over him.

And yes, she'd been wise to decide not to get involved.

If only she hadn't.

CHAPTER EIGHTEEN

ANXIETY, VAGUE BUT INSISTENT, started gnawing at Tom as soon as Reggie pulled out of the driveway.

No...it had started before then. Around the time he'd woken up and felt so incredibly glad to have her there with him.

He went to the back door and called Brioche in from where she was happily digging at something in the grass, growling and pouncing.

"Come on in, tough girl." He didn't particularly want to be alone while he did his small load of laundry and washed his three dishes. He spent the day on edge, and instead of phoning Reggie at the end of it, he phoned Lowell.

"Impatiently awaiting my call?" his friend asked when Tom got him on the line.

"Wondering when I'm leaving. I have to make plans."

"Simone is finishing up the details. How does Wednesday sound?"

"Good."

He needed to get this trip over with, settle his life so he could be fair to Reggie. Who he was just as much in love with as he'd been before going to Spain.

And he didn't know how to handle it.

REGGIE HAD JUST STARTED stirring the paint when she heard someone at the front door. Not Eden; she would have called first. And Justin was actually out on a date on the first free evening he'd had in a long time.

Reggie walked down the hall to the living room, knowing it had to be Tom. But why?

Upon opening the door, she knew why. This was goodbye.

He attempted a smile as she stepped back to let him come inside. It wasn't very convincing, but she didn't feel like smiling, either. She didn't regret their night except in terms of wishing it could have been more permanent, but Tom wasn't wired that way and she wasn't going to try to make a life with a man who was the equivalent of a caged tiger. The tiger would eventually escape, and Reggie would be left with the cage.

"When do you leave?" she asked, closing the door behind him.

"Three days."

"Well, then." She couldn't think of anything else to say. In three days she could start putting her life together without him. It would be more restful. Easier. Emptier.

"Painting?"

"Yes," she answered with a slight frown, glancing down at her clothing. Nothing to suggest painting.

He reached out to touch her cheek, then held up his thumb with a light smear of green paint over it. Reggie put her hand to her face.

"It's all gone," he said, rubbing his thumb and forefinger together. He hooked his thumbs in his pockets. "Want some help?"

"Sure," she said without enthusiasm. There was something bittersweet about Tom helping her paint the nursery. No, make that really bittersweet. Now, instead of focusing on the one positive aspect of this situation, preparing for her baby's future, she was again dealing with unfinished business, unsettling emotion.

They walked together down the hall to the baby's room, where newspaper covered the hardwood floor and all the trim was taped off with blue painter's tape. Just having him here, in the room, was difficult.

This was not the same man who'd made

love to her. Already he was withdrawing, as he had the last time he'd left. Only this time she knew the drill, and he was leaving her on better terms. Then he'd come back. She knew he would. And leave again. Her child would be raised that way, and would hopefully think it was normal—as long as Tom didn't make promises he had no intention of keeping. As Reggie's father had done.

"It's not the color you picked," Reggie said. "But it's still green." Crisp Granny Smith apple green.

"I like it," Tom said, studying the open container. "Stimulating and soothing at the same time."

"Yes." She picked up her brush. "Maybe you could roll and I'll do trim?"

He began to pour paint into the tray, and Reggie had to stop him before he poured too much. When he slopped the roller in, she realized that Tom had never painted before. Biting her lip to keep from saying anything, she started carefully painting around a window as he taught himself the ins and outs of rolling paint. She realized too late she should have offered him an old shirt, since he soon had a fine mist of apple-green over his white T-shirt. When she mentioned it, he looked down, shrugged, then started on the next wall.

Focus. Reggie ran the brush down the edge of the window. Carefully. Trying to avoid the odd swell of her heart as Tom ineptly slung paint.

It took less than an hour to paint the room despite Tom's lack of skill, and then he poured the extra paint back into the container and sealed it while Reggie disposed of the roller covers and washed the brushes. When she was done she came back to find Tom critically eyeing his work.

"I messed up along the ceiling," he said, pointing out where the roller had left green marks on the white paint.

"I'll touch that up tomorrow."

He put an arm around her shoulders and she leaned her head against him, squeezing her eyes shut. She wished they could be just a normal couple getting their baby's room ready. But no.

And she didn't know why. What was this thing that kept all the pieces from coming together smoothly? Why couldn't she figure it out?

"I'll come in to the kitchen tomorrow and

Tuesday," he said. "I don't have anything else to do, and the last time you kicked me out, I went nuts hanging out around my place all day."

"I'd appreciate that. Eden just booked a last-minute cocktail party for Wednesday. Appetizers and desserts." So civil.

Damn, but Reggie wanted to sleep with him. One more time before he left.

"I'll be there," Tom said. He stepped back and when, throat dry from nerves, she was about to ask him if he wanted to stay with her, he said, "I need to go. Brioche is in the house and her bladder is only so big."

"Where will she stay when you're gone?" Reggie asked, knowing the answer.

"The boys," he said. "Frank and Bernie."

"How long will you be away?"

"Two weeks maybe?"

"And then you'll know."

"Then I'll know," he echoed softly.

A moment later he left, kissing her at the front door. She could tell it was only supposed to be a quick goodbye kiss, but it got away from him, grew in heat and intensity, and for a brief moment, as he pressed her to him, Reggie thought she was going to get a proper goodbye. Instead Tom reluctantly pulled back and leaned his forehead against hers.

"I'll see you at the kitchen," he said, his voice slightly husky.

He wanted to stay, but his instinct to leave was stronger.

Moments later, despite her intentions to remain logical, she felt a swell of frustration and anger as she watched him walk to his car.

She pressed her fingertips against her temples. Hard.

TOM BOUGHT A COPY of the *Reno Standard* on his way home from Reggie's, and there was no mention of him being at the Reno Cuisine, no phone photo of the newly shorn Chef Gerard. Apparently he really was old news. It was a good feeling. But he'd buy another paper tomorrow, just to make sure they weren't saving him for a slower news day.

He spent the next day, as promised, in the Tremont kitchen, helping Reggie prep for a luncheon and a cocktail party, while Eden caught up on the office work. Reggie was making a chicken empanada and Tom showed her a filling using chorizo and freshly ground chicken.

"Love it," she said when he offered her

a taste, after turning the heat off under the pan. She met his eyes briefly, smiled a distant smile.

Everything between them was false right now. His actions, her reactions. No, not really so much false as forced. A front they were both using to protect themselves from reality.

"I'd like to use that for the appetizers."

"I'll grind up a batch tomorrow." On his last day at the kitchen before leaving the country.

But he'd be back to take care of Brioche and his belongings. And then he'd leave again, because if Lowell offered him this job on terms he could accept—which was just about any terms at this point—he had to take it. Remake himself. Tom hoped Reggie would understand that it was better for her and the baby if he shook this rogue reputation he had.

He left the kitchen early and went home, surfed the web and called Lowell to firm up plans. Then he kicked around his lonely house with Brioche, who must've sensed something was up. She was shadowing his every move. Frank had finally agreed that he could live with the dog as long as Bernie vacuumed frequently and she slept in the utility room.

She was going to hate that, but Tom had

a feeling she'd be warming Bernie's feet before too much time passed. Bernie was a soft touch.

Tom scooped the dog up and ruffled the hair on top of her head. As was he. That would have to change, pronto, if he was going to command one of Lowell's cutthroat crews.

The next morning, his last day working at Tremont, he got up early after a sleepless night.

He popped Brioche out the back door, started the coffee and sliced a piece of bread, which he covered with marmalade. He read the news as he ate, then turned on the shower. While the water warmed, he walked back into the kitchen and opened the back door to call Brioche.

But she wasn't waiting there, ready to shoot in.

Tom's stomach knotted as he stepped out into the very empty backyard and saw the fresh hole under the fence to Frank and Bernie's. Heart in his throat, he strode over and peered into his neighbors' territory. Their gate was open and the yard was empty.

Brioche was gone.

REGGIE PULLED BEHIND THE kitchen on Tom's last day of work, but the spot where he usually parked was empty.

She poked her head into the office, where Eden was tying on an apron. "No Tom?"

Her sister shook her head. Patty was chopping away at vegetables, using the technique Tom had taught her, and Justin wasn't due in to make desserts until early afternoon.

Reggie put on an apron and went into the kitchen, where she started the preliminary work for hot appetizers, and wondered where he was. She'd counted on him this one last day.

The phone rang and Eden, being closer, headed for the office. A second later, she came back and handed Reggie the cordless phone. "Tom."

"I'm going to be late," he told her.

"Flat tire?"

"My dog is gone. I need to find her," he said, as if he'd lost his socks and needed a few more minutes to get ready. "Can you do without me for a while?"

"Sure, Tom." There was no other answer Reggie could give. Besides, after today, they'd be handling everything without him. All the time. It was just that she'd counted on him today. And now she needed to make a chicken empanada filling.

After she hung up, she called Patty over

and had her go to work on the appetizers while she went into the cooler and came back with the chicken. She started to break it down.

"What's with Tom?" Eden asked.

"He lost his dog."

"Oh, no." Eden put a hand to her chest. "A little dog like that? Lots of things could happen to her."

Actually, Reggie was more worried about Tom. He hadn't sounded right. He'd been too matter-of-fact. No hint of emotion.

For a guy who blew up in the kitchen so often, there were times when he retreated.

Focus. You have a professional commitment here.

Reggie did focus—for almost half an hour. No call from Tom, which meant he hadn't found his dog.

She made it another half hour, putting together her own version of chicken filling, then she gave up. Yes, they were busy, but an emergency was an emergency.

"I have to help Tom look for Brioche," she said, pulling off her apron. "I'll work late tonight. I just…have to go help Tom find his dog."

"It's about time," Eden replied, taking Reggie's apron from her. "Patty and I can finish most of the prep."

Reggie hurried to her car and was inside before she realized she was still wearing kitchen clogs.

She drove slower once she got within a few blocks of his house, looking for Brioche. What she saw instead was Frank on one side of the street and Bernie on the other, peering into bushes and over fences, calling and whistling. Her heart sank.

So much for the hope that Tom was late because of a happy reunion with the dog he'd pretended he didn't care about.

Reggie pulled into Tom's driveway and parked. The house was empty, as she'd suspected, so she started down the driveway and turned in the opposite direction from Frank and Bernie, calling Brioche's name over and over again.

She'd made a circuit of the block, then started up the next street when, in the distance, she saw Tom walking toward her cradling something to his chest.

Reggie hurried to meet him, jogging awkwardly in her clogs.

"I thought you were overloaded in the kitchen," he said when she stopped in front of him, reaching out to pat the little dog, who was panting after her big adventure.

"I was worried about Bree." Tom met her eyes briefly, then focused back on the animal.

Bernie rounded the corner, then broke into a smile and waved for his brother to join them.

"So there you are, you little escapee," he said when he got close enough to pet her. He rubbed the dog's silky ears, oblivious to the fact that Tom wasn't smiling like the rest of them. "Where was she?"

"On a playground," Tom said, his expression taut. He started walking and the others fell into step. Bernie and Frank began making plans for an escape-proof yard as they traveled the three blocks home.

"It's easy," Frank said to Bernie. "I read it in the *Family Handyman.* You bury chain link along the edge of the fence."

"Sorry about this," Tom finally said to Reggie in a low voice as the men debated the best kind of chain link to use. "I overreacted. I'll just grab a shower and head down to the kitchen."

You didn't overreact. You reacted normally.

But for some reason, he wouldn't or couldn't acknowledge that.

"Thanks," Reggie said. "I wasn't able to figure out the chicken sausage filling." She'd made her own, but wanted his recipe.

"I'll write it down when I get there."

Once they reached Tom's house, he thanked Frank and Bernie, who headed off to their place, and told Reggie he'd be at the kitchen within the hour.

She started for her car, then stopped as the thought that had been nudging at her brain finally took form. How on earth could she have been so dense?

TOM STOOD UNDER THE SPRAY longer than necessary, despite the water stinging the healing cut on his side and back. What had started out as a quick shower ended up being a fight with himself.

Reggie had made it more than clear from day one that she didn't want him in her life, because she believed he'd put his career first. And he was doing just that.

Was he running out on her?

She'd never wanted him to stay.

But if he worked a year or two without getting fired…well maybe he could then get a job in the States, close to Reggie and the kid. See if he could get to know his child. It probably wouldn't be too late…would it?

He'd loved his father, respected him, even if he hadn't been able to spend as much time with him as he'd wanted. Even though Tom was just a kid, he'd understood. Would his kid understand and love him? It seemed reasonable, given his own experiences.

But the one thing he was absolutely certain of was that he had to go. It was time. Whenever he considered not leaving, his anxiety spiked.

He needed to put his career on track, then work on everything else. Try to repair his life one aspect at a time.

When he came out of the bathroom, tying the towel at his waist, he almost dropped it when he saw Reggie sitting on the bed, her feet crossed at the ankles, her hands in her lap. Brioche was curled up in a ball beside her.

"Damn it, woman. You scared me." He hitched the towel higher.

"Second time today."

"How so?"

"Brioche," she said, stroking the dog's head. "That had to have been frightening, having her disappear like that."

"I wasn't frightened," he said dismissively.

"I was concerned. She's small, you know. Big dogs and fast cars out there."

"I see," Reggie said, in a tone that put his back up.

"Do you?"

"Mmm."

"Why aren't you at the kitchen?" he asked.

"Because I've spent too much time there, using my business as a shield."

"From what?" he asked, dropping the towel and grabbing a pair of boxers off the top of his suitcase. Reggie kept her eyes on his face. Mostly.

"Anything I didn't want to deal with. It's so much easier to focus on the urgency of getting ready for an event. But you know what? Eden and Patty are capable of prepping." She touched her belly. "And I need to get used to believing they can function without me, just like we managed to function without Eden."

Tom stepped into his cargos, then shrugged into a white T-shirt. "Well, maybe we better get down there now."

"Bury ourselves in work and avoid everything else?"

"However you want to put it," he said impatiently.

"You're worried about more than Brioche and the job, aren't you?"

He stared at her. How in the hell was he supposed to answer that? "Look. In hindsight, it was probably ridiculous to get that upset over a dog."

"Really?" she asked flatly, her expression radiating disbelief. "Come on, Tom."

"What do you want, Reggie? Should I break down and sob or something? Would that satisfy you?"

"I want you to answer the question," she said with maddening calm. "What else is bothering you?"

"The baby, damn it. All right?

"There hasn't been a guy alive who hasn't felt some kind of trepidation at the prospect of fatherhood. So, yes. I'm a guy. I feel some nerves in that regard. *And* I'm concerned about putting my career back on track."

She cocked her head, telling him she wasn't satisfied with his answer. Tough. It was his answer. A solid, truthful answer.

And it was all he was giving.

"Let's go," he said, stepping into his canvas shoes. Reggie got off the bed, but Brioche stayed there, curled up, watching him.

He was leaving her in the house. No more

chances. And before he handed her over to Frank and Bernie, they had to swear that their fence was unbreachable. As he'd told Reggie, Brioche was a small dog and there were a lot of dangers out there. He felt responsible.

THE TALK WITH TOM HAD BEEN just as frustrating as Reggie had anticipated. But she'd lobbed the first volley. Another would follow. She could be stubborn, too.

As promised, Tom wrote out the chicken sausage recipe as he made it. Otherwise, he said, he'd forget a step, because he tended to cook on autopilot.

After he was done and had stored away the trays of empanadas they'd made together in stony silence, he asked Reggie if she needed more help. It was only eleven o'clock and yes, she did need more help, but he was so closed off that it was uncomfortable having him around—especially when she needed to think.

She shook her head. "No. I think we have it from here."

He also had things to say—she could see it in his expression—and quite possibly had no idea how to say them.

Good. He needed to mull this through, as did Reggie.

"I'll see you later," she said as she walked with him to the rear entrance. "Thanks for coming in." He stared down at her, his mouth held in a tight line. She put a palm on his chest, felt the rhythm of his heart, then slid her hand up and around the back of his neck, pulling his head down for a kiss. When his lips touched hers, she felt the heat, but he was holding back. Retreating.

Fine.

For now.

After Tom left, Reggie worked quickly to get the rest of her prep done. Yes, they could have used him, but she wanted him out of there while she settled a few things in her head. She worked with intense focus, ignoring Eden until her sister finally said, "What gives?"

Reggie looked up from the olives she was pitting for tapenade. "I'm plotting."

"Something to do with Tom?"

Reggie finished the last olives, then went to rinse her hands. "You know...it's funny how you can get your mind set in one direction and just keep chugging along, twisting everything around to fit this theory. A theory that, on the surface, seems solid."

Eden twisted her mouth sideways. "Uh,

yes. Like when I believed that if I made cheerleader I could win David Summer's heart?"

"Something like that," Reggie said. "I thought I knew Tom. We lived together for a year. Planned this business together."

"And then he left you."

Reggie took Eden by the shoulders, leaving wet finger marks on her blouse. "I missed the boat, Eden." Her sister frowned when Reggie didn't elaborate, but instead shook her again.

"Just...you missed the boat? No explanation?"

Reggie let go and went back to the counter, where the pitted olives lay waiting on a cutting mat. "All that bluff and bravado? Smoke screen."

"For what?"

Reggie reached for the sharpening steel to take the burrs off her knife. "Fear. He's afraid, Eden."

CHAPTER NINETEEN

TOM WAS PACKED. IT HADN'T taken very long, he was leaving one of the two suitcases of clothes he'd brought cross-country in the house, and taking the other one with him.

Frank and Bernie had agreed to let him drop Brioche off in the morning, and to keep her inside until the fence bottoms were secure. In return Tom would bring them back French postcards…if such a thing even still existed.

And he'd see Reggie when he got back. They would set up some kind of an account for medical bills, child support, etc. He'd do his best to get back to the States for the birth of his child. He couldn't miss that.

Nope. And maybe by then…

He wasn't going to delude himself. Reggie was right. His career would always come first. He was exactly like his father.

Tom sat on the futon and stared across the room. He needed to jump into action, do something to stop the raging anxiety inside him, yet had no idea what he could do.

The rattling of the front storm door sent Brioche on high alert, all the hair standing up on her neck as she poised stiff-legged on the futon, ready to attack.

Reggie. He knew it was her before he opened the door. She stood on the porch, looking up at him without saying a word. She was dressed in a smock thing. Looser than necessary for the small bump she'd developed, but a reminder of what was to come. What he would miss.

Brioche peeked between his legs, then turned a circle. Reggie was welcome.

"Come on in," he said, gesturing with the hand that wasn't holding the door.

"It's good to see you two together."

He smiled tightly. "Is everything okay?"

She ran a palm over her opposite arm, her green eyes wide and serious as they met his. "No, Tom. It's not."

His heart skipped, thumping against his ribs. "The baby?"

"Is fine. You and I are not."

He closed the door. This was not going to be a quick visit to say goodbye.

"Do you love me, Tom?"

That stopped him dead in his tracks. "What?"

"Simple question." She sat on the futon, the picture of analytical calm, which only made him feel more rattled.

"What if I said no to your simple question?"

"I don't know that I'd believe you."

"Pretty sure of yourself," he muttered, still standing. If he sat, he'd have to sit beside her.

Her chin rose slightly. "I think you loved me when you left seven years ago. I think you love me now."

TOM'S FACE WENT BLANK, WHICH made Reggie want to grab him by the front of his shirt and shake him. He had no idea how much it cost her to sit on the uncomfortable futon and pretend to be calm.

"And if I do?"

"Then we have to face some issues and make this work."

"What issues? My job? It's who I am. You have to admit that I'm not a catering guy. It isn't like I can just settle in Reno and become part of the family business."

"I agree." A month of Tom in the kitchen had convinced her that while they were better off with him there, it wasn't the right job for him.

"And I can't start a restaurant."

"Why not?" Reggie asked.

He sent her a weary are-you-kidding? look before saying, "No one will back me, with my rep. Pete made that quite clear to me. And my people skills suck." The words came out of his mouth with rapid-fire delivery, as if he'd said them to himself over and over again.

"Agreed."

"I left you," he pointed out, as if she wasn't ultra-aware of that. She nodded, which seemed to make him even more agitated. "We lost contact. I disappeared out of your life."

"Before I could disappear out of yours."

He stopped moving. For a minute she thought he'd stopped breathing as he studied her, so tightly closed off that she didn't know if she would ever be able to break down the wall between them.

Then he rubbed his hand over his head and turned away from her, toward the window, and stared out to the lamplit street. Brioche trotted over and sat on the carpet beside him.

Reggie rose and walked toward him, stopping a few feet away, sensing that he needed his distance, that his defenses wouldn't allow her any closer.

"Who's in your life today, Tom, who was

also in it twenty years ago? Or even fifteen?"
Who hasn't left you?

He turned back to her and laughed harshly. "Psychoanalysis, Reg? Really?"

"Just an observation," she said. She wasn't so foolish as to think she could undo a lifetime of conditioning in a night. But she could crack the surface, give him something to think about.

"It's just my nature to push people away. I'm a loner."

"I need you to stop being a loner."

He gave a dismissive snort. "As if it's that easy."

"It *won't* be easy," Reggie snapped. She took a breath, willed herself not to let her emotions get away from her. She reached out and took his hand, placed it firmly against her abdomen.

"This," she said, holding her hand on top of his, "is scary. There's a risk of loss. But people keep having kids. Some things last."

Tom shook his head.

Reggie took a step backward, releasing him. She'd done what she could. Delivered her message. The rest was up to him. She started for the door and was almost there when Tom said gruffly, "You know I love you."

"Yeah."

He took a few steps closer. "But you have your support system here. The business you grew. Everything you've worked for. You're a success, Reggie."

"And you wouldn't ask me to leave that." Too much distance still separated them. He started to speak when Reggie interrupted him to say softly, "Just like you didn't ask me the last time…no matter how you remember it happening."

"I thought it was understood."

"Did you?"

He rubbed a hand over his face. "I don't know," he finally said.

But he did. She could tell. And he knew she knew.

"Look, Reggie," he finally said. "This isn't going to work."

"What?" she asked softly.

"You. Me. Maybe you're right about this psychoanalysis, but I can't help the way I react. I try to be normal and it just doesn't work. All I'll do is disappoint you when you need me."

"You're choosing to leave rather than try?"

He nodded. "I'm trying to do what'll work for both of us."

"You're a coward, Tom."

"And who," he asked quietly, "wants to hook up with a coward?"

FOUR DAYS PASSED WITHOUT A word from Tom. That was okay, because Reggie was so damned angry with him, with herself—and the universe in general—that she probably wouldn't have listened to him, anyway.

She hadn't expected him to instantly accept what she'd had to say, to believe that important things could last. But she'd thought they could open a dialogue. Fear factor or not, she hadn't expected him to walk away, and then not contact her. The silence was killing her.

But she was giving him grudging points for honesty. He thought he would hurt her, and he was removing that possibility. She'd told him from the beginning that she wanted to raise the baby alone. Wish granted.

And then, on that fourth night after he left, while she was lying in bed and stewing, she felt the baby move. A flutter deep inside her. A butterfly's touch.

At first she thought it was wishful thinking, but it happened again. An odd fluttering tumble. Her baby…Tom's baby…making his or her presence known.

Making her believe in miracles.

For a few minutes, anyway.

REGGIE SPENT MOST OF THE NEXT day putting her hand to her abdomen every few minutes and waiting to feel the flutter. It made it very hard to cook. But every now and then she was rewarded, and that night, the first since Tom had left, she fell asleep almost as soon as she got into bed—only to be startled awake by the phone ringing.

Mims raised her head and blinked as Reggie snapped on the bedside lamp, then felt around on the comforter for the phone she'd dropped in the process. She'd barely gotten it to her ear when Eden said, "Reggie. You made the tabloids."

"I what?" She pushed herself upright.

"You're not on the newsstand, but you are on one of the big websites. Here. I'll send you the link. Call me back."

A second later the email zinged into her phone's internet in-box. Reggie opened it and followed the link to the site. She enlarged the text and started to read, her heart beating faster as she scrolled down. And there she was—with Tom, of course—at the Reno Cuisine, packing up.

That reporter, Christine, must have found a camera with a longer lens than her phone's. The headline read Volatile Celeb Chef Surfaces at Cooking Competition with Pregnant Girlfriend.

Pregnant Girlfriend?

Sure enough, in the telephoto blowup shot Reggie was no longer wearing her chef's coat, and the breeze had plastered her thin, white cotton T-shirt against her small baby bump as she stood looking up at Tom. If that wasn't obvious enough, there was a pink arrow on the photo pointing to her belly.

She quickly read the article, which was nothing but speculation, and not very flattering speculation, about why Tom had disappeared. Apparently, the only job he could get was with his pregnant girlfriend. Okay, there was some truth to that. He'd cut his hair to hide his identity...more truth there, too. But in general the article was just plain nasty.

Reggie called Eden. "I'm the pregnant girlfriend," she said.

"Not that many people read these things."

Oh, yeah. That was why they were so popular.

"Do you think the paparazzi will stake out

my house?" Reggie asked as she started to get a handle on the situation. This was unexpected and unsettling, but also pretty far down on the page. The reporter had probably made a few bucks from the photo, which was why she hadn't put anything in her paper... but that must be coming.

"Only if some other celebrity fails to sneeze," Eden said. "Don't worry about it." She paused for a moment, then said, "You aren't worried about it...are you?"

"No. I'm good. Maybe it'll bring in new business."

"Do you want me to come over? Because I can come over."

"No," Reggie said, scratching Mims, who was settled on the baby. "I'm fine. It's really not that big a deal." Even if, truthfully, it pissed her off having someone shoving her nose into their private affair. For money.

REGGIE WASN'T DUE AT THE kitchen until late the next morning, since she'd caught up on most of the paperwork, including thank-you notes, during her sleepless nights. She made the most of her morning at home, shopping online for baby furniture, ignoring the unsettling feeling of being on a national gossip website.

She was putting on her makeup when someone knocked on her door, and she slapped on lipstick fast, just in case whoever it was took her photo. But it wasn't the paparazzi at the door. It was Justin, looking like death warmed over. But what was new?

"This is a surprise." She stepped back as he came inside. "Have you, uh, gotten any sleep?"

He shook his head. "Nope. But I thought I'd stop by and see how Tom Gerard's pregnant girlfriend is doing."

"She's well," Reggie said noncommittally.

"Patty's been getting calls at the kitchen from various newspeople. She's fended them off masterfully."

Reggie tried to smile, "I guess she knows I'm pregnant."

"Yeah." Justin sat on the edge of the sofa and rested his forearms on his thighs, clasping his hands together. "This is none of my business, but…what's going on with you and Tom? Is he going to move to France? Are you staying here?"

Reggie stood behind her recliner, facing Justin, but looking at the pattern in the upholstery. Then she raised her eyes.

"I suspect the answer to both questions is yes. Has Eden been talking to you?"

"She has."

"And you're here because…"

He pulled off the white cotton stocking cap he wore when he baked. "We can run the business without you."

"So…you're giving me permission to go?"

"I'm removing one of the excuses not to go."

"Thank you." Reggie bit out the words. "But I might be a little lonely in France, unless something changes."

"You can make things change."

For a moment Reggie stared at him. Where was her protective brother?

He let his head drop. "A baby needs a father."

"I know," Reggie said with a frown. Justin was more serious than she'd seen him in… well…ever.

"Not to get all tough on you or anything, but Reggie, if you can make this work, do it. Forget all the shit that happened between you two before, and give your kid a dad."

"Justin…I'd do that in a heartbeat. But the thing is, I can go after Tom." Whom she still hadn't heard from. "But I can't force him to stay with me."

And she wasn't going to break her heart trying. She was done.

TOM LOVED FRANCE, AND AS LUCK would have it, Lowell's restaurant, in a converted stucco house with a courtyard behind it, was excellent. Tom was quartered in one of the three upstairs rooms and spent his first days there discussing business strategies and menus, meeting potential employees and flirting with Simone. She loved to have Lowell glare possessively at her.

Tom was miserable.

He shouldn't have left Reno. The plane had barely lifted off when he realized that the gnawing anxiety hadn't abated, it had simply changed sources.

And he was still dealing with Reggie telling him that he'd never asked her to come to Spain. Somehow it had never played out that way in his head. She'd given the ultimatum, and he'd taken it—gratefully, as he looked back on it. He may have even pushed her to offer it, giving him the frantic out he needed as the fear of losing her built.

She'd been right on the money with her analysis of him. And the same scenario was playing out with the baby. He wanted to be part of his kid's life, but he was afraid to be. Hell, he was afraid to become attached to a freaking dog…but he had, by lying to himself for a month.

As he'd lied to himself for years.

So here he was—across an ocean, with as much distance as possible between him and Reggie. And his kid.

He wasn't loving it.

Lowell being Lowell, hadn't laid out his offer yet. Tom had over a week left in the country, and he hoped that he wasn't going to be hearing the terms at the last possible minute. He wanted time to negotiate during the first days of his stay.

As if he had any power to negotiate. But he'd give it a shot. Lowell would think less of him if he didn't.

Guests were coming over that evening, people Tom hadn't seen in more than a decade. Simone was cooking and Lowell was off buying booze in copious quantities, leaving Tom with a couple hours to kill before the indulgences began.

He settled in the small courtyard with his laptop, paid a bill, checked his email. An automatic alert that his name had cropped up on the internet was waiting for him. He clicked it and followed the link, wondering what kind of trouble he'd gotten himself into now.

Oh, shit.

For a moment he simply stared at the photo of Reggie looking up at him in the Reno park after the catering competition, the pink arrow pointing at her belly. Then he slapped his computer shut and leaned his head back against the stone fence that surrounded the courtyard, staring up at the cerulean-blue sky, the muscles in his jaw working as he ground his teeth together.

If those bastards started bothering Reggie...

Logic told him that wouldn't happen. He knew how fast these things blew over. He wasn't that newsworthy anymore, not having thrown a public tantrum in over a month. But, still, if those bastards started hounding Reggie...

He got to his feet and reached for his phone. Stopped.

He'd pretty much excused himself from her life. If Reggie had a serious problem, she would have contacted him. By email if not by phone. Wouldn't she have?

At this point Tom didn't know, but he was overwhelmed by the need to make sure she

was all right. The urge to be there and protect her.

Would this feeling fade in time?

Did he want this feeling to fade in time?

The wonderful smell of roasting duck hit
him as he went in and up the stairs to his
room. He sat on the narrow bed and dialed
Reggie's number. She took her sweet time answering the phone and then, when she did,
her voice cooled several degrees when she
realized it was him.

"Tom…what a surprise."

"I, uh, called about the article."

"The girlfriend?"

The fact that she responded so quickly
made his gut tighten. He knew the hell of
being hounded, but he'd always rather enjoyed
the battle. Reggie…she wasn't that way. "That
one. Have people been bothering you?"

"No." He waited for her to elaborate and
she didn't, so he tossed out another question.

"How are you feeling? Is everything all
right?"

"Everything's fine. How are you?"

*I'm going crazy with this stilted conversa-
tion.* "So far, so good."

"Well," she said coolly, "let me know how
it all works out. Anything else?" She sounded

as if she was talking to a client. No—she would have been warmer to a client.

Oh, yeah. He'd burned a bridge here. But wasn't that what he'd been trying to do?

"If you do start getting harassed—"

"I don't see that happening, Tom. I'm in a meeting and have to go."

"Reggie—"

"What, Tom?" Her voice softened a little, giving Tom a glimmer of hope, but no answer to her question. What, indeed? What could he say to her over the phone while she was in a meeting? The truth. "You were right about a lot of stuff."

There was a very healthy silence, and then Reggie said quietly, "I guess the question now is what are you going to do about that?"

He didn't answer immediately, because he didn't yet know.

"We'll talk when you get back. Goodbye, Tom. I really have to go."

CHAPTER TWENTY

REGGIE WAS WORKING ALONE IN the kitchen when her cell phone rang. Wiping her hands on a towel, she walked into the office. She hoped it wasn't Eden with some emergency at the reception buffet she and Patty were serving that afternoon.

It wasn't.

"Hi, Reggie." Tom sounded nervous—as well he should, since he hadn't called her as promised when he'd gotten back from France. Over a week had passed since his scheduled return to Reno, and not one word.

"Where are you?" she asked. *Why haven't you called? What gut-wrenching news are you about to impart?*

Okay, maybe she hadn't been exactly warm and encouraging when he'd called during the client meeting, but that was no excuse for him not to keep his promise.

"Actually...I'm sitting in the parking lot."

"You're what?"

She went into the reception area and peered

out the window. Sure enough, there was a nondescript midsize car with a rental plate in the small lot. Tom stood beside it, phone to his ear.

"I wanted to talk to you alone and I didn't want to just burst in unannounced."

Ah, yes. That unannounced part. That lack of communication part.

She was starting to feel a slow burn. He was supposed to call when he got back in the country and he hadn't. "Where have you been?"

"Do you have a couple minutes?"

Reggie looked around the kitchen for an out, feeling contrary. Nothing.

"Maybe."

"Can you come here? I have something to show you."

Reggie frowned. "Fine."

She took off her apron and laid it over the counter, smoothed her dress over the baby bump, then let herself out the front door, locking it after her. Tom was already halfway across the lot. When he was within a couple feet of her, he stopped. "Are you doing okay?"

"Uh…yes." He looked tired. Careworn. She probably looked the same to him. Sleep had not come easily lately.

"No reporters?" he asked.

Reggie crossed her hands over her stomach, a protective move that was now instinctive. "None to speak of. I had a couple calls from local papers and refused comment."

"Good." He gestured with his head toward the street. "I have something to show you."

"You mentioned that." They started walking toward the car. To Reggie's surprise they walked past it to the sidewalk.

"Only a couple blocks," Tom said. They turned at the next street and went two more blocks to a tiny, run-down brick bungalow sitting next to a weed-choked lot.

"Why are we here?" she asked, trying to make sense of what was happening.

"I bought this house, Reggie."

"You're crazy," she said automatically, the words tripping off her tongue of their own accord.

"I guess, because I'm pretty much sinking every cent I have into the renovation."

"Renovation?"

"Come on," he said, taking her hand in his and going up to the battered door. He pulled a key out of his pocket.

He couldn't have closed the deal this quickly. "How'd you get a key?"

She was truly afraid to speculate.

"I was nice to the real estate lady," he said with a smile that didn't ease any of the tension in his face. "The paperwork on the sale is still pending, but—" he held up the key "—for once I tried sugar instead of vinegar. If it hadn't worked," he said as he inserted the key in the old-fashioned lock, "I would have gone for the vinegar."

"No doubt." Reggie somehow kept herself from recoiling as they walked into the dilapidated, damp-smelling living room. "I hope you didn't pay much."

"I bought the lot next door, too, so I have some change sunk into it." He pushed the door shut. The rattling sound echoed through the empty house.

The empty wreck of a house.

The walls had holes, the ceiling was stained, the woodwork seriously marred. The flooring was worn through to the subfloor in places, and impacted with grime.

"*Why* did you buy this place?" Reggie asked.

"It's a commitment."

She tilted her head, her lips parting slightly. "How so? Are you going to live here?" With small furry creatures that no doubt lived here, too. Craziness.

Tom shook his head. "I'm going to work here. This," he said, "will be the main dining area once we knock out that back wall. I think we can get ten tables in here." He walked her into the next room. "The banquet area for private parties. Everything else will be kitchen, prep and storage facilities."

"You don't have to do this," Reggie said abruptly. "You can probably stop the sale."

A shadow crossed his face. "I don't understand."

"You put me through hell, Tom. And now you buy what may one day be a restaurant, and everything is supposed to be all right? You left me. Told me it wouldn't work."

"You always knew I was leaving. You *told* me I was leaving a couple hundred times. I'm trying to come back!"

She stepped forward and poked a finger against his chest. Why couldn't he see what he'd done to her with days of silence? "Communication, Tom. If you do something like this, you communicate about it. You don't just spring it on a person. I've been lying awake at night, wondering if you were ever going to get your head together, and you're merrily carrying on without me."

It was just too much to process. She needed distance. Space.

She marched out of the house, down the creaky steps onto the cracked sidewalk. It was going to take a boatload of money to bring this place up to standards. She was halfway to the street when he called her name. She stopped abruptly, closed her eyes, then turned back to him. "What?" she asked. Tom stood on the porch of the dilapidated house, looking very much like the captain of a sinking ship.

"Don't leave me."

Reggie's mouth opened, then closed again as she swallowed.

"I know I left you, but…give me a chance," he said. "We're running out of time, Reggie. We need to settle things before the baby comes."

She pressed a hand to the side of her head, then let it drop loosely to her side. "Yes. We need to settle things, but I *don't* want you pretending to change if you can't. I don't want you to try to be something you're not. Like you said before, it just won't work." And she'd be here picking up the pieces.

"But…" he descended the steps then and

walked toward her "…would you mind if I worked hard to become something that I *want* to be?"

For a moment she stared up at him, took in the weary lines around his dark eyes, the grim set of his mouth.

"You want this," Reggie stated flatly. "How many times have you told me you couldn't run a restaurant? That you lacked the people skills."

"Damn it, Reggie. Yes. I want this. I can learn people skills." He took a breath, then reached out to take her by the shoulders, making that contact she hadn't realized she wanted so much. "I've been telling myself over and over that I can't run a restaurant. And I finally realized that I'm afraid to run a restaurant…because I'll have to learn a lot of new skills. Take advice from others. Basically stop being pigheaded."

Reggie nodded, because she wasn't touching that one.

"I have no track record. In relationships or, honestly, in my profession. I'm good." He smiled slightly. "No, I'm great, but I have no history of longevity and I've made some big mistakes. Because of those two things, I can't get financial backers, so I sank everything I have into this place. It's mine alone. No one to answer to. If I fail, then it's all me."

"Why this place?" she had to ask.

"The price. It has room for parking," he said. "It's close to you. And even though it's an eyesore, the foundation is strong. Everything else can be fixed."

"How do you know that? About the foundation?"

"Frank and Bernie."

Reggie stepped back. "They knew you were here before I did? They already toured this place?" Once again, she was ready to turn and walk…or was she just scared, too?

"I live next door to them, Reggie. I had to get my dog…and I needed their help. I wanted to come to you with a plan."

"They're your renovators," she guessed.

Tom nodded. "I'm going to work with them, too. Sweat equity. I'm not starting this place until I've helped rebuild it. Just like I want to rebuild with you."

Reggie started walking then. Everything he'd said made sense. He'd actually come up with a plan. He was trying to stay.

Tom caught up with her, matched her pace, but she didn't slow down, didn't look at him. Instead she focused straight ahead, but saw nothing.

Okay. Maybe it made some sense for him to present this solution fait accompli. That way she'd know he was serious. That he was honestly trying to put down roots.

"I'm sorry I didn't tell you I was here," Tom said. "I tried to think of the best way to do this." She gave a curt nod, but continued to march back the way they'd come. Back to her kitchen. To her safe life where she never had to take any chances or risk getting her heart broken. And she realized she was behaving exactly like she'd accused Tom of behaving.

She stopped suddenly, turning to Tom, who also stopped, a wary expression on his face as he tried to gauge what her next move might be.

"You think we can?" she asked in a low voice.

"Rebuild?"

"Yes."

"I love you, Reggie. Always have. I think *our* foundation is strong." He smiled. "If it wasn't, we wouldn't be making each other so miserable."

She couldn't help smiling back. "Good analogy, Tom."

He reached down to tip her chin up. "I'm a chef, not an analogizer. You get my drift, right?"

"I got it."

"What do you think?"

Reggie took a deep breath. What did she think? That Tom was trying damned hard to do the right thing, to face down his demons.

"Reggie?" he said softly when she didn't answer.

She met his eyes, saw nothing but sincerity and perhaps humility there. And she felt herself go mushy. Tom was trying. She had to meet him halfway, believe in him. "Renovations take time. I'm not going to hurry this one, even if we're running out of time."

"No hurrying," he said. "On the renovations, that is."

"We can't screw up again." To make her point, she reached out and took his hand, placed it on the baby. Tom shifted so that he had a hand on either side of her small belly. Seconds later the baby twitched and he raised a startled gaze to hers.

"It moved."

"Showing definite signs of impatience."

He bent his head lower to kiss her lips, his hands still on her belly. It felt…right.

"We communicate," she said, kissing him back.

"I won't withhold anything."

"If you feel a knee-jerk urge to flee, tell me."

"Done." He took her into his arms, looked her straight in the eye and said, "I'm scared, Reg. I won't lie. But I want to succeed in this. I want to succeed with you."

She leaned back to take his face in her hands, looking him square in the eye. "Then I promise you that you will succeed, because I'm going to be with you, every step of the way."

She dropped her hands and leaned into him, wrapping her arms around his waist. She relished the feel of his long hard body against her own, the baby between them.

"I love you, Reggie," he murmured against her hair as his arms closed around her.

She smiled into his shirt. "And that is why you're going to succeed in this, Chef Gerard."

* * * * *